Pump Prout

Pump Prout

A Little League Story

A. R. Pressman

To Bob, a great storyteller and friend) *[signature]*

Little Compton 7/12/11

illustrations by Peter Aldrich

book design by Jeannet Leendertse

ISBN-13: 978-0615471648
ISBN-10: 0615471641
LCCN: 2011905403
BISAC: Juvenile Fiction / Sports & Recreation / Baseball

Pressman Press
7 Standish Street
Cambridge, MA 02138-6816
www.pumpprout.com

For Robert, Caleb and Noah
A.P.

For Widgie, Thomas, Charley, Thea and Amanda
P.A.

Contents

1
Everyone Has to Start Somewhere   1

2
Scouted Out   5

3
The Real Thing   10

4
Fourth Inning   18

5
Between Seasons   24

6
The Second Season   26

7
The Minutemen   33

8
Opening Day   38

9
Between Games 47

10
Target Practice 62

11
The Muskets 73

12
No Mercy 89

13
A Kind of Victory 100

14
Back to Earth 107

15
The Show 115

16
Thrown a Curve 121

17
Minutemen on Maneuvers 125

18
The Second Half 133

19
Muskets Misfire 139

20
The Revolutionaries 148

21
A Day Without Baseball 152

22
A Second Shot 159

23
How to Clean a Musket 174

24
The Taste of Victory 189

25
The Pilgrims 194

Everyone Has to Start Somewhere

"THIS IS THE WORST DAY of my life," Pump Prout muttered from the back seat of the car. His mother drove along in silence until, finally, she seemed to hear him.

"The worst day? Why the worst day?" she asked.

"Because I have to go to T-ball," Pump groaned.

"But, sweetheart, you love baseball. You'll like T-ball. It's where you learn how to play baseball. You learn how to hit and how to catch."

"Mom!" Pump was exasperated. "I already know how to play baseball and I like it a lot. So I won't like T-ball."

Pump felt he had made his point. It was clear to anyone with half a brain.

When he got to the field, kids were already swarming around the diamond. They were wearing blue t-shirts with the words *Canterbury T-ball* across the chest. Each player had a matching blue baseball hat with a big *C* for Canterbury on the front. Pump liked the look of it, but he wished they had real uniforms.

The coach, carrying a clipboard, introduced himself to Pump and checked off Pump's name on the list of players.

"Go get yourself a shirt and hat and take a place in the field. Do you have a glove?" the coach asked.

Pump showed him his mitt.

The coach smiled. "You're all set. Head on out to center field. You guys in the field will be coming in soon. Then you'll have batting practice."

Pump ended up in center field with two other players. What was this? Three center fielders? Is this what they call baseball?

A girl carried a bat to the plate. Right on the plate sat the tee, a stand on which the ball lay like an egg in an eggcup. The girl took a few practice swings, then whacked the ball off the tee. The ball arched and landed just beyond the pitcher's mound. Some of the many infielders lining the base paths tried to stop the ball but it rolled slowly through their legs and past their gloves until it came to a stop in the grass.

Pump dashed forward, scooped up the ball and looked to throw to first base. There was no one covering first base. The batter was on her way toward first. Four five-year-olds were on the base path between second and first but none of them seemed to take any notice of what was happening. So Pump ran to first himself and got to the bag just before the girl reached it. He looked for an umpire to call the runner out. There were some parents hanging around not paying any attention to what was happening at first. So Pump called, "You're out!"

"What do you mean?" the girl demanded.

"I tagged you. You're out."

"I am not!" she declared.

"Are, too."

"Am not!"

Pump looked around for the coach. Then he gave up, shrugged his shoulders and started back to center field. This was the weirdest way to play baseball, he thought.

By this time another batter had tapped the ball off the tee and was trotting to first base. He'd just hit a slow grounder and he was *trotting* like he'd just blasted it out of the park and had all the time in the world. Pump remembered there wasn't any pitcher. He sped to the ball as it rolled over the pitcher's mound, grabbed it without stopping and raced to first. He touched the bag to make the out, but this time, just to be sure, he tagged the runner, too.

"You're out!" Pump shouted.

The runner burst into tears.

Pump stared at him in amazement. He spotted the coach nearby. His heart sank. Now the coach would think he'd done something and he'd get in trouble.

The crying boy sniffed. "I can't be out. You can't say I'm out."

"Why not?" Pump wondered.

"Because there are no outs," the boy said.

"No outs?" Pump echoed. "There have to be outs."

The coach approached the boys and heard Pump's remark.

"This is T-ball," the coach said. "There are no outs in Canterbury T-ball."

"How's the game get over, then?" Pump asked.

"It doesn't," replied the coach. "We don't really play games. This is for practice. It's a chance to hit the ball without worrying about being put out. No strikeouts, no walks, no outs. The sides aren't retired, we just switch positions."

The coach stepped back, clapped his hands and shouted, "OK, players, all the fielders in to bat and batters out to the field. Move it, now."

So Pump, who had been playing baseball with his brother since he was three, had his turn at the tee. Pump felt he could blast the ball over the fence, only there wasn't any fence. He did manage a hefty line drive to the outfield which gave him a chance to round all the bases and come home. He called it a home run when he told about it. He didn't bother to mention the tee.

Pump's real name was Nicholas. When he was a bald baby, his family called him Pumpkin and the name stuck until his favorite baby-sitter shortened it to Pump. Pump Prout. It sounded like the Real Thing. Real baseball, that is. Which, in Pump's mind, T-ball and the name Nicholas were not. Now he wanted to skip T-ball and go straight into the minors.

In the car on the way home Pump announced, "I'm not going back to T-ball!"

"Not next time?" his mom asked.

"Not ever!" Pump exclaimed. "I won't play until I can play real baseball."

So Pump settled in for a long wait.

Scouted Out

ALL SUMMER PUMP THOUGHT about playing baseball the next spring. His big brother, Luke, was 11. Luke had started Little League when he was nine. He had played for the Patriots in the minors for two years, and now he was a pitcher for the Dodgers in the Canterbury major league. All autumn Pump dreamed about playing for the Patriots. All winter Pump waited for the spring season to begin.

At school, Pump worked hard at reading so he could read the sports section of the newspaper every morning. Even though he lived in Canterbury, Massachusetts, Pump's favorite team was the New York Yankees. The same baby-sitter who had called him Pump had grown up in New York and was a big Yankees fan. Pump loved listening to him talk about the Yankees. Pump's favorite Yankee was Babe Ruth, who started out with the Red Sox in Boston. Pump taught himself to switch-hit so he could bat lefty, just like Babe Ruth.

More than anything else, Pump wanted to play baseball. He practiced all the time. He played the outfield by himself, making amazing plays. He pitched shutouts, like the Babe. He swung and swung the bat, hitting invisible balls into the stands, out of the park. Sometimes he hit line drives, sometimes sacrifice bunts. The roar of the crowd filled his ears.

The season started right after school vacation in April. Pump's mom learned that players who were Pump's age had to start in the Farm League before they could qualify for a minor league team. Pump's friend, Ken Ames, had played in the Farm League last year and this year was expecting to play on his brother Charles's team, the Muskets, in the minors.

Pump was crushed by this news. As usual, his mother tried to make it seem like it wasn't the end of the world.

"It's not the end of the world," she said as she came over to give Pump a hug. "It's all right."

His entire baseball career had just ended and she was saying it's all right.

Pump's mother continued, "Farm League is like the Double A farm teams for the pros. You'll get a chance to practice fielding and hitting before you move up next year."

Pump gave her a baleful look and went to his room. He stared at his Babe Ruth poster on the wall.

"Farm League?" He gulped. He looked the Babe in the eye. "Well, why not?"

The Canterbury Farm League had practices Wednesday afternoons and Saturday mornings. The practices were held on the field behind Pump's school where there were three diamonds. On Wednesdays, the practice for Farm League took place on one diamond while Little League used the other two diamonds for their games, one for the majors and one for the minors.

Pump was excited before his first practice. Farm League sounded like real baseball. He had high hopes—and butterflies in his stomach—as he waited for the practice time. When he felt excited and nervous, Pump was grouchy. His sneakers wouldn't stay tied, everything anyone said sounded stupid, and his brother really got on his nerves.

Finally, it was time to go to the field. Pump couldn't wait to get there. He was one of the first kids to arrive. He was handed a red t-shirt and a red hat with a *C* on it. The shirt said *Canterbury Farm League* in small letters over the left chest. Pump's mouth fell open. This was *not* real baseball. This was little kids' baseball. Coach O'Connor, a big man with short sandy hair, shook Pump's hand. The coach looked like an umpire to Pump, mainly because he wasn't wearing any uniform except for a black Farm League t-shirt. He sent Pump out with a few other players and a father who softly hit balls for the boys to catch. After awhile, Pump's group moved to the infield where four kids lined up at each base and took turns fielding the balls the coach hit out to them.

Half of the kids wore red shirts and hats and the other half wore black. That raised Pump's spirits. Two colors must mean that the Farm League had teams. And if there were teams, they might actually play games.

Pump was right. After forty-five minutes of practice in the field and switching bases, Coach O'Connor called everyone in. He divided up the teams, red and black. He went over some basic baseball rules and a little bit of strategy, like how to follow the play, when to run, and what to be ready for. Pump was picturing all sorts of plays in his head: Pump making a home run; Pump, the first baseman, catching a line drive headed for deep right field; Pump, the shortstop, throwing for a double play. Pump, the pitcher, throwing strikes.

Coach O'Connor's voice broke into Pump's thoughts. "Remember, always listen to your coaches. They tell you what you need to know and what you need to do."

The coach took the mound. The batter would get four swings. If he didn't connect with the ball, the batter would hit from a tee to start play. Pump was put in as shortstop, which was enough for starters. He wanted to play right field, just like the Babe. He wasn't so sure about being a pitcher.

Pump knew baseball was a slow game but this was even slower than he'd expected. It was hard for kids to catch the ball or even to stop it when it was rolling. Pump felt lucky each time the ball came toward him. When his turn to bat finally came, he connected with the second pitch to hit a looping fly ball that landed just beyond second base. By the time he reached first, the infielders were swarming around the ball right next to second so he knew he needed to pull up. That felt good. Maybe Farm League wasn't so bad after all.

For the next few weeks, Pump went to all his Farm League practices. On Wednesday afternoons, Luke sometimes played on the field next to him, and when practice was over, Pump would watch Luke's game and cheer for the Dodgers.

The Little League season was seven weeks long. On the morning of the fourth Saturday practice, Pump was the first baseman and his team was first in the field. These games were not entirely satisfying. No score was kept. Each inning lasted as long as it took to go once through the batting order of each team. Pump supplemented the action by pretending he was a sports announcer.

Pump's mother was watching from behind the fence near first base. Two men Pump didn't know walked over and one of them started talking to her. Pump had noticed these men watching the practice and talking to Coach O'Connor but Pump was concentrating on the action on the field as well as in his imagination and paid little attention to them. When he saw one of the men talking to his mother, Pump became curious.

After the game, Pump came over to his mother. The strangers were still there. The shorter man gave Pump a friendly look and smiled.

"Pump," his mother said, "this is Gary Kennedy, the coach of the Canterbury Yankees and his assistant coach, Fred Namath. They'd like to talk to you."

Coach Kennedy extended his hand to Pump until Pump cautiously put forth his own hand which Coach Kennedy grasped firmly.

"Glad to meet you, Pump," he said. "Like your mother was saying, I coach the Yankees. Fred and I were looking over the Farm League here today. We're scouting out someone to come up to the minors. The Yankees have an opening now. We've been watching you and we think you'd make a great Yankee."

Pump stood still, blinking at this short, heavyset, smiling man. Coach Kennedy's eyes were twinkling but his face was serious. Pump understood this was an important, man-to-man talk.

"Now, like I was saying to your mom," the Yankees' coach continued, "this is up to you and your family. The Yankees need a good player and we'd like you to join us."

Pump's heart thundered in his chest. He shot a glance at his mother. She grinned at him.

"Is it OK, Mom?" Pump asked, his voice squeaking a little. "Can I do it?"

"If you want to, it's fine with me," she said.

"Wow! Yup. Awesome," murmured Pump.

"Great!" announced Coach Kennedy. "I hope we'll see you at practice tomorrow at four o'clock right here at the field. Our next game is the day after that, Monday. Glad you'll be with us. See you tomorrow."

Pump's heart soared. He could only nod. Coach Kennedy walked off with his assistant coach.

Pump's mom smiled. "I think Coach Kennedy is pretty pleased with himself. He nabbed you now so he doesn't have to wait for next year's tryouts to compete with the other coaches for you. He sort of jumped the gun. You should feel honored."

To the tips of his toes Pump felt honored.

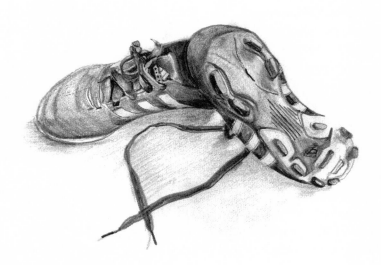

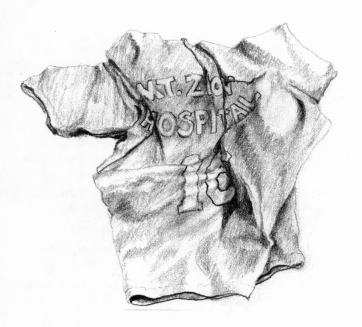

The Real Thing

WAITING MORE THAN TWENTY-FOUR HOURS to start what Pump felt was finally real baseball was not easy. He couldn't believe how slowly the clock moved ahead. By lunchtime on Sunday, Pump was sure time had almost stopped. Finally, he was able to set off for practice.

As soon as he got to the field, Pump was given a blue hat with a white *C* on it, a pair of tan pants with elastic at the cuffs, and a blue shirt with *Yankees* written across the front and the number 16 on the back. Where Pump expected *Prout* to be printed across the back between the shoulders, above his number, he found *Mt. Zion Hospital*, the name of the team's sponsor. He pulled the shirt on over his own t-shirt and adjusted the cap to fit his head. He carefully bent the brim of the hat to just the right curve. He tossed the pants to his mom and tried not to smile when he met her eyes. Pump grabbed his glove and ran to join the other Yankees as they huddled around the coach for instructions.

Coach Kennedy brought Pump into the circle as he ran up.

"Yankees, I want you to meet Pump Prout," the coach announced. "You all know we've been down a player since Jake left. Once we almost had to forfeit a game because only eight guys showed up to play. Prout is joining the team to give us a full squad of twelve. I went down to the Farm League yesterday on a scouting mission and discovered this well-guarded secret. He's little, but he's got what it takes. So he's moving up and we're proud to have him. Let's welcome Pump Prout to the Yankees!"

Everyone clapped and cheered. Pump studied his cleats while his heart leaped and his mouth twitched.

"Now, what's it take to make a ballplayer?" the coach shouted.

"Practice!" yelled a few Yankees.

"What else?" called the coach.

"More practice," screeched the entire team laughing and giving each other high fives. Pump smiled happily as his new teammates slapped him on the back.

"Remember," Coach Kennedy said, "practice is where you get to play. Games, you get bored or you get lucky. Only once in awhile do you get to play baseball."

The practice got underway. Pump loved it. There was batting practice without a tee in sight. The assistant coach, Fred Namath, pitched to them. Coach Kennedy kept yelling, "Watch the ball. If you can see it, take it. Swing at the good ones. I'd rather see you go for anything you can hit than watch a ball go by just for the sake of a walk. Go down swinging. Don't spectate!"

Coach Kennedy seemed to keep track of everything that was going on. He kept coming over to where Pump was at bat or on the field to give him useful tips or just to tell him what a great job he was doing.

At first, Pump froze every time he spotted the coach looking at him. He was afraid the coach would change his mind. Pump still couldn't believe he really had a place on the Yankees. Whenever the coach encouraged him, just a word here and there, Pump felt stronger, and safer. Pump noticed that throughout practice Fred Namath kept a close eye on his own son, Freddy, one of the pitchers on the team.

At the end of practice, Coach Kennedy called in the boys.

"Monday we play the Pilgrims," the coach said as he looked from one player to the next. "They beat us nine to two in our first game with them but we're three weeks stronger now and have a lot more practice under our belts."

On Monday morning, Pump woke with a start. He was certain it must be time for school so he got dressed and went to the kitchen. It was strangely dark and silent. Pump looked at the clock and saw it was only five o'clock. He was up two hours early. He prowled through the back hall and went outside to throw balls into the air for himself to catch. The sun was just coming up.

After school, Pump felt a cramp in his left side and butterflies fluttering in his stomach. They got worse on his way to the field, but, once he arrived and saw his teammates and coach getting ready to warm up, he felt calmer. The butterflies swooped back when he saw the other team across the field.

Coach Kennedy looked up from the roster of players and called out the lineup. At the end he added, "Penny Weiss and Pump Prout warm the bench for a few innings. Rookies just play two innings for their debut," the coach explained to Pump. "Sometimes for the whole season."

Pump ran out to the field for warm up. He was so excited he had to remind himself to focus on the ball.

"Game time! Get the equipment into the dugout," the coach yelled, "We're the home team so out to the field, Yankees. Take your positions."

He clapped his hands and Pump felt his stomach do a somersault.

Pump's position was on the bench so he trotted there against the tide of his teammates jogging out to the field. He jostled against Penny as they arrived at the bench at the same time. Pump saw Penny sit down and he did the same, hoping his excitement didn't show. He sat forward to watch.

The Yankees' starting pitcher, Ted Montgomery, looked determined as he faced the Pilgrims' first batter. A swing at the very first pitch knocked a blooper down to short where it bounced off Freddy Namath's shoulder for a single. The next batter, facing a 3-2 count, hit a ground ball that looked like it would bounce past Annie Maloney, but she snagged the ball and touched second base for an out.

The third batter hit an easy grounder to third. Danny Flagan

scooped up the ball and spun it to Annie Maloney who stuck out her glove and looked stunned when she made the catch. "First, first," everyone was yelling. She looked at the ball, then jumped into action, stepped on the bag and threw to Everett Martin who made the last out. The Yankees erupted into cheers. Pump was thrilled. A double play. What a team!

By the end of the second inning, the Yankees were leading, five to three. The team was bursting with excitement. In their first four weeks of the season, they'd had only one win. Now they were ahead and playing strong.

"In and out, in and out," called Coach Kennedy. "Jill Maloney, take the bench. Nice job out there." He turned to Pump, "OK, Pump, in you go for Jill. Right field. Hustle up."

With his heart pounding in his ears, Pump leaped up and dashed to right field. Everything looked different from Pump's new viewpoint. Now he could see the parents sitting on bleachers or standing along the fence, the two teams' benches, and the backs of the Yankees' infielders. Suddenly, home plate seemed far away. With relief Pump remembered his cut-off, second base. All he'd have to do would be to throw the ball in as far as Annie Maloney.

The top of the third. The Pilgrims' first batter strode to the plate, knocked his bat on his cleats and took a few swings. Even from right field this batter looked big. He was almost as tall as the umpire and swung his bat with great authority. Pump felt hollow in the pit of his stomach. The pitcher probably felt intimidated, too, because his first three pitches were balls. The next pitch was in there. A mighty swing and a miss. Strike one. Then, what looked like a ball curved in to catch the outside corner of the plate for strike two. Pump swallowed hard. He was hoping for some action but, at the same time, hoping for the action to go elsewhere.

Pitching into a full count, Ted Montgomery threw a hard, straight ball practically onto the bat. With his follow-through, the batter smacked the ball over the first baseman. Pump watched the ball in amazement. It was his! He couldn't feel his feet move, but move they did and with his eyes closed he felt the ball whack against his glove. His right hand clamped over his glove to hold in the ball but the ball had already bounced out of his mitt to the ground. The crowd's cheers dissolved into a groan. Shouts of "Get it!" "Throw, throw!" and "Oh no!" poured over Pump. His ears burned.

Pump tried to retrieve the ball as it bumped along the ground. He finally caught up to it as the batter rounded second. In the throes of his misery he forgot about cut-offs and only saw the runner flashing around the bases. He heaved the ball as far as he could toward third base. It landed near the pitcher's mound and the pitcher grabbed the ball which ended play. In the Canterbury Little League play ends when the ball is back in the pitcher's hands. The base runner had to hold up at third. A home run on errors was avoided. Pump felt his face burn as it dawned on him that he had made not just one, but two errors in one play.

"Attatway, Pump. Great save," Coach Kennedy bellowed above the din. What seemed like a century had really taken less than half a minute.

Pump wanted never to play baseball again. His career was over. He stank. The coach was just being nice.

Right field didn't see any more action that inning. The next three batters drew long, excruciating mixes of strikes and balls. Every time the count reached three and two, the last pitch turned into a ball until, finally, a run walked in to make the score 5-4, Yankees. That woke up Ted from his slump. He struck out the next batter. A grounder rolled between Annie and Freddy. Brian Kennedy retrieved the ball and overthrew to Annie at second while the batter made it to third. That play gave the Pilgrims three runs putting them ahead 7-5. A line drive straight to the pitcher retired the side.

"In and out, in and out," Coach Kennedy droned to his team. "OK, Yankees, this is a close one. Clyde Jones, you lead off. Danny, you're on deck. Ted, double deck." He put his hand on Pump's shoulder, "You'll follow Ted. Be ready."

Pump's heart raced. It was suddenly hard to swallow. He tried to spit which usually made him feel tough and full of baseball confidence. Now his mouth was so dry there wasn't anything to spit. Chances were good that he'd get to bat this inning. There was always the chance that he wouldn't. Part of him wanted to be up, but the other part didn't feel ready. Not just yet. Maybe one more inning. But then he'd have to lead off in the fourth. Wouldn't that be worse? Of course, if he didn't bat this inning, that would mean the team went down one, two, three and that wouldn't be good either. He'd better erase that wish even if it meant for sure he'd be batting...wow...in just a few minutes. The lump in Pump's throat got bigger.

Pump snapped out of his thoughts just as Clyde connected solidly with the ball, driving it high between right and center fields. Clyde streaked all the way to third.

Pump intently watched the plate. Danny Flagan, a tall 10 year-old with a few soft belly folds, stepped up to bat. The first pitch hummed in as a strike, which Danny just blinked at. That made Pump more nervous. His turn was coming. What if he just stood and watched them all go by? How could you be sure if a pitch was a ball or a strike?

"Hey, Pump," called the coach, "you're on double deck. Put on a batting helmet. When Ted is up, you come out to the on-deck circle and get in some practice swings. Like Ted's doing now."

A few batting helmets were scattered in the dirt under the dugout bench. Pump took the smallest but it wobbled forward on his head until he tried it on over his cap. Then it held snugly and Pump could see easily from under the brim.

Pump watched Danny hit a rolling grounder to first for an easy out. Clyde darted home to reduce the Pilgrims' lead to one. Pump saw that even a lousy grounder could become an RBI.

Ted was almost 11 and looked big as he shouldered the bat he had been swinging and trotted to the plate. He gave Danny a pat on the shoulder as they passed each other. Pump moved onto the patch of dirt they called the on-deck circle. Pump recognized in Ted his own imitation of Major League moves. It takes a lot of swagger, spitting and chewing to play hardball. Ted eyed the Pilgrims' pitcher, brought his bat around in a few slow-motion swings and poised himself for the pitch. The pitcher delivered a fastball into the dirt in front of the plate. Ball one. Ted gave a mighty slice at the next pitch and fouled it hard over the third-base fence. One and one. As Ted took some practice swings, Pump took some, too, timing them with Ted's. As the next pitch was hurled toward the plate, Ted's body tightened. His bat caught the edge of the ball, which looped just over the shortstop's reach to drop in for a single.

Coach Kennedy stood behind the third base line, right near the on-deck circle. "You're up, Pump," he said, giving Pump a warm smile. "Remember, eye on the ball, elbow up and choose your pitch. Like I always say, if you're going down, go down swinging."

Pump nodded and trotted to the plate. His tongue stuck to the roof of his mouth. His heart was hammering at full speed. The pitcher glared at him, sizing him up. He wound up and delivered. Pump swung blindly. He could hear his bat slice through the air and click against the ball. Foul ball. Strike one. The feel of the bat nicking the ball brought Pump to his senses. He suddenly knew where he was and what he had to do. His heart dove back into his chest and recovered its regular beat.

"Good cut, good cut," yelled Coach Kennedy enthusiastically.

"Attaway, Pump," shouted Fred Namath. "You got a piece of it, now get the whole thing."

Pump was ready. The next pitch was way over his head, followed by a pitch in the dirt. Pump watched them go by.

"Good eye!"

"That's lookin' 'em over!" some fans cried out. The whole team was clapping.

The fourth pitch came in and Pump swung with all his might. He heard the catcher shuffle for the ball behind him. Strike two.

"Great cut," shouted the coach cheerfully.

Pump was ready for the next pitch which was way outside. The pitcher shrugged his shoulders and puffed out his cheeks. He no longer looked so cool and powerful. Another ball over Pump's head.

"Take your base," the umpire yelled.

Pump tossed his bat toward the dugout and loped to first base.

"Way to look 'em over." Calls and cheers followed Pump to first base. He felt lighter than air. A big weight had fallen from his shoulders.

The Pilgrims' pitcher must have been rattled by Pump's strike zone because he threw three balls to Jeff Leonard before giving him something to swing at. Jeff stood still, staring at the next pitch coming straight in. At the last minute he stepped into a swooping swing that sent the ball soaring, soaring, gone, over the fence! The crowd cheered. Pump was as thrilled as if he'd homered himself. As he trotted around the bases behind Ted, his heart swelled with pride and pleasure. Pump pounced on the plate with both feet as he scored his first run.

The parent crowd was yelling and shouting. A three run homer! A first for the Yankees this season. Jeff beamed as every teammate poured out of the dugout to high-five him. Pump came in for his share of gusto and glory.

Yankees, 9, Pilgrims, 7, and one of those Yankee runs was Pump's. In fact, his was the go-ahead run. Freddy Namath followed all the furor with a fly to left field that was caught to close out the inning.

Fourth Inning

ONCE AGAIN IN THE LEAD, the excited Yankees spilled off the bench to take their places in the field.

As Pump turned to pick up his glove which he had tossed behind the bench, he paused in disbelief. There was his father, standing near the fence, not talking to anyone. His arms were folded and he was looking down.

Pump knew his mother was there in the middle of the other parents where he had seen her talking and smiling. She had certainly seen his walk, and his first run. But Pump had not expected his dad to come. Pump's father had never liked baseball and often said so. He never went to Luke's games. Only once had he ever tried to play catch with Pump and that only lasted a few minutes before he said "enough" and went inside.

But there he was. Not only was his dad there, but, for the first time, Pump saw his dad wearing a baseball cap. Pump noticed how big his dad's head was. Or maybe how small the hat was since it just perched on top of his dad's head. To Pump's surprise, it was his own blue hat from T-ball with the white C in the center.

"Get moving, Prout," Fred Namath barked. Startled, Pump grabbed his glove and ran out to right field.

On his way out to his position, Pump digested the fact that his father was there. He felt himself start to get nervous all over again, just like at the beginning of the game. There was so much to get used to. Pump was just getting used to being a fielder and now he had to get used to seeing his dad at his game. Pump knew he could concentrate better on the game without having to listen to his pounding heart.

By the time Pump turned to face the infield, his dad was further away and looked a little smaller. He stood behind the other parents who clustered at the fence so he wasn't very visible. That gave Pump enough space to get into his own world again.

Standing in right field, Pump let himself feel like the veteran he was. A one-inning veteran. He felt his heart slow down just like he wanted it to. Now he would be ready for anything. Anything. Even the soaring fly a Pilgrim hit to deep right over Pump's head. This time he didn't forget his cutoff as he ran to snatch up the ball. He pegged it to second. The batter, not expecting her ball to be back in play any time soon, had merrily rounded first when she heard her coach shouting and saw Annie Maloney planted firmly over second base with the ball in her hand. The runner stumbled as she tried to stop and turn at the same time. Annie ran forward to tag the runner out. The crowd and the Yankees cheered wildly. Coach Kennedy grinned broadly as he jammed his elbow against his side with his fist clenched in victory. Yes! One out.

The Pilgrims seemed to lose heart. The second batter struck out, stretching his bat up over his head to swing at a soaring high ball. The third batter reached first base on a mis-hit that rolled a few feet like a perfectly placed bunt. Pump was ready, longing to get some action again but the next batter tapped a grounder that the shortstop scooped up and ran in to second for the third out. Pump was starting to see that when the play was tight it sometimes made more sense to get the ball there on foot rather than risk a throw. He understood this but wasn't at all sure he liked it. It was too cautious, expecting the team to make errors rather than to make plays. It was like those batters who never swing the bat, but count on the Little League pitchers to walk them. What fun was that?

"In, out, in, out. Keep it moving, Yankees." Coach Kennedy clapped his hands.

The Pilgrims put in a new pitcher to try to shift the balance back to their team. Pump watched this pitcher carefully as he warmed up. This boy was the tallest player on either team. He tried hard to look like a pro. Before every pitch he picked up dirt and dropped it. He chewed gum. He checked out the bases even though these were only practice pitches and even though, in Canterbury, there was no stealing in the minor league. This pitcher tweaked his cap, shook his shoulders, stared at the catcher, raised his leg straight up, then quickly crooked it high as he flung himself onto that leg and released the ball.

Not only was he big and elaborate, this pitcher wore shades. Pump felt himself shiver. He watched Zach Tuttle, the Yankees' catcher, step into the batter's box. Zach stopped a little further away from home plate than he usually did.

For all his imposing style, the pitcher's balls flew all over the place. Zach swung at the first pitch out of sheer nervousness as the ball whacked into the dirt without even reaching the plate. He watched the next four balls wildly miss the plate. The umpire sent Zach to first with a base on balls.

Brian Kennedy, center fielder, a thin, sandy-haired boy who hardly resembled his Santa-bellied father, the coach, swung his bat, then hunched over the plate. The very first pitch hit him. He fell to the ground clutching his shoulder.

Fred Namath ran over to the plate where the umpire was already checking out a tearful Brian. He stopped crying and stood up when his father walked over.

"Good thing we're sponsored by a hospital," Annie murmured.

With a pat on the rump from his father, Brian trotted off to first. Pump felt it might be worth getting hit when he heard the cheers Brian got for being wounded in action and putting another man on.

The pitcher, for all his dazzle, couldn't get the ball over the plate.

Annie and Everett both walked which brought in Zach Tuttle to give the Yankees another run. 10-7. This seemed to settle the pitcher and he unexpectedly drilled three pitches over the plate to strike out Clyde Jones.

"Prout, double deck."

Pump jumped. The team had batted through the lineup and was almost to him.

Danny Flagan, up next, took some forceful practice swings while he looked the pitcher hard in the eye. The pitcher stared back as if nothing fazed him, but he proceeded to walk in another run. 11-7.

Ted stepped up to the plate. The Yankees' pitcher at bat and the Pilgrims' pitcher on the mound glared at each other. This confrontation seemed to focus the wild pitcher. He threw harder than ever right over the plate. Ted was frozen by the unexpected force of the pitch. "Strike one," the umpire called.

Ted took a few swings to loosen up again. This time he was ready for a fast ball and he swung with all his might. Only this time the pitch was so far outside he didn't come close to it. Next, Ted figured the pitcher was throwing balls again and watched without moving as the next ball sailed gently over the plate. Strike three. Two outs.

Pump watched from the on-deck circle. The first pitch had scared him. He noticed that Ted's reaction to each pitch was based on the pitch that went before and each time Ted guessed wrong. Pump realized you couldn't predict pitches that way.

The coach kept yelling, "Watch the ball!" and "Don't spectate!"

Pump caught sight of his father which flustered him as he walked out to face the monster pitcher. In an unpredictable game, this guy was more unpredictable than anyone Pump had seen. "Don't spectate!" rang in his ears. He wasn't exactly sure what that meant, but he got the sense of it. Don't just stand there staring at the ball, is what it meant. So Pump wouldn't. He took his practice swings, watched the elaborate wind up, then focused on the ball. He watched the ball and didn't move.

"Good eye!" the crowd shouted.

The coach yelled, "When it's your pitch, go for it."

Pump had to resist the wish to let the next one go, hoping it would be a ball, too. If the pitch wasn't exactly on target, it was close enough. Pump swung at it. Strike one.

"Attaway, Pump. Great swing," shouted Coach Kennedy.

Pump furrowed his brow and concentrated. The ball sped toward him. The weight of the bat and the force of his swing spun him in a complete circle. No contact. Strike two.

"Good cut. C'mon, Pump!" the team chorused.

The next pitch was so far inside Pump had to spring out of the way so he wouldn't get hit.

"Good eye! Way to keep cool, Pump!" people yelled.

That inside pitch shook him up a little but it made him even more determined to send the next one over the fence. Pump swung forward to catch the ball early. The only sounds were the swoosh of his bat and the clap of the ball into the catcher's mitt. Strike three.

Pump's shoulders started to droop forward but before they could, Coach Kennedy was energetically shaking those shoulders as he thumped Pump on the back, cheering him up with praise. "Great cut! Super swing! Good jawb, good jawb!" he exclaimed in his strong Boston accent.

Pump felt as if he'd done the next best thing to hitting a home run: he'd struck out! He'd struck out and the world hadn't ended. No one was mad at him. He felt great. Pump didn't see how that made any sense considering he'd just retired his own side. He hoped his dad liked swinging strikeouts as much as Coach Kennedy. Now Pump was, indeed, pumped and ready for more.

Only there was no more for him. As a rookie he only played two innings.

"Penny Weiss in for Pump Prout in right field," barked Coach Kennedy. "Great jawb, Prout. Great beginning. Auspicious! Keep it up. Now, back to the bench."

Once more Pump moved against the tide of his teammates heading to their positions. All the butterflies were gone. And so, he saw, was his dad.

It took Pump a whole half-inning to settle down before he could make any sense of what he was watching. He had to unwind from the excitement of his first real baseball experience. Farm League felt years behind him. By the time the Yankees were up to bat again in the bottom of the fifth, the score was tied, 11-11 and Pump threw his heart into cheering for his team. Pump saw that the Pilgrims' pitcher had lost all semblance of control. The entire Yankees' lineup walked around. Under Canterbury Little League rules, each team was allowed only 10 batters per half inning through the fourth inning. The last two innings could go on until dark. Pump could have waited all night for the end of the game. It felt so good to watch from the bench.

Finally, the pitcher traded places with the first baseman, a girl who'd never pitched in a game but was a terrific player. She took plenty of practice pitches, then settled down to do her job. She walked the first batter but never another.

With hardly a wind-up, she tossed the ball precisely over the plate through the center of everyone's strike zone. It was up to the hitters to connect. Some did but some didn't. Finally, the inning was over with the Yankees way ahead, 19-11

The top of the sixth was played through quickly, and the Yankees claimed their second win of the season.

Pump was indeed happy, but he didn't fully understand just how thrilled his teammates were. He saw them almost explode with excitement, but Coach Kennedy kept them from erupting until both teams had lined up and filed past each other, barely brushing hands to indicate a sporting handshake. With this formality over, the Yankees yelled and whooped and pounded each other on the back. Pump, the newcomer, was pummeled and applauded with the rest.

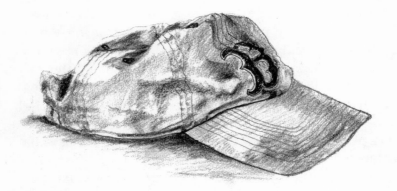

Between Seasons

PUMP THOUGHT HIS ROOKIE SEASON was the most exciting base-ball season there could be. Now that he was part of a team, his mind sailed ahead from the end of his rookie season into the next season, then moving up to the Canterbury majors, then Babe Ruth League, high school, college, and all the way to the pros.

The Canterbury Yankees finished the season with five wins and nine losses, a much better record than they were expecting when Pump joined the team. His dad's appearance at Pump's first game was his first and last appearance for the season. Pump wondered if his dad never came back because Pump just struck out and walked. In other words, he didn't get a hit. People who don't understand base-ball might think it is all about hits. They don't appreciate all the ways a player can contribute to the team.

Pump wanted to know what his father had thought of the game. He wondered why his father had come in the first place and then why he never came again, but he didn't want to ask him. Pump figured the answer might just make him feel bad. Instead, he would forget about it. Clearly, his father had.

Once the Canterbury Little League season was over, Pump turned his undivided attention to the American League East where the Red Sox and the Yankees battled for first place. For three years he had been a Yankees fan but now something strange happened. Pump started to have misgivings.

Now that he had become a real baseball player and a better reader, Pump followed the Red Sox more closely and became more and more attached to his home team. He found he really liked the players and loved reading everything, good and bad, that was written about them. But as long as he was a Canterbury Yankee, Pump wasn't quite ready to let go of his old dream of playing for the big league Yankees.

So that summer and fall he read everything he saw about the Red Sox, who were living, breathing baseball players, while still talking every night to the poster of Babe Ruth that hung on his bedroom wall.

The Second Season

EARLY THE FOLLOWING APRIL, when the Major League Baseball season had just begun, Canterbury Little League was gearing up to start.

The phone rang in Pump Prout's house.

"Pump," his mom called, "Fred Namath is calling you."

Pump ran to his mother and carefully took the phone from her.

"Hello," he said, cautiously. Pump did not do much talking on the telephone.

"Pump, how's it going? This is Fred Namath. I'm calling about this season. We're going to start practice during April vacation. Will you be around?"

Pump gulped and waited for Fred Namath to continue.

"Pump, you there?"

"I'm here," Pump responded.

"Good. Just wanted to check in and make sure you were planning to play this season."

How could there be any question about that, wondered Pump.

"Are you coming to play? Can you make the practices during vacation? Sunday, Wednesday, Friday and Saturday?"

"Yup," said Pump, his heart thumping fast.

"Great. By the way, Coach Kennedy is moving up to help out in the majors this year. His oldest son plays on the Canterbury White Sox. So I'll be coaching. And we're going to have a new name. How does the 'Minutemen' sound?"

Silence from Pump.

"So let your folks know about practice in two weeks, first Sunday of vacation, one o'clock at the field."

Pump hung up slowly. His brother, Luke, noticed his strange expression.

"What's up, Pump?" Luke asked.

"You know what?" Pump said, his lip trembling. "Coach Kennedy is gone. He's going to coach the majors. And, you know what else?" This time his voice really shook. "We're not the Yankees anymore." Tears welled up in his eyes.

"Not the Yankees?" echoed Luke. "Well, what are you then?"

Pumps lips could barely form the words. "The Minutemen."

"The Minutemen?" Luke asked, his voice rising in disbelief.

Pump nodded and rubbed his eyes to try to stop crying.

"The Minutemen," Luke repeated and then snorted. "Yep. That's pretty bad."

Pump gasped a sob and turned away from Luke with his shoulders shaking.

"Hey, Pump, it's not so terrible. These coaches like to name their own teams. So if Coach Kennedy had the Yankees, Fred Namath will want to change it."

Pump looked miserably at Luke.

"It'll be O.K.," Luke said. "Don't you know who the minutemen were?"

Pump shook his head sorrowfully.

"I'll tell you," said Luke, a sixth grader, who was studying American history. "All the team names in the minors come from colonial America, the time when America belonged to England. The American colonists were called Yankees and they fought for independence from

England in the Revolutionary War. But the Americans weren't trained soldiers like the British were. They were just average guys. Farmers and stuff. Kind of like volunteer firemen. When the alarm went out, they had to drop everything and grab a gun. They had to be ready in a minute to fight. So they were called the minutemen."

"I don't want a Minutemen uniform," Pump groaned. "I don't want to play."

"It'll be O.K.," Luke tried to console him.

Pump looked doubtful. "What about Babe Ruth and the Yan...an...an...kees?" He couldn't hold back a sob.

"It's just a name, Pump. Someday, you'll be on the real Yankees. These Yankees weren't the same. It'll be better when you have pinstripes instead of a Mt. Zion T-shirt. Then it will really mean something. Besides, Babe Ruth wasn't always a Yankee. He started on the Red Sox. Don't forget that."

For the next few weeks, Pump was downcast. Second grade felt dull. It was hard for him to cheer up. Even throwing the ball against the wall behind the house felt different.

It took a long time for him to recover, but by the time spring vacation arrived, Pump was tingling with excitement. He couldn't fall asleep the night before his first practice. That felt terrible. He didn't want to be tired for his first practice. He started to worry about not being able to play if he was too tired and being left on the bench all season.

"Pump," his mother said as she peeked in to answer his call at 11 o'clock, "it doesn't matter when you fall asleep. You don't have school tomorrow. You'll just sleep late."

Greatly relieved, Pump fell right to sleep.

The first day of practice was cloudy and cold with a sharp wind that drove the chill right through Pump's jacket. Last year's Yankees were lingering at the edge of the field until a few collected. Then they lazily strolled toward the bench where their new coach was waiting for them. Fred Namath's form was familiar. He wore the same drab pants, windbreaker and blue baseball hat he had worn to their games as Yankees. But now Fred was the coach, the team was the Minutemen and Coach Kennedy was nowhere to be seen.

This was Pump's first real season in the minors. He was no longer a rookie. Neither were Jill Maloney and Penny Weiss, the two other rookies from last year. They were all veterans and all at practice.

Some of the team from last year had moved up to the majors. Everett Martin left first base, Ted Montgomery vacated the spot as strongest pitcher and Zach Tuttle opened up the catcher position as they moved up.

The new rookies were all looking nervous. Each rookie looked over every arriving player trying to figure out who else was new. Pump had never been in exactly that position, since he had joined the team in the middle of the season, but he could tell from their haunted eyes that the rookies were scared.

Pump was a veteran. He knew the ropes, he knew the drills. But he still felt his heart beat hard and fast and his mouth dry up. As soon as he saw Danny coming toward the field, Pump's jitters subsided. The boys walked toward each other. "Hey, Prout," Danny shouted in greeting, "aren't you ever gonna grow? I don't know if this team can carry you. Prout the Sprout."

Danny was pleased with his name for Pump and he smiled as he pulled his hand across the top of Pump's head making the hair stand up straight.

Pump looked with curiosity at the three new rookies. Willie Salvano was tiny. He came to practice in worn-out sneakers. His black hair was long and shaggy and he was really thin. Because Willy was so small, Pump figured that he must be just seven. Pump, himself, would be eight in less than a month and was a seasoned veteran.

Another new player was Josh Gerstein. Pump thought he looked really nervous. His brand new cleats only seemed to make him more nervous and he kept scuffing them in the mud while the team was waiting for the coach to get started. Josh's parents watched tensely from behind the fence. Pump could tell whose parents they were because they kept calling out to ask Joshua if he was cold or wanted his jacket or gloves. Josh pulled up his shoulders to try to hide his head as he ignored his parents.

The last rookie was Bones Bednarski who looked like he didn't want to be there. Pump could be pretty patient with kids who wanted to play no matter how bad they were. But kids who didn't want to play baseball? Well, why did they bother to come? Bones Bednarski's glum, empty-looking face told Pump all he needed to know. Bones wasn't excited about baseball.

Butch Flagan, Danny's dad and the new assistant coach, smiled at each player as he passed out red Minutemen shirts to the team. Pump felt he had to have number 16 again. Luckily, there was one, only Brian got it. Before Pump had to ask, Brian offered to trade the number 16 shirt for the number 2 that Pump had been given.

Fred Namath called the team over. He was standing on the pitcher's mound next to a thick blue disk on legs. The disk had a wide spout pointing toward home plate.

"Glad to see everyone here," the coach began. He nodded approvingly. "It's really satisfying to a coach to see everyone show up for the first practice. Now, one thing this team is going to do is practice. Like Coach Kennedy always said, 'What's it take to make a baseball player?'"

"Practice," shouted some of the veterans from last year.

"What else?"

"More practice!" yelled all the old teammates.

"Then what?"

"More practice!" the whole team howled as the rookies joined in.

Pump shouted with his teammates but he couldn't find the same excitement as last year. Fred Namath was different. He wasn't jolly and easy like Coach Kennedy. He was taut, sharp, and extra watchful. Pump felt sorry for the new rookies who'd never had Coach Kennedy. Pump also felt sorry for himself. He was excited to be playing baseball again, but he missed his old coach. Now he'd have to get used to this new coach, a new team name, new teammates, and that new contraption.

The teammates all chattered together until, one by one, they noticed that their coach was silent and they fell silent, themselves. Fred looked sharply at the team.

"Minutemen," he exclaimed, "tuck in those shirts. If this team is going to work like a team we have to start with the shirttails. When did you ever see a ballplayer, I mean a Major League player, with his shirt flopping out of his pants? You cannot be sloppy and serious. If the outside is in good shape, you'll play with better focus and be a better team.

"Let me tell you what I expect from my team. I expect shirts tucked in, caps with curved brims, everyone listening to what I say. I expect my instructions to be heard and followed.

"If there are any questions, I want them asked. Ignorance is not an excuse for messing up. Questions are important. But I don't want to hear the same question twice. I expect you to listen to the answer. I expect you to listen to each other's questions, too, so you won't have to ask the same question yourself."

Everyone was silent. After a pause, the new coach added, "You can call me Fred or Coach. That's the way I like it."

Fred smiled.

"At ease, Minutemen," he said with a chuckle. "You know, you can still have fun even with your shirt tucked in."

Fred showed the team how the blue contraption, a pitching machine, worked and practice was underway.

Fred showed them how to swing a bat. He showed them how to relax and let their weight and the weight of the bat swing through the ball. He demonstrated how to meet the ball out in front because if they waited for the ball to reach them, it was too late to swing.

Pump's family asked him about his practice when he got home. How could he know what he thought? He was still getting used to the fact that things were different from last year. He hated to admit it, but he was already starting to like the new name, the Minutemen. The coach had told the same story Luke had about how the men fighting for liberty had to be always ready, always prepared.

Pump remembered when the coach had said, "You've gotta know where the play is. If there's a runner on first and the batter hits the ball you want to put out the runner heading from first to second. You want to protect home so you want to do what you need to do to keep anyone from reaching home. A guy on third is closer to home than a guy on second. And a guy on second is closer to home than a guy on first. So, bases are loaded, one out, where's the play?"

The Minutemen, veterans and rookies, had looked at each other.

Pump had been thinking hard when Clyde Jones had answered, "You'd go for the guy running from third to make sure you got him before he made a run."

"Absolutely!" Fred exclaimed. "You got it! You can't always make it happen but it really helps to know where the play is *before* the action starts. You might have to make adjustments after the ball is hit but at least you have more of a chance of doing what you need to do.

"You have to be ready and then act fast," the coach had said firmly.

He'd added, "I don't ever want to see one of you Minutemen dreaming in the field or fooling around on the bench. You can't be a Minuteman if you're not prepared, alert, ready for anything."

Pump had vowed to himself he would be a Minuteman worthy of the name. He'd be awake, alert, ready for anything.

So when his family asked how practice was he shrugged and said O.K. while his heart beat fast, knowing the silent pledge he had made.

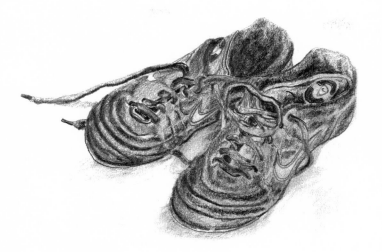

The Minutemen

PRACTICES WITH FRED NAMATH during April vacation amazed
Pump. He saw the group of players he'd known since last season work
together to become a real team. This coach brought a certain urgen-
cy to fielding and batting practice. Pump started to feel that how he
played mattered in a way it hadn't before and he wasn't sure if he liked
that. He still savored the feeling of elation he'd had the first time he'd
struck out. Pump got the feeling that Fred might not be quite as en-
thusiastic about good strikeouts as Coach Kennedy was. Fred shouted more. He didn't bellow like Coach Kennedy, but barked sharply
and unexpectedly. Pump did not want his coach to shout at him.

After the first practice, Fred announced their positions to the
team. When he came to Pump he said, "We need you on second this
year, Prout. You're really coming along with the plays. You're awake.
You can call what's coming." Pump felt flushed as Fred spoke.

Freddy Namath was a year and a half older than Pump, and he
had played baseball with his father since he could walk. Pump noticed at practices that Fred watched Freddy extra closely. He threw

balls to him just a little harder than to everyone else. He'd always go over things again, give Freddy another try if he missed and he always pushed Freddy to improve. Freddy never got a chance to just cool out. He worked all the time. But so did everyone. It was what the coach expected.

Freddy and Clyde Jones were the two best players on the team. This year Freddy, Clyde and Danny would be the pitchers. Clyde was going on 11 and would leave for the majors next season. He was taller than Freddy who was pretty big for his age. Clyde had grown a lot in the past year. Unlike some kids who can't find their balance as they grow, Clyde fit right into his new size. He moved smoothly and ran fast. Pump thought he fielded like a pro.

When Clyde pitched last season, he was either 'on' or he couldn't find the strike zone and walked everyone in sight. In the practices this year, Clyde showed a new assurance, a real awareness of where and how to throw the ball. His pitches were reliable enough now to allow him to go for speed, or to try for a curve ball. If he mastered that, he would be the only pitcher in the minors of Canterbury Little League to own a curve ball.

Fred Namath noticed all these things and barked even more frequently as Clyde, Freddy and the rest of the team improved. Fred Namath ended the last practice the way he always ended practices. He divided the team in half at home plate, six by six. Two runners, one from each group, started at home. They raced in opposite directions around the bases. One ran to first, then second and the other ran to third, then second. Freddy and Clyde started against each other.

"On your mark. Get set. Go!" shouted the coach.

The runners took off. Freddy ran like he was possessed, while Clyde sped around with an easy stride that outpaced Freddy. The two boys scraped past each other at second, but Clyde was ahead and widened his lead to arrive home a whole second before Freddy. Freddy kicked home plate and stomped off. The coach didn't even glance at him.

Next came Annie Maloney, looking tough with short hair, strong arms and legs and a determined face. Annie was at third base this year. She raced against Danny Flagan, first baseman and pitcher, who chugged along to a dead heat at home. Brian Kennedy, the catcher, easily beat the dreamy, gangly outfielder, Jeff Leonard, who galloped with a swaying motion like a giraffe.

Pump couldn't wait for his turn. He would show the coach how fast he was. He was paired against Penny Weiss, this season's center fielder. Though she was not a great hitter, she could sprint. Pump saw her round second ahead of him. He surged forward faster and just managed to beat her home. Both runners gulped air as they threw themselves against the backstop.

Jill Maloney, a thin girl who threw a ball like she was shoving a shotput into the air, came next. She'd be in right field. She was up against the littlest rookie, Willie Salvano. He was small, almost miniature, but compact and well-coordinated. In practice the only ball he could hit was a bunt. He rarely failed with his bunt, but couldn't connect at all with a full swing. Willie sped around the bases, taking two steps for every one of Jill's. Nevertheless, they tied at the plate.

Last came the two other rookies, Bones Bednarski and Josh Gerstein. Bones was round and slow. He had a generous belly that rolled slightly from side to side as he lumbered between bases. He'd almost have to hit it out of the park just to have enough time to get on base, Pump thought. Josh Gerstein had the look of a startled wild animal. His eyes darted here and there as he waited for the signal to start. His parents were clutching the top of the fence looking as nervous as Josh.

"Go!" came the signal.

The boys took off. Bones rolled around first while Josh, his head down, churned past third to second and on toward first. Bones pushed ahead harder until the two runners collided. Josh's head knocked against Bones's chest bowling him over, leaving them both sprawled on the ground. Bones lay flat on his back, breathless, the wind knocked out of him. Josh lay face down in the dust. His mother gave a shriek. Everyone seemed frozen. As Fred Namath ran over, the inert forms began to move. Bones heaved himself up while Josh rubbed his elbow.

The kids knew everyone was fine but Josh's mother railed at the coach, "They're just children. Can't you see how dangerous it is for you to send them *at* each other like that? Why, it's…it's… combat!" She was grabbing at Josh who was trying to wrench himself free.

Practice was over. Fred gathered the team together. The rookies looked worried.

"OK, Minutemen," he said in a low voice. The team gathered closer to him to hear what he said. "After all this practice you guys might feel like we're done. But the season is just beginning. Now is when push comes to shove. Now the learning really starts. You've done a great job but now comes the hard work. Sticking with it when things are going wrong. We'll learn from our mistakes and there'll be plenty of those. Lots of learning material.

"Last year we were the Yankees and had a 5 and 9 season. This year who knows what's in store for the Minutemen. Remember—this is a team of 12 players. No one kid is going to make or break the Minutemen. We all blow plays. We all can make saves. If every one of you stays awake and ready you're doing your part. Then it's all give-and-take, good breaks and bad breaks, repairing damage, holding strong when they're pushing us back. Backing each other up.

"Once a play is over, it's done with. Put it behind you and get ready for the next play. I don't want the Minutemen to live in the what-might-have-been past or in the what-might-be future. On the field you are in the here and now. Be there."

The Minutemen tried hard to listen. Coach Kennedy never laid it on like this. Fred Namath was talking like this was serious baseball. To Pump this felt as close to the real thing as he had ever been.

The coach handed out the season schedules. "We're playing the Colonists tomorrow. It'll be a great game if we keep playing like we're starting to. They've got a bunch of new blood so we can expect anything. Just be ready. Be at the field at five for warm-up.

"Let's hear it for the Minutemen," shouted the coach. Everyone cheered. Caps were tossed into the air and the practice was over.

"At the field by five o'clock tomorrow," Fred Namath shouted.

Pump's mother was waiting to drive him home.

"Hey, Pump," she greeted him. They both noticed little Willie Salvano hanging behind the others. He was the only one who didn't have cleats yet. Pump's mother called to him, "Say, Willie, we've got some great cleats Pump outgrew after the summer. Can you use them? Why doesn't Pump bring them for you to try on?"

"Sure," Willie said.

"Maybe we'll wait and talk to your mom." Relief flooded Willie's face. Then Pump's mother added, "Why don't you two play some more while we wait." Pump couldn't believe his mom was letting him hang out while it was getting dark. She was always in a rush. He and Willie borrowed a ball from Fred Namath who was finishing packing up the pitching machine. They threw the ball back and forth until it was too dark to see.

"My mom's coming," Willie assured them. "It's just lots of the time she comes late."

"We'll wait," Pump's mom said. She asked Willie about his family while they sat in her car and shared the snack she'd brought for Pump. Willie's parents were divorced. In fact, he hardly ever saw his father. Willie loved baseball so his mom let him play but didn't know much about it, herself.

Finally, Willie's mother arrived. She seemed puzzled to find the field deserted. Willie scrambled out of the car and ran to her.

"Yes," she told Pump's mother, "cleats would be great for Willie. I didn't realize he was supposed to have them. Seems there's always one more thing."

Pump went home to get ready for the season opener the next day.

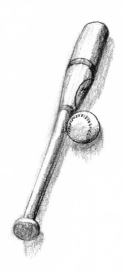

Opening Day

RAIN WAS COMING DOWN the morning of the first game. Pump's heart sank. It had already been hard enough to get to sleep the night before. He couldn't bear the thought of the opening game being postponed. He'd have to go through all those hours of first-game jitters all over again. Pump dragged himself to school, sloshing through puddles. All morning he could pay attention to nothing but the sky. He kept counting the hours.

If it stops raining now, he thought at 11, the field will have six hours to dry and we can play. At 11:30 he thought, if it stops raining *now*, the field'll have five and a half hours to dry.

During lunch at 12, the rain was lightening up and by 12:30 recess it had stopped. Pump went outside with his class, but like a lone old farmer, he paced the yard and surveyed the damage to the land. Pump noted the depth of the puddles and calculated the likelihood of the baseball fields drying enough to be played on.

The sky never cleared which kept Pump tense with uncertainty but it didn't rain again. When it was finally time to set out for the field, the ground was almost dry but the air was damp and chilly.

Pump's mother made him wear a turtleneck under his Minutemen t-shirt. He protested but, in fact, was glad for the extra layer no matter how unprofessional he felt he looked.

Pump arrived early at the field where he saw his friend, Ken Ames and Ken's brother, Charles. The Ameses lived near Pump. They were on the Muskets, the team that won their division of the league the season before. The Ames brothers were pretty good baseball players and never let anyone forget it. Charles was a grade ahead of his brother, Ken, and Pump. Charles praised himself all the time. "Yeah, I'm the greatest. Yeah, yeah, I'm just too good." In fact both brothers showed off all the time. They were nice to Pump but he still felt upset by their bragging. It made it hard to be friends with them.

"Hey there, Pump," Ken called to him.

"Hey," Pump said.

"Who're you playing today?"

"The Colonists," Pump said.

"They were lousy last year," Ken said. "We blew them away. I hit a home run off their best pitcher."

Charles elbowed Ken out of the way and stood right in front of Pump. "I hit an out-of-the-park homer that won the game. Ken just came in on errors."

"Aren't you guys playing?" Pump asked, though he had already memorized the schedule for all the teams.

"Take a guess," Charles sneered. "If we were playing I think we'd be dressed a little different. Like in our uniforms."

Ken interrupted, "We play the Stripes tomorrow. We'll kick their butt."

Pump wished he could feel so confident. Did these boys really know more about this game than he did? He gave up some of his dreams about this first game just talking to them.

Pump loved the sound of his cleats scraping the sidewalk as he trotted over to join his team starting to warm up on the other diamond. He carried his pair of cleats from last season. Willie wasn't at the field yet so Pump dropped the shoes on the bench. The Minutemen called greetings to each other. Pump knew he was a veteran, but he felt as anxious as the rookies looked. Back with his own team, Pump felt his nervousness return, along with the excitement and the dreams. It helped calm his nerves to imagine himself hitting the ball, making great catches and straight, sure throws.

The coaches of both teams arrived and started raking the base paths to get rid of the last puddles. The Colonists had infield practice first while the Minutemen tossed the ball around in the outfield. When they switched, Pump felt himself starting to get his focus. He took his position halfway between first and second and felt his throws become cleaner.

The Colonists were the home team so the Minutemen were up first. Fred Namath, in contrast to his tenseness at practices, seemed cool and calm, even gentle. His voice was low and direct which helped his tight, anxious team loosen up. Pump was glad to see that in tough times, his coach seemed a lot calmer. Maybe Fred wouldn't be so bad after all.

The coach called out the batting order, "Danny Flagan will lead off. Then comes Clyde Jones, Freddy Namath, Pump Prout, Annie Maloney, Brian Kennedy, Penny Weiss, Jeff Leonard, Jill Maloney and Josh Gerstein as D.H. Willie and Bones, you take the bench. Willie, you'll go in for the third and fourth innings and Bones, the last two."

"Whoa," whispered Pump. He was batting clean up. That must mean the coach really thought Pump could hit. Pump started to worry that he might disappoint his coach. But if his coach put him at clean-up…. Pump knew Fred Namath knew everything about baseball and he knew Fred would never have a kid batting fourth who didn't have a prayer of hitting the ball.

Pump shot a quick look at the parents lining the fence. No sign of his father, which was both a relief and a disappointment. He turned around and sat down on the bench.

"Batter up," growled the umpire who had just scraped some mud off home plate.

Danny swung his bat twice, stared the pitcher straight in the eye and watched the first pitch sail by, way outside. The pitcher twitched his shoulders and wound up for the next pitch. This one was right across the plate, slow and direct. Danny threw his weight at it and missed completely.

Danny swung again at the next pitch, which was outside again but within reach. He cracked the ball and went charging ahead toward first base. The ball was a hard grounder that hit the pitcher right in the shins. By the time the ball was located and thrown, Danny was safe on first. The Minutemen cheered. The ice was broken. Pump could breathe again.

Next up was Clyde. He had changed since last year. First of all, he'd grown. Now he was the tallest guy on the team. He seemed more confident in the way he walked to the plate, in the way he handled the bat. Pump tried to figure it out as he watched Clyde wait for the first pitch. Clyde wasn't rushing like he used to. He could wait. Last year, he would've been slicing the air with practice swings. Now he was taking a few easy strokes with the bat before settling down to wait.

The Colonists' pitcher threw a wobbly pitch that Clyde let go by. The umpire called it a strike. The Minutemen shouted in protest. Clyde just repeated his few easy swings to prepare for the next pitch. Last year he would've been all wound up and angry about the bad call. He would have swung wildly at the next pitch without even seeing the ball, trying to prove that the umpire had been wrong. But wild swings don't prove anything except that you're upset, Pump realized as he watched Clyde. Something had really changed for him.

Clyde let the next pitch go. It was too high even for this ump to call a strike. The next pitch came slow, heading straight for the plate. Clyde didn't hesitate. He leaned into his swing, caught the ball dead center and sent it soaring over the heads of the infield, over the left fielder, all the way to the fence. The ball was falling too fast to make it over the fence, but the fielders had to run and scramble to get it. Once they got it, they weren't sure what to do with it. After all, this was the first game of the season. Clyde was heading all the way around the bases for an inside-the-park home run. Danny scored, then Clyde behind him. The Minutemen were shouting and dancing. Two runs and no outs with Freddy up.

The Colonists were restless in the field. Pump could feel their uneasiness as he stepped into the on-deck circle while Freddy moved to the plate. The pitcher just couldn't find the plate. He held onto the ball so long that his throws were looping to the ground before they reached the plate. The Colonists' coach shouted, "Throw hard. Throw to the glove, Bobby," trying to lead his pitcher back into the game.

Plop. The ball hit the dirt for ball four. Freddy loped to first and Pump was up.

A new season, new opportunities, new risks. Pump's heart was beating fast. He swallowed hard and moved his tongue around trying to get his mouth wet again. He scuffed his cleat next to the plate to dig a little hole to support his foot. Pump had grown and so had his strike zone. He wasn't going to baffle pitchers the way he had the season before. The first pitch was high enough not to tempt Pump to swing. Ball one. The pitcher eyed Pump carefully, then threw the ball. Pump felt his bat start into motion as if the bat had decided it was the moment to swing. It was. Pump's swing shot the ball right past the pitcher, past the second baseman. He sped to first base aware that Freddy was moving on to third.

The Minutemen's assistant coach, Butch Flagan, Danny's father, held up his hands as Pump approached first to warn him to stop. Freddy made it to third. The two base runners grinned at each other across the infield as their teammates cheered.

Annie Maloney followed Pump. With a steady eye and sturdy swing she brought Freddy and Pump both home with a heavy line drive right down the middle that scared the pitcher and sent the outfield into crazy maneuvers trying to get their hands on the ball and then heave it to some useful spot in the infield. Annie pulled up at third but Fred Namath, swinging his arm in a circle, sent her home. She took off again but the catcher had enough time to retrieve an overthrow and reach out to touch the plate just before Annie blasted onto it.

"You're out," yelled the catcher. But Annie had played more baseball than the Colonists' catcher.

"You never tagged me," she shouted. "I'm safe."

"You're out!" the catcher screeched. "I touched the plate way before you got there."

"So what?" Annie smirked. "I wasn't forced to run. You have to tag me."

"That's right, son," the umpire agreed. "The run scores."

The Colonists' coach started to defend his catcher but realized it was hopeless. The Colonists' pitcher angrily threw down his glove.

Incredible. Pump couldn't believe it. Another home run. The Minutemen had five runs in the top of the first and no outs yet.

Brian Kennedy settled himself at the plate. The pitcher had been throwing the ball to his infielders in an effort to regain his composure. Now he looked Brian over. Brian was pretty small and didn't look very threatening. He wasn't. His bat came under the third pitch sending the ball in a tiny arc before it landed between the plate and the mound and rolled toward the pitcher who scooped it up and threw to first. One out. Penny Weiss took the plate and swung at everything that came in her general direction. Three slow swings without a thought about whether or not the pitch was good brought the second out.

Jeff Leonard ambled to the plate. He was always an unknown in the lineup. His long limbs were not quite under his own control but sometimes his arms could swing the bat in a wide sweep that connected with the ball to send it arching over the heads of the fielders. But only sometimes.

This time Jeff 's bat swooped and dove and three times a strike was called. The side was retired.

What a sweet game this is, thought Pump as he grabbed his glove and trotted out to take his position. Here it was, bottom of the first, and the Minutemen already had five runs with two homers. Little League homers, for sure, but still homers. As Pump jogged past the mound he heard Fred Namath tell Clyde, "Those pitches need to be good ones. You gotta throw strikes."

Clyde pressed his lips together and nodded. For the first time that afternoon Pump felt chilly and shivered. If someone told him he had to throw strikes he'd be more likely to throw up than to throw strikes, but Clyde looked like he could throw anything he wanted to. That's why he was pitching. Pump became aware of the cloudy afternoon and ran faster to his post. He thumped his glove and caught the ball

Brian threw him from the plate. Pump tossed the ball to Danny Flag-an at first who stuck his arm under his right leg to make the catch like a clown would. That cheered up Pump and he was ready for action.

First up for the Colonists was a big, thick-necked boy who blasted the bat through the air as he took his warm-up swings. Pump looked for a signal from the coach to move back or be ready for something dangerous but Fred just stood there with his arms folded across his chest. Pump swallowed hard. Clyde wound up and sent the ball di-rectly over the plate. The big boy's bat sailed around, inches above the ball. Strike one was followed by strikes two and three. Strikeout number one was followed by strikeouts two and three and the inning was over.

Pump moved in a daze to the bench. He knew he had seen some-thing special. The kind of pitching that Clyde had just produced was not the usual Little League kind of pitching. Not in the Canterbury minor league, anyway. Pump felt grateful that Clyde was on his team. Not just because it meant the possibility of great things for the Min-utemen, but because the last thing Pump wanted was to have to face a pitcher of Clyde's caliber.

The first inning provided the blueprint for the rest of the game. The Minutemen at the top of the lineup kept hitting, while the guys at the bottom kept striking out. Jeff Leonard drifted through the game, waving his bat in some astonishing loops until, in the top of the fourth, and—as it turned out—last, inning, his bat made a surprising swirl that happened to meet the ball and send it soaring for the only out-of-the-park home run of the game.

By the end of the third inning, the Colonists had gone through their three pitchers. They struggled along through the top of the fourth bringing in their catcher to pitch. By the time the Minutemen had batted through their lineup, the score was 20-2.

As he headed to his position at second base, Pump heard the words "mercy rule" uttered by the watching parents. In Canterbury Little League the mercy rule meant that after the end of the fourth in-ning the umpire calls the game if the difference between the scores is 12 runs or more. In the bottom of the fourth, the Minutemen replaced Clyde with Freddy Namath, who pitched faster but more erratically and had given up a lot of walks but only two runs. The score was 20-4. The Minutemen seemed unstoppable. The coach of the Colonists consulted with Fred and the umpire. The umpire held up his hand and announced that the mercy rule was invoked. The game was over.

The Colonists and the Minutemen lined up and filed past each other for the symbolic handshake. As Pump let his right hand slide from hand to hand of the Colonists, he considered how different this year felt from last. A lot more like real baseball.

The outcome of this opening game was not what Pump had expected. Practically a shutout. The Yankees never came close to anything like that last year. Pump himself had accomplished more in this one game than he'd done his entire first season. He had just finished a game without making one error. He smiled at the thought. He had thrown out three players at first base. He had not struck out once.

His new position as second baseman was right in the thick of the action. Last season, right field had felt so scary. There was always so much time to worry and get nervous about what was possibly about to happen. Then, when something did happen, it was always a surprise. A lot of the action in right field came wobbling on the ground, those balls that escaped capture in the infield but ran out of steam in the bumpy grass on the way to the outfield. Those wobblers with their unpredictable bounces and irregular paths were hard to field. Then there were the balls hit high in the air. The worst part about those was that they moved so slowly. All eyes turned to the fielder as he waited for the ball to come down. For an uncertain glove, the pressure was intense.

After the game the Minutemen slapped each other on the back, gave each other high fives and then just poked and punched at each other in giddy joy. The parents were grinning. Some praised the good moves of the other parents' kids and some praised the good moves of their own. Pump's mother gave him a hug and Luke punched his shoulder. His father had not come.

The only frowns belonged to Bones Bednarski's mother who was arguing with Fred Namath.

"Whaddya mean 'mercy rule?'" Bone's mother growled. "I go to all the trouble of getting him out here so he can play just two measly innings, right? Because he's a rookie, you said, right? And now he doesn't even get two seconds out there, because of this, this mercy rule. You never said anything about that. You said rookies were guaranteed—You hear that?—You said *guaranteed*—two innings in the game."

Fred stared out into space somewhere above and behind Mrs. Bednarski's head. She looked disgusted, turned on her heels and walked away.

The game had ended early so the hungry Minutemen, in one voice, shouted for Pirelli's Pizza. Pirelli's sponsored the Muskets, the team the Ames brothers were on. No one ever cared whose sponsors they were except on the days that a team lost to the Muskets. It was understood among Canterbury Little Leaguers that no one ate a piece of Pirelli's pizza if their team lost to the Muskets. After any other game, it was great to go to Pirelli's, to support a sponsor of Little League. It was also great because if Mr. Pirelli, himself, was there, he often gave out packages of cookies for free. The pizza was especially delicious if the hungry team had just beaten the Muskets, but that didn't happen too often. After all, the Muskets had been the West Canterbury champions last year.

But, Pump thought, that was *last* year.

Between Games

AT SCHOOL THE NEXT DAY, Pump tried to look casual as he hung his jacket in his locker. He felt so victorious he wondered if people could tell by looking at him that he had become part of baseball history. Well, his own baseball history, at least. Pump could just hear his father say, "Don't confuse being pumped up with being puffed up." He wouldn't. After all, his name wasn't Pump for nothing.

Ken Ames sauntered over to Pump. He tried to look as if he just happened to be there, but Pump could tell he had been lying in wait to pounce the minute Pump arrived.

"T'sup?" the boys greeted each other.

"Not much. Did you play yesterday?" Ken asked.

"You know I did," Pump replied. "You saw me there."

"How'd you do?"

"You playing the Stripes this afternoon?" Pump asked without answering Ken.

"Yep," Ken said. "We'll kick butt."

"Well, good luck," Pump said as he moved past Ken on his way to their classroom.

"What about your game? How'd it go?"

"Great," said Pump.

"You won? What was the score? How'd *you* do?"

"Mercy rule," Pump mumbled because he really wanted to shout it out. "20-4. Four innings." He swallowed. "Clyde Jones pitched out of his mind."

Ken's eyes grew wide. "Maybe you could come to our game," he said almost wistfully.

"Maybe," Pump said in his normal voice. "Let's see what we have for homework."

"OK," Ken said. "But how'd *you* do?"

"All right," Pump said. "I didn't strike out once."

Pump didn't like anyone to see that he felt good about what he'd done. He knew what he felt like when other kids bragged about themselves. But he wondered if there wasn't a difference between bragging about yourself and feeling proud of yourself.

At recess, Pump passed Clyde Jones in the playground. Pump felt his throat grow tight. He managed to produce a crooked smile. Clyde moved toward Pump and clapped him on the shoulder.

"Pump, my man, slap me five."

Pump slapped Clyde's hand and his smile relaxed. Only if Clyde were Babe Ruth would Pump have been more nervous.

"See ya around, Prout," Clyde smiled. Pump stared after him.

When Pump got home from school that afternoon he sat down right away to get his homework done. He never had much homework since homework in second grade was just supposed to get kids ready for doing real homework in third grade. It seemed to Pump that he was always having to do the imitation, like Farm League, always having to wait for the real thing.

Usually Pump found a way to make homework the last thing he did before bed, but today he wanted to head back to the baseball field as soon as he could. It dawned on him that by getting his homework done early he could do other things. That sounded like something his mother might have said to him and he really didn't want to give in to it. But baseball was more important than anything.

Luke wandered into the kitchen where Pump was bent over his homework.

"Do my eyes deceive me?" Luke gave a low whistle. "Hey, Pumple, what's up? Homework? At 3:30 in the afternoon? Has the sky fallen? I bet you're up to no good."

Pump looked up at his brother. "Shut up," he said slowly and clearly.

Luke narrowed his eyes.

"Oooo, touchy, touchy," Luke sneered and plucked off the Canterbury baseball cap that Pump was wearing. "No hats at the table," chanted Luke.

Pump dove for the hat which Luke held just out of reach. Pump lunged again and again while Luke dangled the hat in front of him, pulling it out of reach each time Pump leaped for it. Luke played Pump like a big fish flopping on a line. They both stopped, out of breath and panting, with Luke still in possession of the hat.

Pump waited until he thought Luke wasn't ready, then grabbed for his hat. His hands closed on the brim but Luke didn't let go and both boys pulled on the hat.

"Let go. Give me my hat," Pump growled.

Luke tried to jerk the hat away from Pump but Pump hung on like a puppy and was dragged around the kitchen as Luke tried to shake him off. A ripping sound stopped the boys short. Luke had held onto the plastic band on the back of the hat that adjusted the size. In the skirmish the plastic band broke and started to tear away from the hat. Luke let go and Pump stood with his mouth open staring at the broken hat dangling from his hand.

"My hat!" Pump wailed. "You wrecked my hat!"

Pump threw himself on Luke and pummeled him with his fists.

"Hold on there, Pump," Luke said as he pulled away from his rampaging brother. "Quit it. Someone's going to get hurt and it won't be me."

"It won't be me, either," Pump yelled as he flailed at Luke.

Luke grabbed Pump's churning fists and pinned Pump's arms around him so he couldn't move.

"Let me go," Pump cried. He saw the hat lying on the floor where it had fallen. He started to cry.

"Don't cry, Pump-O," Luke said. He looked close to tears himself. "Come on, Pump. Let's see if we can fix it. I really am sorry."

"Why'd you do it, then?" Pump sniffed.

"I didn't mean to tear it. I was just fooling around."

"Fred Namath'll kill me," Pump moaned. "He'll tell me I can't be on the team. He'll tell me I'm abusing the uniform and don't have a right to wear it. And maybe he'll be right." Pump's eyes welled up with tears again.

"Bro, if he said anything like that, he wouldn't deserve to coach anybody," Luke said. "I sure wouldn't want to play for a coach who said something like that."

Pump sniffed, "Well, he never said that. I was just thinking what if...." Pump was a little afraid of Fred Namath but he was surprised to find himself so quick to defend his coach, even from his own doubts.

'Well," said Luke, "you know what I think?"

"What?" Pump asked.

"I think we should try to fix your hat."

Luke got some black electrical tape from the tool box in the basement and wound it around the broken band until the band was stuck to the hat again. He measured the cap to fit Pump's head and wound tape around the broken plastic to hold the cap at the right size. From the front the cap looked fine and Pump smiled at his brother who could fix anything if he had to. Pump pulled the hat on and found that it felt rough where the tape was. Not only was Pump a real veteran, he had a scarred hat to prove it.

Pump quickly finished what was left of his homework. It was about 4:30 and the games would start at 5:30 with warm-up at 5:00.

"Luke," Pump asked, "what do you think I should do? I told Ken Ames that I'd try to come to his game today. Mom isn't home yet and I don't know if she'd say it's all right."

"Don't worry, Pump. You know the Ameses aren't the only guys with a game today. I have one, too. I think Mom's coming to watch."

Pump had forgotten about Luke's game. Luke was in his last year of the majors and was the Canterbury Dodgers' best pitcher.

"Wow, you're right," Pump breathed. How could he have forgotten? "It's your first game." Pump wondered if Luke ever felt nervous like Pump did.

"Do you think Dad'll come?" Pump asked.

Luke, on his way to his room, turned around sharply.

"Are you kidding?" he laughed. "Dad never comes. And if he did he'd just say, after my first bad pitch, 'Well, that's it for the Dodgers and he'd go home."

Luke went off to put on his uniform.

Pump realized he had never mentioned to Luke the day their dad had shown up at his game last season. It was almost as if Pump had seen a ghost, a figure who wasn't really there. There was something else that had kept Pump from telling Luke, some feeling that it wasn't fair that their dad, who had never seen one, not one, of Luke's games, suddenly showed up for Pump's first real game. So Pump had put it out of his mind, as if it had never happened. There certainly was no sign of their dad being even remotely interested in this new season. Pump shoved that thought as far away as he could and brought himself back to the present.

Pump loved the feeling he had as he anticipated watching someone else's game. Nothing depended on him. He could just hang out. He could figure out where the next play was but he didn't have to do anything about it.

While Pump wrote a note telling his mother where he was going, Luke clomped back into the kitchen in his cleats. He was ready to play. Pump admired his brother and was happy to ride his bike with Luke to the field. That was something new, too. Pump thought maybe he was ready to ride his bike alone to his baseball games. As he pedaled behind Luke, he admired his hat which dangled from his handle bars.. Pump had bent down the brim on each side to form just the right curve and now the hat had been genuinely wounded. What a great hat!

There were three baseball fields behind Pump's school. One of the minor-league fields shared an outfield fence with the major-league field where Luke's team, the Dodgers, was playing. The other minor-league field had no fence behind left field. Instead, there was a hazy line chalked at the back of the outfield. If a ball rolled over that line it became a ground-rule double but if it sailed cleanly over the line before landing it was considered an out-of-the-park home run. The ground-rule double prevented a home run coming in while the fielders chased down the ball but it meant play had to stop and the runners could only advance two bases.

When the brothers arrived at the fields, Luke sauntered over to the field where his team was warming up. Pump noticed how Luke's teammates stopped their warm-up for a split second to greet him. That's what happened when you were important. Everyone felt good when you showed up. Everyone knew you'd get the job done. Pump locked up his bike and trotted over to watch the Muskets and the Stripes warm up. Ken Ames saw Pump right away and gave him a wave. When Charles saw him he raised two fingers to his cap in a little salute.

As Pump watched the teams tossing the ball around he heard the slow interrupted staccato of a basketball being dribbled on the asphalt court next to the field. He saw Clyde Jones moving in a leisurely walk, dribbling the ball and taking shots from close range. As Pump watched Clyde, he felt his hat get brushed off his head. He turned quickly to find Danny Flagan grinning at him and holding Pump's hat.

"Missing something?" Danny laughed and handed the hat back to Pump. "What's the scoop? Who's going to take this one?" Danny paused for a second and then added, "I guess the real question is 'Who are we for?'"

Pump shrugged.

Danny continued, "Well, if we like the underdog, then we're for the Stripes. But if we want to go with a winner, we gotta take the Muskets. Only I'm sick and tired of them winning all the time. And look at them, those two Ames brothers."

Pump and Danny both watched while Charles warmed up his pitches and swore at his brother who was catching for him.

"Hold the glove up, you moron. I can't pitch if you don't give me a target."

The kneeling catcher shifted his carapace of padding and held up his glove behind the plate. The pitch was hard, fast and so low it smashed into the dirt in front of the catcher's shoes.

"Hold the glove *up*. If you hold it in the dirt my pitches'll go in the dirt, you retard."

Pump and Danny looked at each other.

"Uh-oh, here they go," Danny said. "Ready. Ames. Fire!" He paused, then added, "I think we're for the Stripes today, Pump, don't you?"

"No question," answered Brian Kennedy who had come up next to them.

The three Minutemen nodded agreement. The steady report of the bouncing basketball kept time behind them. Pump felt confused. He wanted to be for Ken, but it wasn't easy. Charles was always nice to Pump, but he could be so mean to Ken. Pump thought that if you knew what it felt like when someone was mean to you or bragged to you, you'd be really careful never to be that way to anyone else. Only Ken, who should have known better than anyone how lousy it felt to hear someone brag all the time, bragged just as much to everyone else. At least he was never mean to anyone. He just bragged, but in a way that made Pump feel small.

There was also a part of Pump that wanted to prove that he was as good at baseball as, and maybe even better than, the bragging Ameses. That part of Pump wanted the Muskets to lose every game. But they never did.

The teams were coming in for their pregame huddle on each of the three fields. Pump strained to see Luke on the distant major-league field where the Dodgers were up first and the Giants were in the field. As Pump looked, the clack of cleats scraped on the asphalt walk behind him. He turned to find Willie Salvano all dressed in his uniform and wearing Pump's old cleats.

The three Minutemen stared curiously at Willie.

"Am I late?" panted Willie.

"For what?" Brian asked.

"For the game," Willie said.

"What game?" the three others said in unison.

"The game!" Willie exclaimed while a look of doubt clouded his face. "You guys aren't in your uniforms. How come?"

"We're not playing. We played yesterday," Danny said.

Willie's lips started to tremble. "Don't we play every day?"

"Every day? Don't I wish," sighed Pump.

"Every day? It'd kill me," groaned Brian.

"Don't worry," Danny said. "We only play twice a week."

"No game?" Willie sniffed.

"No game." Danny confirmed. "But look, we've got a schedule. If you don't have one we'll get you one. Now, let's see, our next game is tomorrow."

"We play the Stars," Pump chimed in.

"So why are you guys here today?" Willie asked.

"We're just chillin'," Danny explained.

"Oh. Me, too," Willie said.

The games started on all three fields. Brian, Danny, Willie and Pump strolled from one field to the other. At the major's field, Luke was the starting pitcher for the Dodgers. He started off the season with some nervous pitches that walked the first batter. Pump could see Luke's face relax as soon as the fourth ball was called. The worst was over and now he could settle down.

Pump loved watching his brother pitch when Luke was relaxed. Then it didn't matter what happened. If he wasn't nervous, Luke could always move on after anything went wrong, a bad pitch, a home run, even a pitch hitting the batter. If Luke wasn't nervous, he didn't feel he had to be perfect. If he was anxious, any mistake left him feeling that he couldn't do anything right. When Luke felt like that, Pump knew he had to stay out of the way. Now Luke was at ease and pitching great.

Pump saw his mother hanging out with the other parents. He caught her eye and she waved to him. He waved back.

With the Dodgers ahead, 3-1, Pump and his teammates moved on to the game between the Patriots and the Pilgrims. The pitching was so much slower in the minors. The whole game was so much slower. There were plenty of walks and errors. Even the strikes were slow. It took the catcher forever to get the ball back to the pitcher. The pace made it hard for the outfielders to stay focused. The right fielder held his glove up to his nose and inhaled deeply the smell of leather and neat's-foot oil. Pump loved that smell, too.

The Patriots and the Pilgrims were both having a hard time in the field and at bat so they were still in the first inning when Luke's team was in the third. Slow as the game was, Pump loved watching. He would spot where the play should be and see if the players followed his game plan.

The boys spent the whole second inning at that game before they walked back to the Muskets and the Stripes. Charles Ames was on the mound in the bottom of the third inning. Willie asked one of the Stripes on the bench what the score was.

"Six, them; two, us," the Stripe replied. Then he clapped and shouted, "Way to look 'em over, Skip. Make him give you one you can swing at."

Charles glowered at the Stripes' bench. He wound up and threw another ball high and outside beyond the reach of the catcher's glove. The batter flipped his bat aside and loped to first.

Charles threw his glove on the ground and stamped his foot.

"Catch the ball, you idiot," he shouted at his brother.

A muffled voice came from behind the catcher's mask.

"Yeow," Danny yelped. "Look at that. Their coach doesn't say a word to him."

"Neither does the umpire," Pump said.

"I bet Fred would have something to say," Brian said. "Boy, we'd be smithereens if we pulled something like that."

The four Minutemen all nodded seriously.

The sound of a basketball as it spanked the pavement right behind them startled the boys. Clyde had come over to take a closer look at the game.

"Hey," Clyde greeted them.

"Hey," they chorused.

The five boys watched Charles Ames hurl a fastball that was the third strike of the third out. The side was retired.

Ken Ames led off the inning. He signaled a greeting to Pump and sauntered up to the plate. He tapped the tip of his bat on the far side of the plate, fixed his eyes on the pitcher and swung the bat a few times.

The pitcher turned his back on the batter for a second, lowered his head and ground the ball into his glove. Then he was ready. He faced the plate and delivered a slow, straight pitch that sailed right over the plate at least half a second after Ken had thrown his weight into a big swing that caught air. The boys standing right behind the backstop could see Ken flush. He took a few steady swings, then watched the next pitch pass on the outside.

"One and one," Danny said. "Let's see what this big boy's going to do."

"One and two," Brian said as Ken took a mighty swing that sent the ball sailing foul.

The Stripes' pitcher was tall and thin. His arms stuck out from the floppy sleeves of his uniform. His pitching was reliable and pretty strong. No one could count on a walk from him. Pump wondered if Ken ever hoped for a walk, like he, himself, sometimes did.

The next pitch looked good but Ken didn't go for it. The umpire called it low.

"Two and two," Pump counted.

The pitcher took an extra second to adjust his stance, then wound up and hurled the fastest ball he'd thrown in the game. Ken swung with all his might and knocked a hard drive over the third base line. Foul ball.

"Two and three," Willie said proudly.

"Two and two," Danny corrected. "A foul ball after two strikes doesn't count."

"You mean you can just keep hitting as many foul balls as you want?" Willie asked doubtfully.

"Yep," replied Danny, "you can just keep hitting them."

"Wow!" exclaimed Willie. "I wonder why people don't just do it all the time. I would, if I could hit that far."

Pump's eyes met Clyde's over Willy's head and they grinned at each other. Danny and Brian both laughed out loud and then stopped short.

A looping pitch landed in front of the plate.

"Full count," said Brian hoarsely.

Pump could feel the tension he saw on the faces of the pitcher, the batter and his teammates. Now that it was a full count, Pump started to hope Ken would get a hit, even a big one. Before the full count he had not felt so generous. Pump had even wanted his friend to strike out, to do something that might stop his bragging. But now that feeling was gone. He saw Ken sweating this one, which meant it wasn't all so easy for him after all.

The next pitch was heading straight over the plate. Ken swung the bat and knocked the ball high in the air arching down to drop into the right fielder's open glove. The glove never closed and the ball bounced out again. Ken started to run fast. He rounded first as the fielder was recovering the ball which he threw to first right after Ken had passed the base. The throw to first wildly missed the first baseman who scrambled to retrieve the ball while Ken passed second. Finally in possession of the ball, the first baseman saw Ken still running and flung the ball in the general direction of third base. The ball plopped down on the mound where the pitcher ran and grabbed it saving the hit from becoming a home run. Ken had to pull up at third.

A triple. That was a sort of compromise between a home run for Ken and a strikeout against him. Pump was relieved that Ken had a good hit and he was also relieved that he hadn't hit a home run. If Ken bragged about his triple, Pump would know that it wasn't a home run, and he would know that Ken knew he knew. That would be enough. Pump waved to Ken on third base and Ken hitched up his pants and dusted himself off even though he hadn't even had to slide.

Pump thought about how much he loved to practice sliding. He slid all the time. On grass, on dirt, even on the wood floor at home. He had an urge to slide right then and started to run before sliding into an imaginary plate on the grass between the baseball field and the basketball court.

"You're safe!" Clyde made the call as he lazily took a shot that slipped off the rim without scoring. Pump got up, his left pant leg smudged green and trotted over to Clyde.

"You're a slider, huh?" Clyde laughed.

Pump waited to feel embarrassed but he didn't. He only felt shy. He nodded.

"Me, too," Clyde said. "Sliding is one of my favorite things about this game."

"Yeah?" Pump said.

Clyde nodded. He pushed a chest pass to Pump. The force of the ball startled Pump for a second but he took the cue and sent the ball back to Clyde. Pump trotted onto the basketball court where Clyde bounce-passed him the ball, then ran down the court so Pump could pass the ball back. Pump tried to make a long throw to Clyde. The ball only made it about half-way, but Clyde ran up, grabbed the ball on the bounce and dribbled down to shoot and almost sink it. Pump had trotted down the court to stay in the game, but Clyde made his own rebound, twirled and tried a hook shot. Pump watched in admiration.

"See how you move a basketball around?" Clyde said. "A baseball is more like a musket ball. That's how I think about it." He smiled. "A single loader. A basketball is different. Repeat firing. You can always get another try. Grab the rebound or dribble yourself out of trouble."

Clyde shot, missed and grabbed the rebound, dribbled around Pump, faked a toss to him, then drove back to the basket and tried again. The ball swished through the net without grazing the backboard.

"Wow," said Pump.

Clyde laughed and bounced the ball to Pump.

"I'm on you," Clyde said as he closed in on Pump. "Try to get past me."

Pump stood for a second holding the ball loosely. Clyde cleanly knocked the ball out of Pump's hands.

"You can't just stand there, Mr. P., my man. You gotta move. Here," he said as he tossed Pump the ball again, "go for it. Make me work."

This time Pump started to move and dribbled the ball trying not to let Clyde's nearness or moving arms distract him. Pump was so intent on keeping the ball moving that he lost track of the basket and ran out of bounds off the end of the court.

"I'll throw the ball in," Clyde said and waved Pump onto the court. "Get ready."

Clyde tossed the ball to Pump. This time, instead of guarding him, Clyde set himself in position to receive a pass. Pump passed, Clyde moved the ball down the court, then passed to Pump who had moved in front of the basket. Pump turned to shoot. He held his breath as the ball hit the backboard and slowly circled the rim before dropping into the net.

"Yes!" Clyde shouted. "That's my man."

Pump was glad they were on the same team. He got into the rhythm of moving the ball around with Clyde. The basket was high. Pump needed more luck than he had to make up for his lack of height and strength, so Clyde was the team scorer. Pump got a lot of assists.

The game was close, with Pump and Clyde getting fouled a lot which gave them chances for free throws. By the time the score was 19 for P and C and 18 for the Invisibles, both boys were panting. They took a time out.

"See what I mean?" Clyde asked as he caught his breath. You get all these chances in basketball."

Pump nodded. He hoped he looked like he understood. He figured if Clyde just kept talking, he'd have a chance to catch on.

"That's what kills me about baseball. Especially batting. No chances. At least it feels that way to me. If you make an out, you're out. If you miss the ball, you're out."

"But you've got three strikes, don't you?" Pump ventured. He also thought to himself that if you made an out, there was always another at bat. But he didn't think that showed enough agreement with what was on Clyde's mind, so he kept it to himself.

"I suppose so," Clyde agreed. "I just wish I could *feel* that. To me it feels like you've got that one shot and once it's fired you have to take all that time to reload. Like a musket. You can't get into the rhythm like we were just doing out here. It all depends on you. No one to pass to and take a breather. It's just you. Well, that's pitching."

"You're an awesome pitcher," Pump said matter-of-factly. "You can do just about anything this year."

"You think so?" Clyde looked at Pump with some doubt.

Pump nodded.

A shout, a mix of cheerful disbelief from one group and mournful moans from the other group, rose behind them. Pump and Clyde turned to see what had happened. From the scurrying around in the field, they guessed a fly ball had been dropped. Sure enough, the batter on the Stripes stood at the plate, the bat still in his hand as he stared open-mouthed at the melee in shallow right field. In a second he saw that the easy catch had not been made. He dropped the bat as if he just realized it was on fire. He headed for first base but it looked like he wouldn't make it.

Wonders did not cease. The second baseman, who had finally subdued the bouncing ball, shot it to first. The first baseman reached to catch it but the ball cleanly passed him, hit the fence and fell to the ground. More groans and more cheers from the two groups. The startled runner dashed on and finally had to pull up at third. The Muskets' shortstop ended up with the ball. He glared so fiercely at the runner that it would have taken more than a third base coach waving him on to budge that Stripe from the base.

At the end of the fourth inning the Stripes had four runs to the Muskets' eight. Pump saw that their game would not end by the mercy rule and he was glad. The roving Minutemen collected back at the major-league field.

"How're the Patriots doing?" Pump wondered.

"They're down, 13-10. It's close. Close and slow. They're only in the top of the fourth," Brian reported.

The Dodgers and the Giants were also close. Close and fast, in the top of the sixth. Luke was no longer on the mound. He was at shortstop. Pump caught his eye and Luke gave him a thumbs-up which Pump understood meant everything had gone well. From the buzz among the onlookers Pump learned that the Dodgers were up by one run, 6-5. The Giants had two outs and a man on first. The Giants' lead-off batter was up. He watched the first pitch go by. A clean strike but the catcher dropped the ball and before he could find it under his legs, the runner had stolen second. The next pitch was a ball, outside. The catcher held onto the ball and the runner retreated back to second. Pump saw that Luke was ready to make a quick tag if the opportunity came.

The next pitch was a little slower and the batter threw his weight into it, driving the ball right past the pitcher. Luke leaped over, snagged the ball and, for good measure, tagged the runner moving to third.

"Four outs?" asked Willie, looking up at his teammates.

"Yup," replied Danny with a straight face. He took a sip of soda but started to laugh as he swallowed. Soda sprayed out his nose and he had a fit of coughing. The boys laughed and pounded him on the back.

"What they can do in the Majors!" Danny exclaimed. "It's really something."

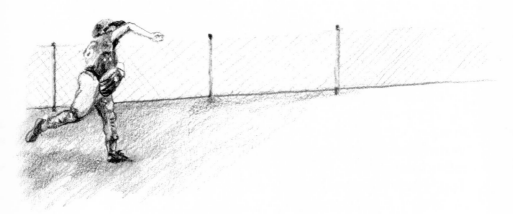

Target Practice

FRED CALLED FOR PRACTICES every Saturday and Sunday morning. Some of the Minutemen thought they practiced too much. Pump, on the other hand, thought there could never be too many practices. He loved being on the field with his team: throwing, catching, batting, sliding. He knew that Danny Flagan didn't like practices because Fred got mad at him a lot for fooling around. But Danny made everyone laugh which was a relief after Fred's intensity. Brian complained about practices, too. Since his father was a coach, Pump wondered if Brian just needed some time away from baseball. Which was the last thing that Pump wanted.

The Minutemen were riding a wave of wins they had not expected. After routing the Colonists, they had gone on to defeat the Stars and the Stripes in easy games. As the team kept winning, Fred got more intense and Pump saw Clyde get more withdrawn.

Clyde had been full of energy at the beginning of the season. The better he pitched, the higher soared the team's hopes. The better he pitched, the more Fred Namath barked at the team. The more the coach barked, the more moody Clyde became, the way Pump remembered him from last season. That wasn't a good sign. The team depended on Clyde now.

Following the game with the Stripes, the Minutemen played the Patriots, who put up a better fight. The Minutemen had come from behind in the top of the sixth with a two run double by Annie Maloney that gave them a one-run lead. The Minutemen needed Clyde to pitch them to safety in the bottom of the sixth.

Clyde walked the first three batters without throwing one strike. The batters didn't move a muscle. Either their coach had told them to look for walks or they were afraid of Clyde's fastball. Then, coming out of nowhere, his thirteenth pitch sizzled through the strike zone. The batter didn't even know the pitch had come and gone. The next two pitches kept the batter so stunned he never moved his bat. The strikeout couldn't have been cleaner.

The entire field and crowd fell silent. The only sounds were the distant calls on other fields and the smack of thrown strikes landing in Brian Kennedy's catcher's mitt. Another out. Clyde threw two more swift strikes before the next batter finally moved his bat. The swing was cautious but the bat made contact sending the ball straight to Clyde who caught it for the last out. The Minutemen erupted with glee but Clyde just dropped the ball on the mound and walked off the field.

In the next game, against the Revolutionaries, Clyde didn't pitch at all. He had pitched his six-inning-a-week quota by pitching the entire game with the Patriots. Pump thought Clyde needed a rest, anyway. He worried that the new relaxed Clyde was fading, giving way to the old moody, unpredictable Clyde.

Freddy Namath took the mound for the first three innings against the Revolutionaries. He threw his usual ferocious medley of fastballs either over the plate or at the batters. Part of his success, Pump felt, came from the terror factor—the batters were afraid of the speed of the pitch and afraid of being hit. At first frozen by the sight of the ball hurtling toward the plate, batters soon learned to swing in self-defense, which generally led to a strikeout. Pump was grateful that he never had to face Freddy at the plate.

The Minutemen swamped the Revolutionaries even though Jeff Leonard pitched the fourth inning and walked the lineup around the bases, which brought in seven runs. Pump and Danny once overheard Jeff's father insisting to Fred Namath that Jeff be put in more often to pitch. "He's got a great arm. He's born to pitch," they heard Mr. Leonard say.

"Born to pitch high and outside," Danny murmured.

Since the league rules said a team could only go once through the lineup for the first four innings, Jeff never pitched after the fourth.

The Minutemen were leading 15-9 at the top of the fifth. Fred put in Danny Flagan to pitch and he purposefully worked his way through the batters, allowing no runs in his two innings. Pump always cheered up when Danny was on the mound. For all his clowning, Danny was a hard-working team player. Pump was as buoyed up by Danny's baseball dependability as by his humor. The combination calmed the team. Clyde looked happy at shortstop as he yelled encouragement to the pitcher. The side was quickly retired.

Pump's team was getting excited. The chatter from the bench grew louder and hits flew off their bats like popcorn. The Minutemen made four runs in the bottom of the fifth and the game was over after the Revolutionaries remained scoreless in the top of the sixth.

After that rout the Minutemen had two games left to play in the first half of the season. There were eight teams in the minor league. Each team played every other team twice, fourteen games in all. The team that won the most games in the season was the division champion. That team got to play against the champions from the three other divisions of Canterbury Little League in a weekend playoff called the City Cup. That was the biggest honor of all.

Even though Pump tried not to think about it, he found himself drifting into daydreams of championship victory. The more Pump slipped into thinking ahead into that possibility, the sharper Fred Namath became at practices and the harsher he seemed after the games they won. Pump guessed that his coach was having the same daydream, which caused him to push the team harder and harder.

Whenever the coach heard the boys talking about their place in the standings, he would snap, "Dreams can't take the place of hard work."

No one said they could, thought Pump. Can't you have both, though, hard work and dreams? What good is work without the dreams to work for, he wondered. This was an important discussion Pump had with himself, since he spent a large amount of time living in daydreams. Most of the hours he put into baseball were spent in his imagination, even when he was right on the field.

The next game was going to be the toughest of the season. The Minutemen were playing the Muskets, the Ameses' team. Pump imagined all sorts of scenarios for that game. He knew it would be a real challenge.

After the Muskets, the Minutemen would face the Pilgrims, who seemed to be improving steadily after a slow beginning. Some teams had more practices than other teams. The Minutemen practiced a lot, which made a big difference, especially at the beginning of the season. The Pilgrims had started the season with no practices at all, but after half a season of games, they were getting the hang of it and playing pretty good baseball.

The game against the Muskets was definitely the Big One. Both teams were undefeated. Since the Muskets were the division champions last year, every team felt a certain rivalry with them. Pump felt both team rivalry and personal rivalry. He didn't want Ken Ames to have a real reason to brag. He couldn't stand the idea of Ken lording it over him if the Muskets won. If the Minutemen won, Pump vowed he wouldn't rub it in. But Ken would know. Maybe that would keep him quiet.

The Muskets game was scheduled for Monday. On Wednesday, the Minutemen would play the Pilgrims. The coach called for two practices over the weekend. Pump could eat, sleep and live baseball. This is what he was made for, he thought.

Fred Namath was fiddling with the pitching machine when Pump arrived at the field for Saturday practice. Now that he rode his bicycle to the field he always came early. It was a big relief not to have to wait for his mother to take him. She didn't seem to understand how important it was to get to his practices and games on time. Now he could get there when he wanted to, which meant he could get there early.

Freddy tossed a ball to Pump while he was locking up his bicycle. Pump dropped his bike but couldn't make the catch. He gathered up the rolling ball and whipped it back to Freddy, who was laughing. Pump picked up his bike and chained it to the fence.

"Sorry," Freddy called, still laughing.

Pump ran onto the field where Freddy tossed the ball to him again. This time they concentrated hard on throwing the ball swiftly back and forth. *Thwap. Thwump.* The ball clapped into their leather gloves.

The other Minutemen drifted onto the field. It was Saturday, the sky was a clear blue, the air was warm. They felt no need to hurry. Fred Namath had a different idea.

"Move it, move it," the coach snapped to his team. "Take your positions. Outfielders, get a move on. No wonder you can't get to those hits. If you can't even get to right field how can you make a play, Weiss?" Fred Namath called to Penny Weiss as she scuffed her feet along through the dirt of the infield.

When he heard the coach single out specific players, Pump swallowed hard. It wasn't a good sign. Pump never knew when he would be yelled at next.

"Prout," the coach shouted "you gotta keep awake. You gotta know the plays. You gotta keep track."

Pump practically jumped out of his skin when Fred barked at him. He never could really hear what the coach said because he'd get too scared to listen. Pump nodded vigorously. Fred went on to yell at Clyde who just stared at the coach. Pump wished he could be that cool. Or was it just that Clyde really didn't care?

The practice would have been more fun if it hadn't seemed so important. The players were all thumbs. Balls refused to be caught. Grounders bounced like jumping beans, impossible to predict. No one could throw or catch.

Pump felt frozen stiff. He actually shivered. It was a sort of inside shiver because it was a hot day outside. He couldn't loosen up. He was like the Tin Woodsman in *The Wizard of Oz*. Pump wished someone could oil his joints.

Somehow Clyde didn't stiffen up like the rest of the team. If anything, he seemed looser than ever. Maybe even too loose. Instead of being jittery, he had melted. His arms were so loose he couldn't throw. His whole body sagged. Pump stared at Clyde and wondered what to do.

Fred called the team in.

"Well, that's about the worst I've ever seen. You just can't play like that if you want to win the championship. The Minutemen are undefeated, only you'd never know it to look at you. What a bunch of clowns."

Fred turned away in disgust. The entire team froze. Pump swallowed hard. He felt like he'd been caught doing something wrong. It didn't matter that he hadn't done anything. Maybe that was exactly the problem. He hadn't done anything. Not a good play to his name. He tried to think of some good baseball he had played, something he had done to contribute to the team. His mind went blank. Pump dared a look at his teammates. Most of them were staring at their shoes. Annie Maloney looked straight ahead bravely while her sister, Jill, squeezed her mitt like a wet washcloth. Jeff Leonard's head hung low between his hunched-up shoulders. Willie Salvano looked curiously at each of his teammates, not really sure what was going on.

Freddy Namath stood at attention like a military cadet, his hands cupped in front of him. Bones Bednarski was biting his cheeks to make sure he didn't laugh. Danny Flagan checked to make sure the coach still had his back to them before he rolled his eyes heavenward and puffed out his cheeks. Penny Weiss and Josh Gerstein looked even tinier than usual as they shifted their weight nervously from one foot to the other.

Josh shot a glance at his parents where they gripped the fence on the sidelines. They always stayed to watch him practice. Pump wondered if they were trying to learn baseball. They never seemed able to follow the game but they loved to clap whenever other people did. At first they only cheered when Josh did something, but as the season went on they had started cheering for all the good plays.

Pump felt his heart miss a beat as he sneaked a look at Clyde. Clyde's face was totally expressionless. Pump wondered if that was how a dead person would look, empty and blank. He wanted to reach over and punch Clyde in his belly to wake him up. The silence weighed heavily on the team's shoulders.

Only Brian Kennedy looked like he always did. His sandy hair stuck out from under his cap and his mouth was relaxed. Maybe it helped to be the son of a coach. Brian's eyes were fixed on Fred Namath as the coach turned back to face the team.

"OK, Minutemen. We'll let bygones be bygones. I've got a new drill for you. A fresh start." He smiled and the whole team sighed in relief.

"Listen up. Everyone take a position along the base paths. Run and find a spot," the coach directed.

The players scattered from their cluster and positioned themselves along the base paths between first and second and between second and third.

Fred Namath shouted, "Everyone hunker down with your back turned to the plate." Fred demonstrated by squatting down with his back to the team. With a little shuffling all the players squatted like catchers with their backs to the coach, who stood at the plate.

"That's it. You've got it," Fred Namath said. "Only now I want everyone to look at me again. I'll be here at the plate and I'll be hitting grounders out to you. You'll have your backs turned to me like we just did. As soon as you hear the bat hit the ball, you turn around and be ready to field the grounder. You can't know where the ball is going until you turn, so everyone has to turn and be ready.

"There're two parts to this drill. First you have to field the grounder. Then, you've gotta make a good throw in to Butch. If he can make the catch, you've completed the play and you're done. Last one in has to put away the equipment."

Pump was ready. He liked Butch Flagan. As assistant coach he usually kept score for the Minutemen and helped out at practices. He was quiet but seemed to like the kids, which meant you could trust him. Pump knew Butch would try to make it easy for the players and try hard to make the catches no matter how badly someone threw to him.

"O.K., Minutemen, take your positions," Fred barked out. He waited until every player was squatting and turned away. Then he hit the first grounder. The players whirled around to look for the ball. It was heading toward Bones, who had barely turned around before the ball bumped past him. He ran off after the ball and finally caught up to it. He was so flustered that his throw only made it to the pitcher's mound. Even sprinting forward, Butch couldn't get to the ball. Bones had to stay in line

At first, everyone was nervous and bungled the ball. Finally, the ball bounced toward Annie who scooped it up and spiked it to Butch. Fred gave her the nod and she came in off the field. Pump's heart was beating fast. He dove for the first ball that came to him but came up empty-handed and had to search for the ball in the outfield. One by one the players started to complete the plays and come in. Most had to try at least three times before earning the right to leave the field.

It seemed to Pump that everyone was getting a chance except him. After his first error, the ball didn't get back to him until there were only five kids left. The others were milling around and making disparaging comments about the ones who were left, but also cheering them on. Finally, a ball hobbled toward Pump. He remembered not to wait for it to reach him and moved forward to meet it . The ball hopped into his glove. Pump fired a throw directly to Butch's glove and he was given the signal to leave the field.

"Good work," Butch said smiling at Pump as he loped to the sidelines. As he ran by the fence, Pump saw the group of parents waiting to pick up their children after practice. Standing apart from the others was Coach Kennedy. Pump slowed down as he passed his old coach.

"Prout," Coach Kennedy called gruffly. "Prout, how're you do-ing? Looking great out there. Remember, when you're famous, you tell them I was the one who spotted you. I was the first. Don't forget."

Pump grinned. Coach Kennedy could still make Pump feel like a million. Even when he wasn't Pump's coach. Pump joined his team-mates. All the heart-racing, dry mouth-making anxiousness was gone. For the first time Pump felt excited about the big game.

By this time everyone was done except Bones Bednarski. The coach stayed calm and patient even though the team was restless and whining that it was late. After six grounders in a row that he missed or fumbled, Bones finally caught the seventh and completed the throw to Butch who dashed halfway from the plate to catch it.

Fred Namath let his eyes scan the faces of his players all grouped in front of him. "OK, Minutemen. We've done what we need to do. We've gotten ourselves in a dead heat with the Muskets. There's still a lot more baseball in front of us. Sure, it would be great to win this game on Monday but whatever the outcome we've got another half season to go."

"Half season and a game," Danny whispered loudly.

Fred shot Danny an irritated look, then relaxed. "That's right," he said, "a half season and a game to go … after Monday.

"Now we got the jitters out and it's time to do our job. Let's say we got the worst over with. The game, well, that'll be different. That's what practices are for. That's why we'll practice again tomorrow.

"And, by the way," Fred added. He waited until the team had quieted down. "The Minutemen *are going to win!*"

As the players walked away, shouting that they would see each other the next day at practice, Fred Namath called out to Bones Bednarski.

"Hey, Bones, not so fast. Remember, last one in on that drill picks up the equipment."

Bones stopped short. He was on his way to where his parents were standing.

"Awww, c'mon, Coach, the practice's over. I gotta go."

Fred Namath frowned. "You know, Bones, there's a reason for everything. If you want to play baseball, want to be on a team, you've got to learn how to put out that little extra when the team needs you to. If you can't put a little more energy into your fielding, like in the drill, then you need to put a little more energy into something else, like picking up the equipment. It's all part of teamwork. Where you choose to put your energy is up to you. I just offer the options."

As Pump unlocked his bike, he saw Bones shuffle out to first base. He stepped on the bag, marking his hit, before he picked up the base and moved on to collect the others. Bones's parents glowered at Fred Namath as he packed up the pitching machine. Pump saw that Fred did most of the work anyway. Talk about extra effort. He just wished Fred would take things a little easier.

Pump pedaled off. He was elated, full of a floaty feeling of possibility. Full of dreams.

Sunday's practice was totally different from Saturday's. The curse of the Big Game was gone. Everyone was excited. Everyone, Pump noticed, except Clyde. The Minutemen went through their regular routines, practicing fielding and practicing batting against the Blue Monster, as they called the pitching machine. Danny blasted a few balls over the fence and so did Freddy.

When Clyde started to swing his bat everyone stopped to watch. But there was nothing to see. Pump could tell he wasn't even watching the ball. He was just going through the motions. He didn't even get his swing going until after the ball reached him.

"Prout," Fred Namath called Pump over. "Take Clyde out and catch for him awhile, will ya? Hold up your glove. Give him a steady target."

Fred tossed Pump a catcher's mitt.

"Clyde, you just throw to the glove. Hard as you can. Nothing fancy. Just get it in there."

Pump felt his mouth dry up. He worked his tongue to get up enough spit to swallow. Clyde picked up one of the balls lying in the dirt behind the plate and walked outside the foul line in left field. Pump trotted right behind him.

"Hey, my man," Clyde said as he turned around, "it won't work if you're right next to me. I can't pitch to you if you're about an inch away from me."

Pump couldn't tell if Clyde was kidding. "Right," Pump said and sprang away until he thought he was about the right distance from Clyde. Then he squatted down and held up the thick glove as much to hide his face as to catch.

Clyde moved with the same dreamy smoothness Pump had noticed before. Pump felt a little stiff as he squatted down, but after just a few pitches catching felt familiar, like he'd been doing it since he was born. It didn't take long for Pump to realize that Clyde's pitching was pretty unvaried, almost as if he weren't trying. Every pitch was the same. Maybe that's what you had to do to practice pitching.

If Clyde wasn't going to throw interesting pitches, Pump thought he would just make some interesting catches. He tried moving his glove around. He tried throwing the ball back to Clyde in different ways.

Finally, Clyde put his hands on his hips and called, "Yo, Prout, you're messing with me. I can't pitch if you're wobbling all over the place. You gotta hold steady."

"Sorry," Pump said quietly.

Pump crouched down again and held up his glove. He wondered how he could startle Clyde out of his mood. Pump couldn't think of anything. Instead, he just caught the balls that Clyde tossed to him.

"Hey, Clyde," Pump shouted as he stood up to throw back the ball he'd just caught. "What about we play like this is basketball? I mean, like we're passing back and forth. The batter is trying to intercept our passes and we won't let him."

"You out of your mind, Prout? Just catch the ball."

Clyde threw a few more lackluster pitches. Suddenly, he threw a wicked fastball that burned Pump's hand. Pump hadn't even been looking at Clyde. He looked up and saw a smile on Clyde's face. He whipped the ball back to Clyde who fired another pitch right into Pump's glove.

They were absorbed in their game until Pump felt someone watching them. He looked over and saw Fred Namath quietly observing. The coach nodded when Pump caught his eye and Pump turned back to his catching. It was great to see Clyde get fired up again. It was also great to see their coach relax. Now the team could look forward to the game tomorrow. If Clyde could just hold it together, the Minutemen could actually win this thing.

The practice ended with the traditional two-at-a-time race around the bases. Pump lost his heat with Clyde, which made him feel great because it meant Clyde was trying again. And that meant the game with the Muskets could be a good one.

The Muskets

PUMP LAY IN THE DARK in his room the night before the game with the Muskets. He flopped around in bed until his blanket and sheets were twisted around him. He felt hot. He kicked off his covers and then was too cold. He jumped up to check the clock on his dresser. Ten o'clock. He moaned.

"Mom," Pump called out. He waited.

"Ma-ahm," he called again, this time louder. Pump heard his mother's footsteps approach his door. Pump always left his door open at night. He liked to hear the noises of his family and know he wasn't alone in the house. He also kept a night light on just to make sure he could see what was going on while he was falling asleep. Or for nights like this one when he couldn't fall asleep.

He heard his mother pause outside his room.

"Mom," Pump said.

"What is it, Pump?" his mother asked as she came in to find Pump lying with his sheets snarled around him.

"I can't sleep," he complained.

"Excited about the game tomorrow?"

Pump swallowed hard.

"It's ten o'clock," Pump choked out. "I'll never be able to play tomorrow."

"Of course, you'll be able to play," his mother said. "It doesn't matter if it takes a while to fall asleep. You can always sleep more to-morrow. You're just excited. I bet everyone is. I wouldn't be surprised if your whole team is awake and feeling just the same way. And the Muskets, too. I bet the Ameses are wide awake."

While Pump's mother shook his sheets and blankets over him and tucked them in again, Pump imagined the Ameses, lying awake, as nervous as he felt about the next day. Before his mother's footsteps had faded away, Pump was asleep.

Pump didn't exactly mean to avoid Ken Ames at school the next day, but he hardly saw him at all. Even the Minutemen didn't meet each other's eyes. Pump felt like they were all in on some secret they weren't supposed to talk about. The strange code of silence lasted all day.

At home after school, Pump sat down to his homework and just nodded to Luke when he stomped into the kitchen looking for action.

"What's up, Brussels Prout?" Luke said as he jabbed Pump in the shoulder with a few sharp pokes.

Pump just looked up at him before returning to his homework. Only he wasn't really doing any work. He was trying to figure out a batting lineup that wouldn't have him leading off in any inning.

"Big game, today?" Luke smiled. "What are you waiting for? Shouldn't you be at the field? It's after five."

Pump's heart leaped. He jumped up and shot a look at the clock. It was four o'clock.

"You ... you ... you," Pump sputtered as he grabbed for Luke.

Luke sprinted away saying, "Whoa, there, Pump. Not so fast. I have a game, too, you know. We start at the same time you do. You're not going to be late."

Pump shrugged and went to get dressed for the game.

He arrived at the field just as the first Minutemen were pulling in. Some were jumping out of cars, and some came on foot, while Pump and a few others rode their bikes. Everyone seemed serious. They greeted each other with curt nods or just raised eyebrows. The silent greetings made Pump's heart race.

The Muskets, in their black shirts with white letters, were gathering like a thundercloud in the infield. They were the home team for this game and had first infield practice. Pump felt a chill, as if the sky really had darkened.

"Where's the funeral?" Danny Flagan shouted as he clacked up in his spikes. "Looks like someone died."

Danny swiveled his head around. Fred Namath was conferring with the umpire and the coach of the Muskets. The three men laughed.

"Look, guys, if our coach is laughing, why do we look like it's the end of the world? Just remember, how many umpires does it take to change a lightbulb? Three. One to hold the lightbulb and two to turn him." Danny guffawed at his own joke.

The Minutemen all laughed and suddenly they were a team again. A baseball team that was about to play an ordinary baseball game with the usual equipment and the rules the same as always. Baseball.

They moved out to the field to warm up.

"Prout," Fred Namath shouted over, "you warm up Clyde, OK? You can take your fielding practice after you come in and catch Clyde."

Pump flushed with pleasure. A wave of confidence swept over him. This had the makings of a great game.

Pump wondered why Brian wasn't catching for Clyde's warm-up, but he let go of the thought and squatted, ready for Clyde's pitch.

"Rebound off the rim," Pump yelled as he shot the ball back to Clyde. Clyde fired back a pitch, his arm loose and flowing, his body coiling and uncoiling with a smooth motion. Clyde seemed to be in pretty good spirits as he warmed up. Pump noticed the coach watching them like he had done at practice the other day.

No one was sure who Fred Namath would put in to pitch this game. Ordinarily everyone took it for granted that Clyde would be the starter for the harder games. But in the last inning he'd pitched, he'd loaded the bases on walks before throwing the most remarkable string of strikes Pump had ever seen.

One of Clyde's pitches got away from Pump. As he scrambled after the ball he noticed Freddy Namath pitching to Brian. That probably meant Freddy would be the starting pitcher. Pump caught Clyde's pitches until the Minutemen came in for infield practice.

Pump trotted to his position between first and second. He felt his heart pound hard in his chest. Danny whipped the ball to Pump who had to take a few steps back to absorb the impact of the throw. Since when had Danny gotten so strong? A few more balls appeared in the field and the players threw them around. Clyde was on the mound.

Moods were infectious. As the teams came in to their benches, Pump had the jitters. He could tell that all his teammates felt nervous, too. Except maybe Bones Bednarski, who looked bored. Josh Gerstein kept pounding his fist into his mitt until Annie Maloney loudly whispered to him to quit it. If Annie, the most easygoing player on the Minutemen, was edgy, Pump knew everyone was at least as nervous as he was.

"Listen up," Fred Namath called out. The players' voices faded away. "I can tell that everyone is feeling the pressure today, and that's all right. But that doesn't mean you're going to let it interfere with your playing. We've had a season that's gone our way. Is that what we thought would happen?"

No one said anything.

The coach continued, "Maybe you guys thought that the Minutemen would be heading into this game undefeated but—and I'm telling you the truth now—I didn't. This season is a complete surprise to me. As far as I'm concerned we've got nothing to lose. We've gone so far beyond expectations that we don't have them anymore. We're just playing as it comes. And that's a great place to be in. No pressure.

"The important thing is to get out there and play like a team. Back to basics. Be ready. Be in the game. Know where the play is. Know where your cutoff is. No heroics. Teamwork. This is where practice pays off. In the game. So everyone put your hand in. Come on Minutemen."

Each player extended a hand into the center of the circle.

"Go Minutemen," they shouted. The players cheered and filed to the bench where Fred announced the lineup.

"We're the visitors today, so we're up first," Fred Namath said. "Pump, you'll lead off."

Pump's mouth went completely dry. That can't be right, he thought. He had never led off. Pump was sure his heart stopped beating. He didn't hear the rest of the lineup until it came to Josh Gerstein batting last as DH.

Everyone else on the team got to hide on the bench for a while. Pump wished he could tuck himself out of sight and bat his usual fourth. Now he was the first to face the Muskets' dreaded pitcher, Charles Ames. Pump walked stiffly to the bats leaning against the fence. He picked one up.

"Loosen up, Prout," the coach shouted to him. "Let the bat do the work. Just start the swing and let the bat finish it. Watch the ball.

"And Prout," he added, "you might want to check your bat."

Pump looked down and saw that he had picked up the little pee-wee bat they saved for Willie Salvano. No wonder it felt so light. He quickly tossed it down and found his favorite silver bat with the red neck and handle.

Pump approached the plate as Charles Ames threw his last practice pitch. Ken squatted behind the plate. Pump braced himself for a taunt from Ken but his friend just smiled behind the grille of his mask.

With his back to one Ames and facing the other, Pump felt strangely calm. After all, he knew these boys. So what if Charles was bigger than everyone else? It wasn't as though Pump were facing Randy Johnson. All he had to do was watch the ball.

Pump stepped up to the plate, took his practice swings and fixed his eye on the ball. His eye never left the ball and the bat never left his shoulder. He completely forgot to swing.

The umpire held up his right hand. Ball one.

"Good eye, good eye," shouted the Minutemen.

Good luck is more like it, thought Pump. He took another two swings to loosen up his arm.

Even before the force of his swing swept him off balance, Pump realized that the pitch was so far away from the plate he'd have had to stretch a mile to make contact. Why did I go for that one? Pump wondered.

"Strike," growled the umpire.

The next pitch arced into the dirt in front of the plate. Even so, Pump almost swung at it. He was so wound up he was having trouble getting his body into a rhythm that matched the pitches. Pump liked those times when his bat felt like it was just a part of his body and what he saw guided how his bat moved. Like a reflex. This was not one of those times.

"Two and one," Fred Namath shouted. "You're ahead of the pitcher."

So I am, thought Pump as the next pitch sailed across the plate at something close to the speed of light. Strike two.

Pump tightened his grip on the bat as if to keep it still as the next pitch passed so far outside, Ken had to chase after it while his brother threw his glove on the ground. It wasn't clear to Pump whether Charles was angry at himself or at Ken.

Full count. The Minutemen were on their feet cheering for Pump. Charles glowered at the batter and the catcher. Pump was rattled but still quick enough to jump back as the pitch whisked past his head.

"Take your base," the umpire growled. Pump tossed his bat aside and trotted to first. Once on base, he was flooded with relief. He was grateful to Charles Ames, who was throwing a minor tantrum on the mound, for not throwing more strikes. Pump could breathe again. He had done his job. The lead-off hitter just needed to get on base. And that's where he was.

From first base, Pump scanned the crowd just for a second to see if his father had come. Not a sign of him. Ever since his dad had come to one game, looking for him had become a kind of reflex for Pump. He always both hoped and dreaded that he'd spot his dad.

Next up was Freddy Namath who seemed reluctant to leave the on-deck circle. He slowly walked to the plate and carefully assumed his batting stance. The first pitch Charles delivered headed right toward Freddy who couldn't turn out of the way fast enough and got hit on the back. He grimaced but then showed no emotion as he trotted to first. Pump, feeling awed by Freddy's courage, moved to second.

Danny Flagan sauntered up to the plate, tapped some dirt from his cleats and took a few swings. Pump imagined Danny walloping the ball to bring Pump home.

"Strike," the umpire yelped.

Danny swung hard at the next pitch and sent it over the fence, foul. The ball bounced in the street, then rolled to the opposite curb. Strike two.

The next two pitches were clearly balls. Danny looked ready at the plate. He met the next pitch with a smooth swing that sent the ball soaring straight up and nearly straight down toward the shortstop, Pete "Pizza" De Souza. Pizza moved in to meet the ball while Charles moved back for it. Pump knew he needed to be ready to tag up in case the ball was caught. Once the ball was caught, Pump could try to make third. It looked like the ball was going to land close to third, anyway, so he would be running into a sure out.

Meanwhile, Danny was churning toward first. Freddy hesitated on first and then, without waiting to see if the fly was caught, took off for second which forced Pump to head for third. Pizza De Souza called for the ball but Charles Ames kept trying to get under it. The two Muskets collided and the shortstop dropped the ball.

Pump ran hard to stay ahead of Freddy who was panting right behind him. Pump rounded third and headed for home while the Muskets scrambled for the ball. Pump slid into the plate. When the dust cleared Freddy was on third, Danny was on second and Pump had scored the Minutemen's first run. He happily dusted himself off.

There was some commotion between the plate and the mound. Charles Ames was stamping his feet and shaking his fist at his shortstop. Fred Namath was listening to the umpire while the Muskets' coach yelled at the two of them. In the midst of the shouting of players, parents and the Muskets' coach, Fred Namath appeared strangely thoughtful.

The umpire motioned Danny off the base. Danny looked confused and didn't move. The parents on the sidelines were bellowing at the umpire. Fred escorted Danny off the field.

Pump was bewildered. He'd slid practically halfway home from third which was the best slide of his entire career. He'd scored the first run of the game, and no one seemed to notice.

Bones's dad, Bub Bednarski, was exclaiming at the top of his voice, "Whaddya mean, 'infield fly rule'? You making this up, ump? What, you got a kid on the Muskets, or what?"

Pump could not figure out what had happened. A fly ball is a fly ball. And a dropped fly ball is just like any other ball. So what if it was an error and not a hit. The base runner can still advance. Pump knew that much.

Pump could hear the parents buzzing behind the backstop.

"The infield fly rule? Sure, well, it's a fly in the infield. Seems it doesn't count," mused Josh Gerstein's father.

"It's that straight-up kind of fly. No one should hit that. It's like the easiest out," mourned Jeff Leonard's father.

"But no one caught it. They dropped the ball," pointed out Mike Maloney, Annie and Jill's dad, a matter-of-fact guy.

Pump recognized the deep voice of Coach Kennedy rise above the clamor, "It's an infield fly, all right. That means the umpire invokes the infield fly rule. When there are fewer than two outs ..." he paused.

There weren't any outs, Pump remembered.

"When there are fewer than two outs, *and* runners on first and second or even bases loaded ..." Coach Kennedy paused again. Pump could still see himself on second and Freddy on first.

Coach Kennedy continued. "In that situation, if the batter hits an infield fly and the team in the field makes the catch, how many outs would you get?"

"One!" declared Josh's dad with a hint of pride.

"That's it," Coach Kennedy announced. "But if the fielder 'drops' the ball, maybe even on purpose, then how many outs can he make?"

Now Pump started to follow the point. If the fielder dropped the ball, the team could make a double play and get two advancing runners out.

"Exactly," Coach Kennedy shouted so quickly that Pump wondered if he had read Pump's thoughts. "So someone made a rule to prevent that kind of intentional error. If there are runners on first and second, or first, second and third, and fewer than two outs and someone hits a fly that would land in the infield, the *batter* is automatically out. The runners can try to advance. They don't have to tag up. That's the infield fly rule, plain and simple.

"So Pump's run counts, Freddy is on third and there is one out. That would be Danny. There it is. The infield fly rule!"

"Learn something new every day," muttered Jeff Leonard's father.

It took awhile for the teams and fans to settle down. Freddy was on third, the Minutemen had one run and one out, and Clyde stepped up to the plate.

Fred Namath shouted, "It's up to you, Clyde. Bring a run home. Let's get things going."

Clyde's shoulders slumped forward and the bat rested practically next to his cheek. His timing was way off. He swung the bat too late, then swung too early on the next pitch. It didn't seem to matter where the pitch was going. Clyde swung at it. Strike three. Two outs.

Annie Maloney drew a walk to put runners on first and third.

"Now's the time, Brian, " the coach called to the next batter. "Give that ball a ride."

Brian nodded like a robot and raised his bat to his shoulder without taking any practice swings. The first pitch caught the edge of the plate for a strike. Brian decided that Charles was throwing strikes, so he pushed his bat forward to reach the next pitch even though it was headed for the ground in front of the plate. He just managed to tap the ball, which rolled about two feet toward the mound.

Brian dashed toward first. The catcher, Ken Ames, lumbered to get the ball and swung himself between the plate and the oncoming runner. He stuck out his hand and thumped Freddy in the chest with the ball. The side was retired. Minutemen, one; Muskets, nothing.

Clyde started throwing his warm up pitches to Brian. So Clyde was the coach's choice after all. Pump agreed with that decision. He just hoped Clyde would pitch the team to glory like he'd done in their last game.

Pump had a funny feeling as he watched Clyde pitch. If Clyde couldn't handle the pressure the whole team would fall apart. Not just Clyde. The team didn't just *feel* like everything rested on Clyde's shoulders, they believed it.

"Come on, Clyde," Pump heard himself shout. He wasn't the usual one to start the chatter. That job belonged to Danny.

Danny took his cue. "You can do it. How's about a perfect game? Don't give 'em nothin'. They got Swiss bats. You know, the kind with holes in 'em. They won't even see the ball."

Danny danced around first base while Clyde methodically threw to Brian.

"Throw hard," Fred Namath yelled. "Right to the glove, Clyde."

Ken Ames led off for the Muskets. He settled in at the plate, gave his bat some swings and held still for the pitch. It looked like Clyde was going to walk Ken. The balls he was throwing were so far outside that it might have been an intentional walk except for the fact that Brian kept hunkering in position right behind the plate as though he expected each pitch to cross the plate. Three balls, no strikes. Then Clyde found the plate with a slow, straight ball that Ken Ames sent in a high arc over the fence. Ken gave Pump a knowing smile as he trotted toward second on his way around the bases.

Ken Ames leading off with a solo home run. Things couldn't get worse than that, Pump thought. And they didn't. Things didn't get any better, either.

Clyde walked the next three batters before an eager Musket swung at three balls and struck out. One out, bases loaded. His next pitch was sent into far right field where Jill Maloney scrambled after the ball in a pantomime of searching for a button in the outfield grass. She finally got hold of the ball, aimed it in the general direction of the infield, but threw it to the startled center fielder. Penny Weiss saw the ball coming, cringed and ducked. The ball dropped onto the grass. Freddy swept out and scooped up the ball. He desperately hurled it toward third where it sailed over Annie's head.

When Pump dreamed about the Minutemen making baseball history, this was not what he had in mind. He couldn't believe how little time it took for a whole season to go down the tubes.

Pump reviewed his team's position. Bottom of the first Muskets lead, 5-1, with one out. The situation didn't look good. It was hard to watch Clyde struggle. Only Clyde didn't really seem to be struggling. It was more like he had collapsed without a fight. Pump felt disappointment rising in him. He felt that Clyde had gotten his hopes up and now was letting them all down.

By this time the Muskets were halfway into their batting order and the big bats were finished. Each batter now was smaller than the last, though none as small as Willie Salvano. If Clyde had been having a hard time finding the strike zone on the bigger players, he was lost with the little guys. The batters stood with their bats frozen to their shoulders while pitch after pitch came in high, low or outside. Anything coming inside scared them into action and they either jumped back or swung wildly. Despite a few inside balls, that turned into strikes, Clyde walked the next three batters. He finished the inning by walking the tenth batter, which brought in the sixth run. Mercifully, that was the last batter in the Muskets' lineup and the first inning came to an end.

The Minutemen were morose as they straggled in from the field.

"Look sharp, Minutemen." Fred's voice cracked over the slouching players. "No time for long faces. We came here to work. Now we know what we have to do. Get the equipment in. Penny, you're up, Jeff Leonard on deck, Jill Maloney, double deck. Get those bats swinging."

The coach clapped his hands with a snap like a popped balloon. The team came back to life.

"Hey, guys," Danny yelled, "it's only the top of the second. Let's get things moving. Come on, Weiss. Clout that sucker."

Penny Weiss blinked at Danny, then blinked at the pitcher as though trying to get him into focus.

"Practice swings," prompted the coach. Penny stared at him blankly.

"Take some," the coach ordered. Penny lifted the bat to her shoulder, then chopped down as if it were an ax.

"Swing, Penny. It's gotta be a swing, not a chop. Think of the Blue Monster. Do what you do with that. Step into your swing," Fred Namath called calmly to the batter. "Go on. You can do it. Just like always."

Danny clapped his hand on his forehead. "'Just like always?' Don't say that. That means she'll never connect," he groaned in a stage whisper to the kids on the bench.

Penny Weiss brought the bat back to her shoulder, gave a shudder and stood perfectly still as Charles Ames threw a fastball, low and outside. From the mound the pitcher tried to convey his disdain for his task. He glared at the batter to indicate how unworthy she was to receive his pitches. Penny hadn't moved a muscle and was still ready at the plate.

Ball two sailed wide. Balls three and four landed in the dirt. Penny trotted to first, forgetting to drop her tightly clutched bat until Butch, coaching at first base, took it from her.

Jeff Leonard approached the plate already swinging. His bat swept back and forth like a scythe. His long legs were straight and stiff while his bat kept moving like a pendulum.

"Bend your legs, Jeff. Fluid, remember? Keep it fluid," coached Fred Namath.

Jeff bent his legs by sticking his rear end out and folding his knees in a sharp kink. He brought the bat to his shoulder.

Charles Ames was having a hard time with the bottom of the line-up. He kept trying to burn the ball past these batters as though to show them how good he was. "Don't play the batters. Just play the bats," shouted the Muskets' coach as he watched Charles throw three more balls.

Finally, a pitch came toward the plate and sweeping the bat like a golf club, Jeff Leonard sent the ball over the center field fence. It was the longest home run in the season so far.

The Minutemen erupted with cheers. The players swarmed to the plate to greet Jeff as he ambled home with his straight-kneed lope. Jeff grinned widely. He kept high-fiving and hugging his teammates until the umpire reminded everyone it was time to continue the game. 6-3, no outs.

Jill Maloney got a base on balls. Josh Gerstein let a strike go by, swung at a high one, then watched a perfect pitch sail past him for the first out.

"That was a ball. That was clearly a ball," muttered Josh's father. "Why don't they ever have impartial umpires for Little League?"

Jill stood right on first base when Pump came to the plate. He tried not to look at Charles Ames's face as he took his warm-up swings.

"Go, Prout," the Minutemen shouted.

The Minutemen fans were clapping and shouting. "Come on, Pump. Give that ball a ride."

Pump could bring the Minutemen within one run of the Muskets if he could really connect with the ball like Jeff Leonard had. Pump could feel his fingertips tingle. Maybe there was some supernatural energy flowing through him. Pump swung. Strike one.

Pump watched a ball float by. You couldn't be a hero if you didn't swing. It was safer to walk but not very glorious. The next ball sizzled toward him. Pump felt the bat vibrate as it connected. In true big-league style, he let go of the bat with his upper hand to let the bat glide around him in one hand.

Foul ball. Strike two.

Pump was no longer afraid of fastballs. But he was afraid of striking out. The next pitch blazed toward him. Pump closed his eyes and swung with all his might.

"You're out," barked the umpire, sounding like a pro. Pump didn't feel like a pro. Two outs.

Freddy stared at the pitcher. Charles Ames wound up and delivered a high ball. Freddy stepped back from the batter's box, took a slow look at his father, who was standing with his clipboard near third base, and resumed his stance at the plate.

The next pitch steamed in and Freddy swung. He sent a high fly ball sailing toward left field. The Musket outfielder backed up to follow the ball. He positioned himself under the ball as it dipped back toward Earth.

"Mine," called out the left fielder.

The onlookers held their breath. Jill Maloney seemed glued to first base until the ball ticked off the top of the fielder's glove. Everyone sighed. Jill lunged ahead to second. Freddy passed first and steamed toward second. The fielder tracked the ball and scooped it up before it came to a stop.

Jill ran as hard as she could to third. She looked relieved and ready to stop when Fred Namath, coaching at third, waved her on. Her face tightened with panic as she sped home. 6-4.

Fred motioned Freddy to keep coming just as he was about to pull up at second. Freddy hesitated an instant, then churned around second to try for third.

The Minutemen fans groaned in bewilderment. They saw the left fielder hurl the ball toward third.

"What's Fred doing?" shouted Bones's father.

"Watch. That fielder is the one that lost the ball. He'll overthrow," said Jill and Annie's father. "That's what Fred's banking on."

The throw was high, but the third baseman stretched up and intercepted the ball as it sailed over his head. He pulled the ball out of the air and lowered it to Freddy's shoulder right before the runner got his foot on the base. Freddy tucked his head down to hide his tears. He slouched toward the bench while the Muskets cheerfully trotted past him on the way to their dugout.

The Minutemen grabbed their gloves and headed to their positions. Freddy shrugged them off when they tried to say anything to him. Pump could see Ken Ames pulling off his catcher's gear as fast as he could. The Muskets were riding the wave.

Before Pump could trot out to his position between first and second, the coach stopped him and turned him around. Fred was holding the catcher's equipment.

"Pump," he began, "I know this is a big change, but I'm going to put you in to catch Clyde. Just for an inning. Or maybe two."

Pump's eyes grew wide and his heart beat fast.

"Catch Clyde?" Pump stammered.

"Yep," Fred confirmed. "I've seen you put some life into him. Some sort of basketball game you two got going.

"I know you never wore this gear before," the coach said as he looked at the mask, chest protector, shin pads and thick mitt, "but it's worth a try. I know you can do it. I'd rather try this than pull Clyde so early. Brian, you'll play second this inning."

Fred helped dress Pump in the catcher's gear, adjusted the mask so Pump could see and put him in behind the plate.

On the mound, Clyde looked startled and smiled as he called, "I don't believe it. Prout catching! OK. Let's do it!"

For an instant, Clyde seemed to be himself again.

Seeing through the mask seemed the hardest part for Pump. But he figured if Ken Ames could catch, so could he. Clyde threw good, solid pitches to Pump in their warm-up and Pump had no trouble catching them.

The umpire called for the batter. Pump squatted behind the plate and realized how uncomfortably close he was to a swinging bat. He hitched himself back a bit.

Ken Ames was the first batter. He laughed at Pump hunkered behind the plate.

"Watch this, Prout," Ken said. "I'll send it over the fence. That'll save you the trouble of having to catch it."

Once the inning was under way, Clyde started throwing balls again. He walked Ken and the next two batters to load the bases.

The coach called, "Prout, get that glove up where Clyde can see it. Jones, throw to the glove."

Clyde walked in a run with the next batter, but this time he got in a few pretty pitches right over the plate.

"Rebound off the rim," Pump shouted. His voice was muffled by the padding of the mask.

When Clyde walked in a second run, Fred Namath motioned to Pump to join him and they walked out to the mound.

"How're you feeling, Jones?" Fred asked his pitcher. "You're looking a little more together. I just wanted to check in. Give Prout a chance to stretch his legs."

"I'm doing OK," Clyde responded. He looked directly at his coach, which Pump took as a good sign.

"OK," Fred approved. He looked at Pump. "Any words for our pitcher?" he asked.

Pump thought a second. He felt tongue-tied until he suddenly said, "Go for a three pointer. Swish it in."

As Pump resumed his crouch behind the plate, he could tell Clyde was more relaxed even though his face looked serious. Pump felt more relaxed, too. He couldn't see the parents even if he had wanted to. It felt good to stop trying to spot his dad.

Pump put up his glove. Clyde went for a three pointer, and he got it. Three strikes in a row for the first out. The batter had expected a free trip to first and the umpire had to repeat, "You're out," before the batter headed back to the bench.

8-4 and one out.

The bases were still loaded. Clyde was getting into a rhythm. His pitches were coming with more certainty. Pump liked the way they smacked into his glove. Another strikeout meant only one more out to go.

Even as Clyde and Pump were working on relaxing, the rest of the team seemed either tight or asleep. The next batter swung at Clyde's first pitch and popped a ball just beyond the infield. That set in motion a lot of scrambling and wild throws. Pump watched helplessly as three Muskets clomped across the plate.

Finally, as the last runner rounded third, Annie managed to subdue the ball. She was too late to get the runner at third, but in time to make the throw home. Pump stood ready to catch it. Annie threw the ball right to him, but Pump felt the ball glance off his padded glove. He totally lost sight of it. The fourth run came in.

The Muskets shouted with pleasure. Luckily, Pump's mask covered his face, which burned with disappointment and embarrassment.

Clyde walked the tenth batter with some lackluster balls and the inning was over. The Muskets were in the lead, 12-4.

"Jeez, you've been out there forever," groaned Bones as the Minutemen returned to their bench. "I can't believe it's just the third inning."

"Yeah, well, you just see if you can do any better," snapped Danny as he tossed his mitt down.

No Mercy

"TWELVE TO FOUR, GUYS," Danny groaned. "12-4. If we keep going like this, we'll be mercied. Mercied by the Muskets. Nothing could be worse!"

The coach flushed with anger. Pump was startled and felt scared. He braced himself for a tirade. Fred took a deep breath.

"OK, Minutemen," Fred paused. "We're not flat on our backs yet. We just need to regroup. New goals. What did we come here to do today?"

The Minutemen shuffled their feet, studied their shoes and stubbed their toes in the dirt.

Danny blurted out, "I know what we came to do. We came to win the game. That's what we were wanting to do."

"That's what I thought," Fred said. "We came here to win, to get to the top of the league. Now we feel things slipping away. So let's grab what we can and make the best of it. Think small, think doable. Don't think home runs. Think base hits. Don't think heroics, think team-work. Don't think 'Uh-oh, it's up to me.' Nothing is up to you. Not alone. You're part of a team. And that team does not want to lose by the mercy rule. And neither do I.

"Get a grip, Minutemen!" Fred exclaimed. "What we have to do now is show that we are a team."

The coach gave his team a hard look and then got back to business.

"Bednarski! In for Maloney in right. You'll follow Leonard at bat," he barked.

"Gerstein!" Fred seemed thoughtful as a look of hope, then fear, flickered across Josh Gerstein's face. "Gerstein, you hang in there as DH, OK?"

Josh nodded with relief.

The umpire had swept the plate clean more than once while the Minutemen talked with their coach. He was getting restless. Finally, he bellowed, "What's going on, Namath? Play ball!"

"OK, Minutemen, time to rumble. Get out there and act like a team. Flagan is first up. Jones, on deck. Maloney (that's you, Annie), double deck."

Danny swaggered to the plate. He gave the pitcher a long hard look before taking his warm-up swings. The first pitch tore toward the plate. The ball was at head level but Danny didn't even flinch. Ball one. Danny glared at the pitcher and took a few steady, deliberate swings.

The next pitch headed straight in. Danny's bat swept through the air and took the ball with it. The pitcher stretched to intercept the line drive but it passed him and the shortstop before landing deep in the outfield. The center fielder ran in a circle around the rolling ball before picking it up and throwing to first, which Danny had already passed. The first baseman wasn't ready for a throw and the ball bounced past him toward the plate. The catcher chased down the ball and threw it to his brother on the mound, which forced Danny to pull up at third. Fred met him with a high five. Danny adjusted his pants and crouched a little, ready to run.

Clyde walked cautiously toward the plate, placing his feet carefully as if he were treading a booby-trapped path. He faced the pitcher without even bending his knees and watched two strikes sail by.

"Give it a ride, Clyde," yelled Danny. "Let one rip."

Clyde hunched up a little, bent his knees a little, and swung his bat more than a little.

"Good cut," boomed Butch Flagan from near first base.

"Strike three! You're out!" called the umpire.

Clyde shrugged and turned back to the bench.

It hadn't looked to Pump like Clyde was really going for that ball. His swing hadn't carried him off balance. It was more like he'd taken a good practice swing, just for the feel of it. He must've liked the feeling because his face had lost its frown.

Annie Maloney attacked the first pitch with a mighty swing that missed the low ball.

"Eye on the ball. Great cut," shouted Fred.

The next pitch sailed by for a ball. Annie settled herself, balanced on both feet. With a hefty swing she knocked the next ball high into the air. She started to run while everyone watched the ball sail over the low fence and bounce to a stop in the next field. The Minutemen were on their feet cheering wildly. Some of the parents were bouncing up and down on the sidelines. Fred was smiling in a satisfied way as he slapped Annie's hand when she trotted by third.

The score was 12-6. Nowhere near the mercy rule cutoff. Pump felt so relieved. He started to picture the runs that were about to pile up this inning. He figured if he got up to bat this inning the team could have gotten anywhere from one to five more runs. Now anything was possible … even the idea of Josh getting on base.

Pump's calculations were interrupted by Brian Kennedy's pop fly to right field for the second out. Then Penny Weiss struck out and the side was retired.

The Minutemen trotted out to their positions. Freddy took the mound, Clyde was at shortstop, Brian returned to catching and Pump was back at second. Pump felt exhilarated and hopeful. The Minutemen trailed by only six runs. They had added two runs to the awful margin that separated them from the mercy rule. Pump bounced to second base, straightened the bag, then slid over to his spot just behind the baseline between first and second.

Ken Ames was swinging two bats in his hand before he flung one aside and took his stance at the plate. Freddy looked cool on the mound. The haunted looks were gone from the Minutemen's faces. The thought that his team was relaxed made Pump feel even calmer.

Despite the pressure, Freddy's delivery was smooth. His first two pitches were outside. The third pitch came right over the plate to take Ken by surprise. Two and one. Freddy threw one more ball and then burned in two identical scorchers that sent Ken down swinging.

Ken bounced his bat on its end on the ground and stomped off, which delighted the Minutemen. Pump met Danny's eyes and they grinned at each other. Pump was glad he wasn't the only one who was relieved that Ken hadn't hit another home run. In fact, Ken had struck out, just like Pump.

The Muskets' second batter was Blaster McGarry. Fred Namath signaled to Freddy on the mound. The pitches that followed had so little on them that three of them didn't reach the plate. The next three looked like they would make it across and Blaster took the bait. He stretched forward to try to hit them and missed them all. Two up, two down.

Freddy walked Charles Ames and the batter following him. The fifth in the lineup hit a solid low fly to left field. Jeff Leonard missed the catch and loped after the ball as it bumped away from him. By the time he had tamed the ball, which seemed to buck in his hands, one run had come in, the second was rounding third, and the batter was running past Clyde at short. With a cry, Jeff whipped the ball to third where it flew beyond Annie's reach and over the fence. The last runner trotted home.

The next batter drew a walk. So did the two who followed. The fourth walk brought in the Muskets' fourth run of the inning. Freddy frowned and turned his back to the plate as the Muskets' DH took some swings.

Bones moved closer to Pump to whisper loudly to him, "Hey, Prout, here we go again. Mercy rule, watch out."

When Freddy turned back, the frown was gone. He threw a fine pitch in for a strike. The next pitch was straight in again and the batter popped it up. Pump called for the play and made the out. The side was retired.

Pump tossed the ball to the umpire as Danny Flagan joined him on their way to the bench.

"Who's Frankenstein over there?" Danny asked.

Pump followed the direction of Danny's nod and saw … his father. Pump's father was tall with a long face. His brow was furrowed in a frown so deep, it looked like a scar across his forehead.

"That's my dad," Pump said.

"Hey, forget the Frankenstein crack." Danny slapped Pump on the back. "He just looks so serious."

Pump wasn't listening. He felt a little thump in his chest when he figured his dad must've seen him make that last out.

"Move it, Minutemen. Let's hustle," Fred Namath clapped his hands. "Listen up."

The whole team gathered around their coach. "Good job, guys," he announced. "I like what I'm seeing. So what's different?"

"The score," muttered Bones.

"Yeah, the score is different for starters. What is it?"

"Sixteen to six," called out Mr. Gerstein. His wife jabbed him with her elbow and he clapped his hand over his mouth.

Fred Namath continued, "The Muskets got six runs in each of the first two innings. This inning we kept them down to four runs. What else?"

"We got two runs," Annie spoke up.

"Right," nodded Fred. "So our defense is improving and our offense is holding steady. Only I thought it had a better feel this inning. Before you all seemed paralyzed. I like the way you're starting to move. I can see you working. That's all I ask. Keep it up."

"What about that mercy rule, Coach?" asked Bones, his eyes wide in mock innocence. "We're 10 runs behind in the third."

"Well, we've got another inning. We're getting better all the time. Just do your job, Bednarski. You might be surprised what can happen."

"Seeing is believing," Bones muttered under his breath. Pump thought it was loud enough for the coach to hear but Fred looked calm and quiet. Either he hadn't heard or he really didn't care. Pump was too busy keeping an eye on his father to follow what was going on. He made himself pay attention.

"Leonard's first up, followed by Bednarski on deck. Gerstein, double deck. Remember, think basic. That means think getting on base. You gotta swing the bat. You gotta be serious. I'm with you all the way."

Pump couldn't believe the level tone of the coach's voice. There wasn't any anger and here they were, down 16-6. Pump just hoped Fred's quick anger wouldn't come back. He wished it were more predictable. Since Pump didn't know when it was coming, he waited for it all the time. Fred Namath's words echoed in Pump's head, "I'm with you all the way." The Minutemen needed to know that.

Jeff Leonard was at the plate. His practice swings showed Pump that he was trying to recreate his home run swing from the second inning. This time he never got the chance to use it. Charles Ames walked him in four straight pitches. The pitcher stamped his foot on the mound as Jeff trotted to first.

"Prout, double deck," Fred Namath called out.

Bones Bednarski watched a strike go by. Then a ball, high and inside, forced him to jump back. Maybe that's what started him moving, because he gave a lazy, early swipe at the next pitch and actually connected with the ball sending it in a perfect arc just out of reach over the first baseman's head. It settled in the grass after a single bounce made the right fielder scramble after it. Huffing, Bones pushed himself onto first about a second before the first baseman got the ball and turned to tag him. Bones stood on the base and panted. The Minutemen cheered. Fred jabbed both his thumbs up to praise Bones's hit.

Josh Gerstein stood at the plate. His face was pale. He looked startled and frozen. Before every pitch he would roll his eyes toward his parents at the fence, then back in the direction of the ball. Pump knew that desperate feeling and wondered if he looked like that at the plate. He'd never thought about it before. Nothing could be that bad. Not even striking out.

But Josh didn't strike out. He walked. Charles Ames muttered things under his breath. Pump wished he could hear what Charles was saying as Josh almost skipped to first to load the bases.

Pump moved from the on-deck circle to the plate, his heart pounding. He felt a lump in his throat that made it hard to swallow.

Here he was, up to bat, bases loaded, no outs, a tiring pitcher. Four potential runs at one blow. And his father was watching.

Pump swung the bat stiffly. Practice swings were supposed to loosen you up, but Pump felt nothing could loosen him up. The only thing loose about him was his mind. Visions of glory flashed before him. So did visions of disaster. He could save the game with a grand-slam homer. Or he could strike out. His hands were clammy as he tightened his grip on the bat.

"Play the ball, not the pitcher," echoed in Pump's head. He closed his eyes for a second to shut out Charles Ames. When he opened his eyes, the ball was coming at him. He didn't have to try, it was all he could see. His swing was simple reflex. It worked.

Pump hit a solid low, deep fly ball out to left field. Blaster McGar-ry looked startled and tripped as he backpedaled to keep up with the ball. Pump dashed to first where Josh Gerstein stood frozen while he looked toward left field.

"Move," shouted Pump.

At the same instant Fred Namath bellowed, "Tag up, everyone, tag up! Touch the bag! Get your foot on the bag, then go. Go, runners!"

Josh trembled on first. Pump shoved his arms in front of him as he ran. Josh saw the fierce look on Pump's face and took off.

As Pump heard his coach's command to tag up and run, his heart missed a beat. "Tag up" meant only one thing. It meant someone caught a fly ball. And the only ball in the air was Pump's.

Pump looked up and saw the left fielder, Blaster, curling up to throw. He must've caught Pump's hit. Pump slowed up as he rounded first, right on the heels of Josh Gerstein. That was it. His fly ball was caught. He stopped running.

"Home, home!" shrieked the Muskets' coach.

"Home, home!" yelled Fred Namath.

Rushing to get rid of the ball, Blaster hurled it to second base. The second baseman was still on the base path between first and second, so the ball flew all the way past the first base foul line.

A cheer went up. Jeff Leonard had just crossed the plate.

Bones rounded third. His face was flushed. His cheeks puffed out and in like bellows. Fred Namath and Butch Flagan were both motioning like windmills to keep the runners moving while the first baseman retrieved the ball.

"Home, home!" screamed the Muskets.

"To the pitcher!" yelled their coach, desperate to stop play.

Another cheer erupted amid the general shouts as Bones Bednarski heaved himself across the plate.

"All the way," called out Fred Namath as Josh Gerstein hesitated at third.

"To the pitcher," pleaded the Muskets' coach.

"Home! To the mound!" The Muskets shouted a garble of conflicting orders.

Now that he saw the end in sight, Josh turned on speed no one could have guessed he had. He whizzed over the plate just as the ball dumped into the dirt at the pitcher's feet. The pitcher picked up the ball and, with an angry shout, threw it high to the backstop which clanged with the impact.

The Minutemen were beside themselves. They bounced up and down and slapped each other's back or hands. Pump was cheered and pounded as if he had hit a home run.

A three-run sacrifice fly. If that wasn't baseball history, Pump didn't know what was. Three runs and not one of them Pump's. But they were all Minutemen runs and that was almost as good. Pump knew he was supposed to feel that that was even better, but somehow, in his deepest hidden heart of hearts, he would have rather hit a home run. But so what? The Minutemen had nine runs now and only one out. Pump tried not to notice that that out was his.

But Pump couldn't help but notice that his dad was gone. Had he seen Pump's fly ball? Did he know it brought in three runs? Or did he just see it as Pump's out? Pump tried to shake off these thoughts and focus on the game.

Freddy walked to first. Pump could practically see steam coming out of Charles Ames's ears. The pitcher lost it completely when Danny drove in another run with a clean double to center field. Clyde tried his best to strike out by taking some half-hearted swings at two outside balls. The third pitch was inside and hit Clyde in the arm, putting him on base in spite of himself. Clyde smiled over at Danny at second. Pump saw that flicker of the confident Clyde and smiled, himself.

The game stopped while the Muskets changed pitchers. Ben Bracken, a short, solid boy, stepped in to relieve a muttering Charles Ames, who took his place at first.

After warming up, the new pitcher faced Annie Maloney. Ben was steady from the beginning. He was not necessarily going to be giving out free trips to first.

The Minutemen's spirits seemed to lift once Charles Ames was off the mound. Annie swung with conviction as she took her practice swings. Her brisk grounder bumped between the pitcher and first baseman. The second baseman threw himself on the ball, jumped up and snapped the throw home. Ken made the catch but was just too far from the plate to reach Danny as he slid home. 16-11. The Minutemen were closing the gap. Still only one out. Pump's out.

For the first time in the game the top of the lineup was standing firm. Brian Kennedy was next up. Inspired by his teammates, he looked hungry for a hit. If you're hungry enough, anything looks good. Brian swung at everything he was served and struck out in three swings.

Penny Weiss drew the last walk of the inning. This was the first inning that the Minutemen got through the whole lineup, 10 batters, to retire the side. Pump knew if they made it to the fifth inning, the teams could bat until they were put out with three outs.

"Nice improvement in the offense department, Minutemen,"

Fred Namath said as the team picked up their gloves from the bench. "Now tighten up the defense, and the mercy rule won't stop us."

The Minutemen trotted out to the field.

Ken Ames led off for the fourth time. Pump hoped Ken wouldn't notice that the Muskets had batted through their lineup every inning. But he probably did since he led off. At least in the third inning, the Minutemen had made the Muskets' third out. The last out was the 10th batter anyway so it looked the same. Pump would have to point that out to Ken.

"Let's go, Freddy. Throw as hard as you can. Right to the glove," called out the coach. "Hold your glove *up*, Brian. Give him a target!"

Freddy looked like he was trying too hard. He was looking for a strikeout and was coming up with a walk by throwing too hard and sacrificing control.

Ken walked to first.

"Ease up, Freddy," Fred called to his pitcher. "Make him come to you."

Freddy followed his father's advice. Blaster took huge swings and struck out.

Charles looked bored at the plate. Freddy threw steady pitches. At the three-and-one count Freddy tried a curve ball, which startled everyone who noticed and made it in for the second strike. Charles almost swung at the next pitch, which was high. Another walk.

Bones sidled closer to Pump so he could say in a loud whisper, "Both Ameses got walked. Uh-oh."

Pizza De Souza was up next. Freddy hung his head while he composed himself. Then he wound up and threw a fine pitch in for a strike. His next pitch was straight in. The batter got under the ball and lifted it for a shallow fly to right field, just over Pump's head. Bones had never moved back to his position, which left him standing right under the falling fly ball. He held his glove out and the ball settled into it. He stared in amazement at the ball in his glove.

Charles had taken a lead off first but hadn't tagged the base before taking off for second after Bones' catch. Fred as well as Freddy and several of the other players and parents saw this and called urgently to Bones, "Get him. Throw him out, throw him out."

Bones heard their cries and looked up in confusion. Danny kept one foot on first base and stretched his arms to receive the throw. Instead of throwing to Danny for the automatic out, Bones hesitated and hurled the ball as hard as he could right at the runner. A direct hit. Charles grabbed his right shoulder where he'd been hit and stopped running to shout in the direction of Bones and Pump. The fury on his face scared Pump.

"You're out," shouted Bones.

"You're out," yelled Charles. "Outta this game, you geek." He stalked toward Bones who cowered behind Pump. The umpire and the two coaches ran over to hold the two boys apart. Charles made threatening motions toward Bones, holding up his fist ready to throw a punch. Bones made himself as small as he could.

Ken Ames had completed his trip home and came out to see what was up. Pizza came running out to see if maybe his out didn't count and he could go to first. The umpire held up his hands.

"The fly ball was caught for the out. The runner was struck by the ball, so he takes a base. Get yourself to second, son," the umpire said.

"I thought it was a double play," Bones muttered.

"It could have been," sighed his father from behind the fence.

"Two outs, runner on second. Batter up," roared the umpire. He adjusted his chest protector and stood behind the pitcher, which Canterbury umpires often did. Pump didn't like it.

Freddy didn't seem to mind. He struck out the next batter to retire the side. 17-11. A spread of six. Nowhere near 12. The Minutemen had made it. No mercy rule. Now, thought Pump, it was time for a comeback.

A Kind of Victory

"YOU'RE LEARNING, BEDNARSKI." Fred Namath clapped Bones on the back. "Whether you like it or not. Now you can take a rest and absorb all that learning."

Bones looked up at the coach who shouted, "Fifth inning. Last rookie replacement. Willie, you're in for Bednarski. Gerstein, take a breather. Jill Maloney, you take over for Weiss. Weiss, why don't you bat DH. Hustle in, guys. Leonard, you're up. Salvano, on deck. Weiss, double deck."

Ben Bracken threw slow and sure pitches that invited the Minutemen to swing. Jeff Leonard kept swinging with all his might but without watching the ball. He struck out.

Willie stood at the plate for the first time in the game. He watched the first pitch sail by. It looked good but the umpire called it a ball. Willie shifted his slight weight and crouched down. The pitch was high but this time the umpire called a strike. Pump thought the umpire would do better if he stood behind the batter, especially one with such a tiny strike zone. Willie swung neatly at the next pitch. He sent a slow grounder toward third base. The third baseman waited too long to see if the ball was going to roll foul. It didn't, and Willie beat the throw to first.

Everyone cheered. Willie bounced up and down on first. It was his first hit not only of the season but of his entire career. He kept grinning as Penny Weiss stood stiffly at the plate, watching the pitches sail by. With a two-two count, Penny impulsively poked her bat forward, connected with the ball and popped up a fly that floated toward first base.

Charles Ames stood behind Willie waiting to make an easy out. As the ball dropped toward first, Willie shoved both hands upward and plucked the ball from the air.

"I got it," Willie shouted in excitement. He held the ball over his head to display his trophy. A look of dismay crossed Willie's face. "Uh-oh," he groaned, as he realized what he'd done.

Everyone stared at him in wonder.

"That's an out," shouted a Muskets parent.

"Interference," called Bub Bednarski.

"Two outs," yelled the Muskets' coach.

"Hold on," called out Fred Namath.

The umpire shrugged. "Beats me," he said.

Pump couldn't think of what the call should be. The ball touched Willie so that would be an out—except his foot, both his feet were on the base. Wouldn't that make him safe? Had he made an out against his own team? Or was that interference? And if it was, what did that mean? Take the whole thing over?

"When in doubt, you're out!" the umpire growled at everyone. "You're out!" he declared pointing at Penny who had run to first just in case the out didn't count. Her lip trembled as she tried not to cry.

The umpire turned and pointed his finger right in Willie's face, "And you're out," he shouted. "Everyone's out. The side is retired."

"Now wait a second," Fred said calmly.

The umpire frowned and scratched his head. The crowd babbled in pandemonium. The Muskets' coach was pacing up and down. He stopped in front of the umpire, jabbed two fingers at him and said, "Two outs, Jim. Don't be stupid. Two outs."

"Watch who you call stupid," the umpire roared. "One out it is."

A big grin lit up Fred Namath's face.

The umpire saw the smile and turned red. "So, Namath, you think you've pulled a fast one. OK. It's gotta be two outs. The batter is out on the caught fly. The kid on first is out because he interfered with play. The side is, like I said before, retired."

Pump watched from the on-deck circle before he walked back to the bench. Penny picked up her bat on her way to the bench. Willie walked back in a daze.

When Willie reached the bench, Danny greeted him with a clap on the back.

"Way to go, Salvano!" Danny exclaimed. "Your first hit of the season! And the only sacrifice catch in history. You are our secret weapon."

Willie looked woefully at Danny. He wasn't sure if Danny was kidding or not. Danny reached out and patted Willie. "You did good, son," Danny added with a wink.

Willie smiled doubtfully. He carefully took off his batting helmet, picked up his glove, and trotted out to right field.

17-11. Despite all the action, the score hadn't changed. Pump tossed his batting helmet into the dugout, grabbed his glove and trotted out to his position. He'd had great plans for his at bat. They would just have to wait.

In the bottom of the fifth, for the first time in the game, the strongest part of the Muskets' lineup wasn't leading off. Danny Flagan walked to the mound. Pump heard Freddy complain, "Oh, Dad, you always do this. It's not fair. I'm just getting warmed up. I can do it. Give me a chance."

"Save that energy for first base. The team needs you there right now. We'll use you in the next game this week," Fred said to his scowling son.

Danny threw his usual steady pitches to Brian for warm-up. The batter stepped into the box. Danny's straight, predictable pitches gave the batters plenty to swing at. The first two batters swung but they went down swinging.

The next batter decided it was safer not to swing and he walked.

The third batter connected on his first swing but hit the ball right to Freddy who, in one motion, caught the ball on the bounce, grazed the bag with his foot and started in to the bench. The score held steady.

"Minutemen, keep it up," said Fred Namath. "I like what I'm seeing. Now we've got some catching up to do. Remember: think base hits.

"You're first up, Prout. Then Namath, then Flagan. This could be interesting."

Here was Pump, leading off again. He wondered why he felt nervous when he was first up. Maybe, he thought, because no one was on base. But when he was second up and the first batter had made an out, he didn't feel as scared as he did when he was the very first batter. So he pretended that someone had just struck out and now he was up. He felt less jittery.

Ben Bracken gave Pump a nice fat pitch, right down the middle. Pump couldn't believe his luck. He threw himself into his swing and missed. There went his chance. The next pitch was just as ripe for the picking as the first. Pump watched the ball and stepped into his swing. The ball shot up the middle, past the pitcher.

As Pump ran to first, Butch Flagan motioned for him to keep going. Pump sped toward second. He saw the center fielder scoop up the ball, so he dropped into a slide. Pump slid more than a whole body length, his leg stretched toward the canvas base. As he touched it, the loose base slid out of his reach. Pump swam through the dirt. In two strokes his foot was on the bag. A breath later, Pump felt the ball pressed against his arm.

"He's out," shouted the Muskets' coach.

The umpire crossed his arms in front of his chest, then scissored them downward and open. Pump was safe. The Minutemen yelped with joy.

"You're nuts, ump," shrieked Tony, the Muskets' coach. "He was out by a mile."

"Take a hike," grunted the umpire as he shifted his chest protector and hitched up his pants. "He's safe."

As the crowd settled down, Freddy moved to the plate. He looked determined to do something big. Pump could hear the air move with Freddy's warm-up swings. He knocked the first pitch as hard as he could and lifted it high enough to sail over the right fielder and drop before it reached the fence. Freddy's triple brought Pump home.

17-12. No outs.

At the plate, Danny's expression was unusually serious. He tore at the first pitch and just caught the ball from below. A high pop foul over the backstop. The next pitch got the same treatment.

"You got a piece of it, now get the whole thing!" Butch called out.

Danny nodded. He shifted his weight, then swung. He got the whole thing.

The ball sailed high and over the fence. Freddy cantered home in front of Danny, who chugged solemnly as far as third, then broke into a grin and trotted home. He was met at the plate by a swarm of his teammates. The Minutemen jumped all over Danny and each other. 17-14 and still no outs.

Clyde stepped up to the plate. His face was without expression. Pump noticed that this time Clyde bent his knees slightly. That was an improvement from the straight-legged stance he'd been using for the past few games. Ordinarily, if there was one thing Clyde was good at, it was bending his knees. Clyde could look relaxed as melting ice cream and then instantly dash to make a play faster than anyone.

Ben Bracken looked calm as ever on the mound. He threw the same tempting pitches, but Clyde didn't take the bait. He looked the balls over and drew a walk.

Annie Maloney went after the ball with too much excitement for two quick strikes. Then she calmed down which seemed to trouble the pitcher who lost the plate and walked her.

Brian Kennedy came to the plate.

"Tie it up! Tie it up!" The Minutemen chanted in a chorus. "Tie it up!"

Brian drew the third walk in a row while his team kept chanting, "Tie it up."

Bases loaded

Jill Maloney appeared at the plate and the chanting stopped.

"Come on, Jill," the team shouted. "Make him pitch to you. Wait for your pitch. Look 'em over."

Jill looked them over and she waited for her pitch. Her pitch never came and she struck out. One out.

"Tie it up! Bring them home!" chanted the Minutemen as Jeff Leonard swayed to the plate.

"Remember the second inning, Leonard!" exclaimed Freddy from the bench.

"Give it a ride," yelled Bones.

"Take your time. Watch the ball, not the future," called the coach.

Pump couldn't bear to watch. They had a chance not only to tie the game but to go ahead if Jeff could surprise them all again.

That's what baseball is about. There's always room for surprises. You just keep trying and hope for some luck. Pump closed his eyes and wished for luck until the umpire yelled, "You're out!"

Pump sighed and raised his head. Two outs.

Willie Salvano continued to mystify the pitcher with his tiny strike zone. He drew a walk, which brought in Clyde for the 15th run. Now a grand slam would put the Minutemen in the lead. Just two more runs to tie it up. Was that asking too much?

Apparently it was asking too much, since Penny Weiss kept the bat on her shoulder using her statue strategy and, on the fifth pitch, struck out.

The game was over. The Muskets won, 17-15. The Minutemen's sixth inning rally didn't win them the game but it brought back their good spirits and the will to try again. After all, not being mercied by the Muskets was a kind of victory.

When the teams lined up and slid their hands across the vertical palms of their opponents, Pump made himself meet Ken's eyes as they passed each other. He tried to pretend it was just another game. But it wasn't. It was their first loss of the season. And it was to the Muskets.

"Good game," his mother said as he tossed his glove to her and ran over to join his team as they huddled around the coach. Pump wasn't sure that he wanted to hear anything his family might say to him right then. He preferred Fred's post-game wrap up. At least all the Minutemen were in this together.

No pizza at Pirelli's when you lose to the Muskets, Pump knew. He didn't feel hungry anyway. At dinner that night, Pump hardly ate anything. His mother kept smiling at him, which made him mad. Pump knew she was trying to cheer him up.

His father didn't seem to notice him, which also made him mad, even if he was afraid to talk about the game to his dad. Pump wondered why his dad had left and he even wondered why his dad had come. Pump thought if he talked about the game, his dad would warn him about not letting his hopes run away with him. His dad would say a loss was either a wake-up call, which meant you weren't really trying your hardest in the first place, or it was the end of any hope for success.

"Well, that's it for the Minutemen," he could imagine his father saying.

And, Pump worried, maybe he'd be right.

Chapter 14

Back to Earth

THE NEXT MORNING Pump moved slowly to delay his inevitable arrival at school. He couldn't think of anything that would cancel school for the day.

"Welcome back to Earth, spaceman," Luke greeted him when Pump finally came into the kitchen for breakfast.

Pump glared at his brother. He tried to give Luke a don't-mess-with-me look. Luke continued, "It's tough coming back to reality, isn't it?"

Pump tried to ignore him. Luke wouldn't take the hint. He pushed further. "It's rough to see the undefeated season go up in smoke. The truth is bitter. Poor guy." Luke shook his head without meeting Pump's eyes. "I wonder what the Muskets are feeling like right now?"

Quick as a striking rattlesnake, Pump slugged his brother right between the shoulder blades, then jumped out of the way as Luke grabbed for him.

"Quit it, boys!" yelped their mother. "Luke, you leave Pump alone."

"Me?" shrieked Luke.

"Stop goading him."

Luke clenched his teeth and squinted his eyes in Pump's direction.

Pump looked down at his cereal bowl. He pushed some Cheerios down under the milk and watched them pop back up to the surface. He didn't meet Luke's eyes.

Pump wasn't hungry. The sunny day seemed dull and cloudy. At the end of the game yesterday he had been sure the Minutemen were coming back. But today the Minutemen's chances seemed dim. Luke was right. The season was as good as over. The Minutemen played like a bunch of rookies.

And what about Clyde? What had happened to Clyde? He'd looked like he was going to be the best their league had ever seen. He was going to carry the whole team on his shoulders. Every game would be just another chance to break records. Now look at them. Bedraggled, lousy and discouraged.

Pump's father came into the kitchen, poured himself a cup of coffee and joined the boys at the table.

"What happened yesterday?" he asked. As if he hadn't had the whole dinnertime last night to ask that or to notice something was wrong, Pump thought.

Luke told how his team had been robbed of a win by a crummy umpire, who clearly favored the other team. The Dodgers had lost a close game.

"So what," Pump blurted out, "You weren't undefeated in the first place."

Luke and his father turned to Pump.

"Oh, yes?" his father said, "Your team, as I remember, was undefeated, wasn't it?"

"Yeah," Pump muttered, looking at his cereal bowl.

"And that leaves the Muskets still undefeated?" Pump's dad asked.

Pump nodded forlornly.

"Well," his father said as he stood up and put on his coat, "There's always next year."

As soon as his mother followed his father out of the kitchen, Pump popped up, dumped his cereal into the sink, and washed it down the drain. He grabbed his backpack and headed out the door. Luke let him leave without any comment.

Pump liked to ride his bike to school, but today even his bike didn't lift his spirits. When he got to school, he found he had forgotten his bike lock at home. He could either ride home and get the lock, which would make him late, or he could risk leaving his bike unlocked.

Pump parked his bike in the bicycle rack where he always did. He just hoped it looked locked up. The old bike rack shook when Pump kicked it and growled, "Rats." As if everything weren't already going wrong, Pump realized he'd forgotten his lunch. He'd left everything behind today, at least everything beginning with *l*, he thought to himself as he hoisted his school bag over his shoulder. Lock, lunch, and luck.

Walking into school, head down, Pump didn't notice someone fall into step with him. They took a few steps in stride together before Pump realized that Ken was beside him.

"Yo," Ken greeted Pump. Pump braced himself for a flood of bragging. He barely nodded to Ken.

"Sorry about the game," mumbled Ken.

"Sorry?" Pump could hardly believe his ears. "Did you say 'sorry'?" He gulped. "Hey, there's nothing for *you* to feel sorry about. You played a great game. If we'd just had one more inning … "

He laughed for the first time all morning.

"Whaddya think you woulda done with one more inning?" Ken laughed with Pump.

"Well, we were on the way back," said Pump.

"Yeah, on the way back to the cellar." Ken grinned. "No, really, that was a tough game." Ken paused.

Pump just said, "I gotta go. See ya later," and headed to his classroom.

Pump's class was studying Africa. Their big project for the week was working on African masks they were making out of paper. There was a box of bark, feathers, beads, straws and all kinds of odds and ends to use on their masks. Pump took aluminum foil and made a set of jaws with sharp-looking aluminum teeth for his mask. He was feeling ferocious and his mask was looking fierce.

Fierce was better than gloomy. It meant you had plans to fight back. Pump squeezed a pond of glue onto the cheeks and chin of his mask. He piled wood shavings into the glue. He looked with satisfaction at the teeth gleaming out through the curly beard.

The class had learned that the Africans who make masks use symbols in their masks to signify important aspects of their lives. Pump used his most significant symbol. He cut a *C* out of white construction paper, a hat shape out of red and pasted the *C* onto the hat. "Pump!" His teacher's voice startled him. "I've never seen you so focused. What a mask!" she exclaimed and held it up for the class to see. Pump was embarrassed but pleased.

At recess, Pump checked the bike rack and saw his bike was still there. Pump suspected that his mask really did drive away harmful spirits. By the time he left school he was once again happy to see Ken Ames.

"Nice homer, yesterday," Pump blurted out.

"Hey," Ken said, "thanks. It's my first, you know. First ever."

To hear the way he usually talked, you never would have known that, thought Pump, but, of course, it was true.

"Well, it won't be your last," Pump said, feeling generous.

Ken beamed.

The boys reached the bike rack together. While Ken unlocked his bike, Pump went over his with his hand, like he was inspecting his horse.

"Good game, though," Ken said once they were riding. "You guys almost took it away from us."

"Next time," Pump vowed.

"Maybe. Maybe not," Ken replied.

Pump finished his mask on Wednesday, the day the Minutemen were playing the Pilgrims. The Pilgrims were an unknown. They had four wins and two losses going into the game with the Minutemen.

As the teams gathered at the field and game time drew near, Pump felt excited and nervous. Some of the good feeling of the last half of the Muskets' game seemed to have stuck with the Minutemen.

While the teams warmed up, Pump saw no sign of Clyde. No one knew where he was. By the time the teams collected at their respective benches, Clyde still hadn't shown up. Fred Namath gave his usual pep talk with no mention of Clyde's absence. Finally, Danny spoke out.

"Where's Clyde?" he asked.

Fred shook his head. "I don't know. But I'm not surprised."

"Can we delay the game?" Jeff Leonard asked hopefully.

"We're all set," Fred said without concern. "We've warmed up. We know what to do: stay focused, be ready, know where the play is. Just like always. When Clyde comes, we'll be glad to see him. We always like to have the whole team. But we can do fine if someone, anyone can't make it. This is a team. We're ready. We're the Minutemen."

Pump's heart thumped fast as he realized the game was starting without Clyde. Through the whole first inning, Pump kept a lookout for Clyde. He hoped he'd catch sight of Clyde's face coming through the crowd. Pump imagined so hard that a few times he thought he saw, out of the corner of his eye, a flicker of Clyde's shadow. But Clyde didn't come.

Pump had to lead off. He was still distracted by his search for Clyde. Leading off seemed less important than locating Clyde. With the count at 0 and two, Pump pulled his attention back to the game, but he went down swinging. The rest of the team was a little more focused and brought in two runs. The Pilgrims made two runs in the bottom of the inning and Pump hardly noticed. Luckily, the ball did not come to him.

In the top of the second the teams were tied at two apiece. With two outs and Penny Weiss on first, Pump came up for his second at bat. He swung hard at the first pitch. The ball skimmed past the pitcher to become a bumpy grounder for the shortstop, who took so long to subdue it, that Penny brought in a run. Pump pulled up at second just a few feet from the shortstop, who was circling the ball like a dog chasing his tail. The Minutemen cheered and whistled. The Pilgrims' shortstop pulled his cap low over his face but Pump could see his chin trembling.

Pump crouched, ready to run as Danny took his practice swings. Danny walked, putting runners on first and second. Freddy reached for a high ball and managed to launch a slow fly that baffled the right fielder, who dropped it. Pump sped around third and landed on home with a clap of cleats. Danny came churning toward third but somehow the right fielder had gathered the ball and thrown to his cutoff at second base, who actually threw all the way to third in time for the tag. Danny was out. Pump forgot about Clyde. The Minutemen were ahead by two. In the bottom of the inning the Pilgrims surged one run ahead.

The game stayed close. Freddy had pitched three innings in the last game and Danny had pitched two. Each player could only pitch six innings in a week. Freddy was the starter and had finished his three remaining innings after the top of the third. Danny was available for four. That would cover the pitching even without Clyde and without having to call on less certain pitching options, like Jeff Leonard.

In a way, Pump felt more relaxed with Clyde absent. Fred Namath seemed less tense, too. How could it be that when the team's best player is out, everyone is more relaxed? Pump was puzzled. But he shook it off. There was a baseball game to play, and they were in the thick of it. The Pilgrims were playing well, better than the Minutemen would have predicted. But the Minutemen were playing about a hundred times better than they would have predicted without Clyde.

Freddy only hit two batters in his three innings on the mound, which was evidence of his improved control. Danny pitched two solid innings after a shaky fourth in which he walked in two runs. In the top of the fifth, the Minutemen broke through to take the lead, 8-7. From then on the Pilgrims lost their momentum. They made more errors, flailed more at the plate. The Minutemen stayed focused in the field and at bat.

The final score was the Pilgrims, 8, and the Minutemen, 12.

Danny burst into a huge grin as the last Pilgrim swept his bat above a low ball for the last out of the game.

"That's what I call a real game!" shouted Mr. Bednarski slapping Fred on the back. "Now *that's* baseball!"

The Minutemen slipped their hands over the hands of the Pilgrims before sitting on the grass for their wrap-up with Fred. Finally the teammates took off by car or on foot or bike for Pirelli's Pizza. Pump walked to his bike. As he bent over to unlock it, the streetlights flashed on and a shadow fell across him. Pump looked up to see Clyde standing near him, his head haloed by the streetlight. Pump straightened up.

"Hey," Clyde said. "Not a bad game."

"Not bad," Pump echoed. "Clyde?" his voice trailed off.

"Yeah, Prout?" Clyde responded.

"Where were you? You missed a great game."

Clyde shrugged, "Probably just as well. It wouldn't' have been so great if I'd played," Clyde sighed heavily.

"That's crazy," Pump protested. "Who says so?"

"I say so," Clyde said. "And I should know. I'm no good now. I gotta face the facts."

"Hey," Pump declared, "that's no fact. Where were you? Why'd you miss the game? How much did you see?"

"Just about the whole thing," Clyde admitted. "I just couldn't play."

Neither of them spoke for a while. Pump started to walk with his bike. Clyde fell into step alongside him.

"It's worse to know I'm letting everyone down," Clyde eventually said. "Is everyone mad at me?"

Pump met Clyde's gaze. He shrugged and answered, "I don't think so." After a pause, he added, "I'm not."

Clyde kicked a rock. He remained silent.

Pump spoke again. "You know, when you didn't show up I was sure we'd lose. But look what happened. We didn't. Look at Freddy. He only hit two Pilgrims. That's a record low for him. He really performed."

"Yeah," Clyde agreed. "Better than I could do."

"I didn't say that," Pump protested. "That's your idea."

Pump could hardly believe he was talking to Clyde the way he talked to Luke.

Clyde continued as if he hadn't heard Pump. "Seems like sometimes I even surprise myself with what I throw when I'm in the zone. It just seems to happen. I can't make it happen. I wish I could.

"But everyone, Fred and the team, seem to be counting on me to pitch great every time. Today I just couldn't face it."

Pump protested. "You've got it wrong, Clyde. Look what we did today. We had to play even if you weren't there, and we had to play better *because* you weren't there. So we did. But just because we *could* play without you, doesn't mean anyone wanted to!" Pump concluded with feeling.

"Hey," Clyde said, "that is quite a speech. Quite a speech for a sprout."

Relieved by the change in Clyde's tone, Pump said, "Come on. Let's go to Pirelli's."

Clyde frowned in doubt. "No, I gotta go. See ya around."

Clyde ran off. Pump got on his bike, turned on his light and rode to Pirelli's in the dusk.

Chapter 15

The Show

THE CANTERBURY LITTLE LEAGUE SEASON usually started out with frigid weather, icy rain and cold winds, while the second half of the season brought warmer and warmer days. Finally, it was May. The weather was improving, and Pump's birthday was coming. He was going to be eight on Friday. The Red Sox were playing a series against the Yankees at Fenway Park that weekend, and Pump's family was taking him and a friend to the game to celebrate his birthday. Pump couldn't wait. It was his first real baseball game, his first in-person look at major league baseball, his first appearance at The Show.

Pump had decided to bring Ken as his invited friend. He hoped Ken wouldn't forget about him because Luke was there. Luke could treat Pump's friends like they were friends of his and Pump's friends ate it up. Pump hated that.

Pump's mother had gotten the tickets before the season started and before the Canterbury Yankees had become the Minutemen. Now, no longer a Yankee, himself, and closely following the Red Sox, Pump was ready to take the plunge and join his brother as a Red Sox fan. After all, Babe Ruth had started out on the Red Sox before he got traded. The Babe had helped them win the 1918 World Series, the last one they had won for the next 86 years until 2004.

Pump would just go in the other direction, moving from the Yankees to the Red Sox. And this night, going to his first Major League game, his first visit to Fenway Park, he would go as a Red Sox fan.

Two things worried Pump. First, he didn't want anyone to make fun of him for switching. Since his brother and his friends always teased him for being a Yankee fan, he knew they might tease him more for becoming a Red Sox fan, maybe call him disloyal. Second, and just as important, he didn't have a Red Sox hat.

As they were getting ready to leave for the game, Pump looked for Luke and found him in front of the bathroom mirror.

"Luke?" Pump said.

Luke gave one last pat to his hat and turned it around on his head so the brim faced backward. "What is it, lil' bro?"

"Luke?" Pump began again.

Luke raised his eyebrows and looked at Pump.

"Yeah?"

"Luke, you know I've been a Yankees fan …" Pump's voice trailed off.

Luke nodded, then turned his hat around, and took it off.

"Well," Pump continued, "I think I'm ready to be for the Red Sox. Ever since my team changed its name, it doesn't seem so important to be a Yankee anymore. In fact, I'm hoping, more and more, that the Red Sox will make the playoffs and then make it to the series. Do you think it's all right for someone to change teams? Would you be mad at me?"

"Well, I dunno," Luke said, his face serious. Then with a yelp he grabbed Pump and spun around with him.

"Mad at you? You're crazy! I've always known you were really a Red Sox fan, deep down. You were misguided, a brother who didn't know his true destiny. Welcome back, you goon.

"Hey, you can't be for the Red Sox without a hat. Here you go." Luke took his hat and thumped it on to Pump's head. "Just in time for your birthday."

The game would start just after 7:00, but the Prouts arrived early enough to watch the Yankees take batting practice. They entered Fenway Park at the gate, then followed the curving concrete canyon that circled the field under the stands. Pump felt they had walked forever before they reached the stairs that led to their grandstand seats.

Stepping from the cave below into a blast of light and green, Pump almost gasped. He felt he had crossed some magical threshold. Even though he could see the blue sky above, lights already blazed around the field. Fenway Park was vibrant. The grass was an intense green. It was perfectly trimmed as if a barber had just finished shaping it. The base paths were rust-colored settings for the sparkling white bases that lay in the corners. The big green wall known as the Green Monster was the boundary for deep left field. Pump thought the Green Monster was as famous as most of the players and he felt awed to see it in person.

The players looked huge, definitely larger than life. They were so close and so big, Pump felt like he could reach out and touch them. He swallowed hard.

As Pump adjusted to the magic of the park, he scanned the players who were already on the field. Some were stretching, some were sprinting. A batter was at the plate while a pitcher, standing behind a metal frame with nets draped over it, sent even, straight pitches over the plate. The batter whacked one ball after another casually sending them deep into the field. A lot of balls soared into the stands.

Pump watched number 2 drop to the grass for a series of push-ups. His biceps bulged, his back and legs were straight. It was Derek Jeter himself.

Lost in reverence, Pump could hear his name being called. He looked up to find that his family had not stopped to stare in awe at the Yankee shortstop doing push-ups, but had moved on toward their seats. Pump waved. Soon Luke and Ken rejoined him. The boys moved down to just above the Yankees dugout where they watched the rest of practice hoping they would have a shot at getting an autograph.

Jeter sauntered over to two of his teammates who were standing to the side of the batter practicing at the plate. Jeter laughed as he took a batting helmet brought to him by a batboy. Pump wondered why they called them batboys when this guy was clearly a grown man. Pump wished he could be that close to the players.

Jeter stepped up to the plate, where he took a long set of swings to loosen up. The pitcher started with a big windup before sending over the first ball. Jeter swung like he had all the time in the world and sent the ball over the fence and into the net that kept home runs from dropping to the street. Pump could hear Fred Namath saying, "Don't rush your swing." Jeter was not rushing his swing and look at what he could do.

The pitcher and Jeter struck a rhythm. Quiet wind-up, pitch, smooth swing, gone. Again and again.

At some invisible signal, like a change in the music, Jeter relinquished his helmet and bat to the batboy and jogged up the foul line before veering back toward the dugout. As he approached the boys, who stood squashed between the larger men and autograph seekers, Pump's heart beat so fast he stopped breathing.

Voices called out, "Over here, Derek. Over here, Jeter."

"Hey, Derek, over here," shouted a deep, grown-up voice.

"Just one, just one. Aw, come on, just one," growled another.

"Up here, Mr. Jeter," called Luke.

But Jeter avoided looking up and ducked into the dugout. Pump gave a weak smile and heaved a deep sigh.

"I'm ready to sit down," Luke announced. "Let's get back to our seats."

The boys worked their way to their parents. Pump's mom waved to them. She had brought a jacket for each of them, which accounted for the stack of jackets heaped on the seat next to her. Folded blankets teetered on top of the pile. Pump's father sat reading a book. Pump of-ten wished that his dad could get into the game the way he could see other fathers did, but tonight he was just glad his dad had come. After all, it was Pump's birthday.

The game was like a dream. Pump felt surrounded by baseball, inside in his heart and all around him. He had heard people de-scribed as living and breathing something. Well, he was living and breathing baseball. The more baseball he gobbled up, the hungrier he was for more.

The game was close. The boys teased each other a lot but some-times were silent with tension they shared with thousands of other fans.

In the ninth inning, with the Red Sox leading by one run, 5–4, Derek Jeter was up. He had already struck out, flied out to shallow center field and hit a double that bounced off the fence. Now, with two outs and no one on base, Jeter looked like he meant business. No smiles. His eyes burned as he squinted at the pitcher. He let the first strike go by. On the second pitch he got a bead on the ball coming low. With a perfect swing, he brought the bat under the ball and swept it high over the field, just like in batting practice. That ball was gone.

Pump punched Luke in the arm. Luke slugged him back and glowered at Pump.

Luke hissed, "Are you forgetting you're for the Red Sox now?"

"It was still a great hit," Pump muttered as he rubbed his arm to erase the throbbing and stinging left by Luke's knuckles.

The next batter was put out at first to retire the side. The Red Sox remained scoreless in the bottom of the ninth. The game went into extra innings. By the end of the 12th inning, Pump was glad to be sharing the blankets his mother had embarrassed him by bringing.

In the top of the 13th inning, the Red Sox seemed to get a sec-ond wind. Three outs came quickly and the team sprinted in from the field. With a runner on first, David Ortiz swayed to the plate. He swung two bats, then dumped one on the ground.

"Papi! Papi!" shrieked the fans. Ortiz stepped into the batter's box. The first pitch smacked into the dirt and caromed off the front edge of the plate. The runner dashed to second. Ball one. Balls two and three followed quickly. The pitcher settled down and threw two successive strikes.

Full count. Ortiz shook the air with his practice swings. At the next pitch he flung his weight into the swing. His bat connected and the ball soared past the glaring lights, deep into the black sky and over the wall. David Ortiz trotted around the bases.

Pump felt his heart soar skyward with Ortiz's ball as the crowd went wild.

"Papi! Papi!" the crowd cheered as Ortiz crossed the plate where his teammates swarmed around him. Pump, Ken and Luke pounded each other and jumped up and down. Pump was glad and proud he was a Red Sox fan.

The boys were sleepy. It was 11:30 and Pump's birthday was almost over. All three boys fell asleep in the car and snuggled into sleeping bags on the floor of Pump's room without really waking up.

Thrown a Curve

THE NEXT DAY was Saturday. After a late breakfast of pancakes, then playing catch outside, Ken and Pump were getting restless and decided to ride their bikes.

The two friends pedaled up and down the streets between Pump's house and school. They went down the streets they didn't usually follow on their daily route to school. The familiar places looked strange when the boys approached from a different direction.

While they cruised, Pump thought about baseball. Until the week before, Pump and Ken each played on an undefeated team. Now the Minutemen had lost. Catching up seemed harder than staying even.

Pump liked the feeling of moving through space, his legs churning, the wheels spinning.

He pretended he was in a tickertape parade after winning the World Series. He'd be in the white home team uniform, tipping his hat to the crowds.

Suddenly, Pump felt his bike spin to the left. The wheels stopped turning and skidded sideways. He squeezed the brake handles with all his might but couldn't stop the skid. His bike started to topple and he tried to jump free. But when the bike crashed to the pavement, Pump went down, too. He was dazed but sat right up.

A woman with a look of horror on her face sat inside her parked car. When Pump saw her frightened look, he felt like fainting. The woman's hand still held open the door that had caught Pump's bicycle wheel. She had flung open the door of her car without looking and the door had struck Pump's front wheel sending the bike careening.

"Are you all right?" she asked, frantically, as she jumped out of the car.

"Oh, my god, Pump! It's you! Are you OK? Maybe you'd better lie down."

The woman was Willie Salvano's mother. Pump saw Willie sitting in the front seat, peering up over the dashboard.

"I wasn't thinking. I just opened the door. I could've killed him," Willie's mom muttered to herself.

Willie looked more pale and scared as his mother continued to mumble. A little color started to rise in Pump's very pale cheeks. He wasn't badly hurt and was beginning to realize how lucky he was.

Meanwhile, Ken Ames had been calling back to Pump about his last baseball game and didn't notice that his audience was gone. He turned around to force a comment from his silent friend, only to find no one behind him.

Ken looked back and saw a crowd of people collected in the street. He spun his bike around and raced back. Ken found Pump sitting on the curb. Someone had picked up Pump's bike and propped it against a lamp post. Pump wore a dazed expression as he stared at his bike with its twisted wheels.

Ken hopped off his bike and ran up to Pump.

"What happened?" Ken asked. "What's going on?"

Ken was breathing hard.

Pump looked up. "I got knocked off my bike. When that lady—I mean Willie's mom—knocked me off."

"How'd she do that?" Ken demanded. "Are you OK?"

"Yeah, I think so," Pump replied.

"You're bleeding," Ken observed, looking more closely at Pump's arm and elbow.

Pump looked down. "Hey, I'm all scraped up." He winced. "Man, it stings now."

The scraped skin was starting to ooze. The right knee of his pants was torn.

"Wow, this could've been bad," Ken said with awe.

"I'm OK," Pump declared. He tried to push himself up but could tell his legs weren't going to hold him so he stayed where he was.

"What a relief," exhaled Willie's mother. "I am so sorry Pump. I should've been more careful. I'm always telling Willie that. Willie, watch out! Willie, be careful! But here it was me who wasn't careful."

She started to cry. Willie shriveled up in his seat.

Pump felt really uncomfortable. He stood up fast, felt dizzy and sat back down.

"Take your time there, Prout." The familiar voice of his coach sounded over Pump. "Take it slow."

Fred Namath gave Pump a hand and helped him rise slowly to his feet. Pump's scrapes were stinging, but nothing else really hurt. The worst part was the sight of his bicycle, its frame and both wheels bent and useless.

To cry in front of Ken would be bad enough, but now with Ken and the coach there, Pump just wouldn't cry. He bit the inside of his lower lip until the crying feeling passed.

"That was really careless of a driver to open the car door without looking first," Fred Namath said angrily. "Do you feel OK, Pump? No broken bones? Did you hit your head?"

Pump shook his head.

Ken Ames, glad to have a grown-up in charge, blurted out, "Nope, cap'n, it's only a flesh wound."

Pump smiled.

"Here, Pump," the coach said, looking at Pump's bike, "let me put that into my car and I'll drive you home. You need to get those scrapes cleaned up. I was on my way to get in some pitching practice with Freddy and Clyde before our team practice at two."

Pump slapped his forehead. "I forgot!" he exclaimed. "What time is it? Did I miss practice?"

Fred smiled. "You are a little shaken up. No, you have plenty of time."

"Hey, Fred," Willie's mother said in an anxious tone, "let me take Pump home. I am so sorry. This is all my fault. Let me do something."

Fred's angry frown softened, and he said in a calm voice, "That's OK, Mrs. Salvano. Freddy and I can take him home. You look pretty shaken up yourself. Pump's all right. Anyway, we all need to be more careful about car doors. Just get Willie to practice at two."

Fred turned to his wounded player. "Hey, Pump, Freddy and I can take you home to get cleaned up. Then maybe you'd like to come with us to the field."

"Sure, I would," Pump said eagerly. Ken hovered behind Pump. He was suddenly shy.

"Coach," Pump said, "can my friend, Ken, come, too? He lives right near me. We were riding bikes."

"Sounds good." Fred Namath agreed immediately, then added with a wink, "Even if he is a Musket."

Freddy was standing next to Pump's bike, admiring the unnatural kinks in the front wheel.

"Impressive," Freddy said when his father and Pump came over to him.

As Fred picked up the bike he said, "We're all lucky, Pump. This could've been a lot worse. You kids have to be really alert on your bikes, especially in the city like this. And, for crying out loud, keep wearing your helmets!"

Fred shook his head as he opened the back of his car and fit the bike in. He couldn't fit Ken's in, too, so they decided Ken would meet them at the field. He was sent off to tell Clyde, who'd be waiting for them, that they'd be there soon.

Ken furrowed his forehead to show how seriously he took his assignment. He reached up to pat his helmet and headed off on his bike.

"Careful, now," shouted Fred Namath. Ken nodded vigorously to show he'd heard and would be, absolutely, careful.

Minutemen on Maneuvers

EITHER BECAUSE FRED NAMATH WAS THERE or because Pump
was actually wounded, Luke didn't tease his little brother when he arrived home with his broken bicycle. Their parents were out doing errands. Pump ran upstairs to wash his wounds.

His pants were torn. A rough welt blazed his left leg. His arm was
raw where it had been grated by the street. Pump studied his arm. He
watched the straw-colored ooze seep out where the skin was scraped.
Blood had welled up and dried along the wound. Pump checked the
injury in the mirror and saw his pale, smudged face grimace as he
looked at the mess of his arm. He started to feel a little faint, again,
when a knock on the bathroom door distracted him.

Fred Namath appeared in the doorway with Freddy looking over
his father's shoulder with wide eyes.

"How're you doing?" Fred asked in a gentle voice.

Pump's lips started to tremble and Fred quickly stepped into the
room. Pump's coach flipped on the water in the sink, put an arm
around Pump to help prop him up and stuck Pump's arm into the

sink. Very gently he washed Pump's arm with soap and water, all the while holding Pump firmly.

"Does it hurt?" Fred asked when he saw Pump's tears.

Pump shook his head. He was afraid that if he tried to speak his voice would shake.

"You'll be OK," Fred assured Pump. The coach looked carefully at him.

"You know you were so brave out there when you got knocked off your bike."

Freddy nodded behind his father. Pump felt color flood back into his face.

"So now that the danger is past," Fred continued, "you realize you could have been really hurt, so you're scared and relieved at the same time."

Pump nodded and blinked hard to keep back the tears. He couldn't quite do it and tears quietly flowed. Fred patted Pump on the back, then, with the towel, patted Pump's arm dry. Pump washed his face. By the time he was cleaned up and dry, his tears were over.

"Do you have any stuff to clean cuts?" Fred asked.

Luke pushed past Freddy. He opened the medicine cabinet and pulled out an old brown bottle of Mercurochrome that their mother liked to use on their cuts because it was orange. Fred Namath painted Pump's arm orange. Then Pump's leg. He and the boys admired the result.

"Hey," Freddy burst out, "we'd better get to the field. Clyde's waiting for us."

"We're all set." Fred said. He bumped into Luke as they tried to get out of the bathroom at the same time.

"Luke, think you could help out at practice?" Fred asked.

Luke looked pleased. "Sure, I'll get my glove."

"Mine, too," called Pump.

Luke hesitated.

"Just this once," Luke called back.

The boys tumbled out of Fred Namath's car at the field. They found Clyde and Ken tossing around a pink foam football they'd borrowed from two little kids who were busy somersaulting in the grass. Fred brought an extra glove out of the trunk for Ken.

Clyde was laughing as he danced past Ken's hands to run a touchdown over the goal. As soon as he caught sight of Fred and the boys, he stiffened up. He looked as if he had been caught doing something wrong. Pump heard Fred sigh. Freddy ran forward.

"Pass to me. Pass to me," Freddy called out.

Clyde, still in possession of the ball, flipped it halfheartedly toward Freddy. The ball fell short. Freddy tried to keep the game going, but, suddenly, no one seemed in the mood.

Ken ran over to admire Pump's glowing orange arm.

"What's up?" Luke asked Clyde.

"Not much," Clyde muttered and looked away.

Pump saw his brother look puzzled. Luke shrugged and walked over to Ken and Pump.

"What's with him?" Luke asked, bending his head toward Clyde. "He's so, well, so deflated."

Pump thought he could answer that but he wasn't sure he was right. He didn't want Luke to tease him. It seemed weird. But Clyde did look like the air—the life—just went out of him whenever he was around their coach.

Fred didn't act like he noticed, but Pump thought he had heard Fred sigh.

Fred called the boys over to him.

"O.K., this is just a small practice situation," Fred said. He pulled his cap on over his sandy-colored hair. "I get the feeling the fun is completely gone for some of you. So we need to get the spirit back in the game.

"Clyde," Fred directly addressed his pitcher, "I think you know what I mean."

Clyde stared at Fred. His dark eyes focused on the coach.

"That's right. I like to see your eyes on me when I'm talking to you," Fred said. Immediately Clyde's gaze wandered off again.

"Clyde," Fred said sharply, then his voice softened. "We've got to keep this in perspective. Is this the Canterbury Little League or the

American League? No one's paying you guys to play this game. You're doing it, or you're supposed to be doing it, because you like baseball. Because you like to feel the bat connect, like to try and like to see yourselves get better at it."

Pump worried that this kind of talk would just make things worse but he saw that Clyde was listening, his eyes sharply on Fred.

"No one is expecting you to be perfect—you've gotta remember that. So don't expect that of yourselves. If you're feeling off or like you're in a slump, then it's not your turn, not for that game or a whole string of games or maybe not even for an entire season. Baseball is a team sport. Your coach is the guy who sets the strategy. The strategy is to maximize your strengths and cover your weaknesses. No one ever carried a team singlehandedly. Not even Babe Ruth.

"Clyde and Freddy and Pump, you are members of a team. If I ever thought I had to carry a whole team, I'd give up on the spot. That's a weight no one could possibly bear.

"Though I have to say," Fred spoke quietly, "I think we all got caught up in pennant fever. And, I have to admit, I was probably the worst of all." Fred laughed and shook his head before he continued. "We spend too much time watching the Red Sox. It's those dreams of glory you've gotta watch out for. They can cloud your vision.

"OK. Enough talking. I wanted you out here to work on basics: hitting and throwing. That's all. This team can be so good. It's tantalizing. Makes my mouth water. So don't make me starve. I want the same thing for breakfast, lunch and dinner. Just give me your best effort and I'll be satisfied. Got it?"

Fred looked around. Pump had never seen his coach so happy. In fact, he'd never seen his coach happy, period.

Fred sent Freddy back to his car to get some old plastic hula hoops from the trunk. He tossed one to each boy.

"I was saving these for team practice later. But let's try them now to see if you can do it. If you guys can't get the hang of them, the rest of the team never will," Fred said.

Fred demonstrated how to get the hoop spinning and how to keep it twirling around his waist by rocking his hips forward and back, shifting his weight.

Pump stepped into the middle of his hoop, which happened to be pink. He tried not to look as embarrassed as he felt to be cursed with a pink hoop. At first, it seemed impossible to get the hoop to work. If it was so easy, how come the hoop kept dropping to his feet every time he tried?

All the boys had the same trouble. Their hips moved in jerks and the spinning hoops slowed, then clattered to the ground.

Luke gave a shout. "I got it, I got it! Look, Fred."

Luke had it, all right. His hips rocked and the hoop spun around his middle. In less than a minute the hoop slowed down. Luke shoved his hips crookedly in an attempt to get control over his hoop while the other boys stared at his contortions. Pump looked at Clyde and they started to giggle. Luke twisted and jerked trying to keep the hoop off the ground.

As the plastic hoop clattered to his feet the other boys burst into laughs. They couldn't stop. Clyde, Ken and Pump reeled around, laughing too hard to breathe.

"What's so funny?" demanded Luke. Then a snort rumbled through his nose, which set everyone laughing again.

Pretty soon Luke was back on his feet. This time he got his hoop going more easily. It stayed up longer and longer each time he tried.

Clyde was the next to get his hoop turning around his waist. Clyde and Luke tried to outlast each other, seeing who could keep the hoop up longest. Eventually, Freddy, Pump and Ken got their hoops going, too. They joined the competition.

While the boys were mastering the hoops, Fred had taken some ropes and tied a hoop so it was hanging from a tree branch. To anchor the hoop, Fred tied one end of a rope to a brick on the ground, and the other end to the bottom of the hoop.

The boys were reluctant to leave their hoops, but they came over when Fred called them.

Fred laughed. "Good work, boys. Did you notice how fast you learned that hoop? And, then, how fast you found a way to turn it into a game? That's what playing sports is about. Baseball's no different.

"So, now, I want you to see this hoop as a big, very generous strike zone. You each get nine pitches. First to get three strikeouts ... that's

every pitch in the strike zone … wins and the game is over. When your turn is over you go collect the balls."

Luke went first. He got six strikes on his first try. No one else came close. On his third turn, Luke pitched a perfect inning. Fred retired him permanently and set him to calling encouragement to the other pitchers.

Freddy kept hitting the hoop. Pump was amazed. It was actually hard to hit the hoop. How did Freddy do it?

"Hey, Freddy," Fred called out. He sounded excited. "Freddy, what are you looking at? Think. Do it again. Throw the ball. Go ahead! Pitch. But don't look at the hoop. Look at the *hole*. Go on. Throw."

Freddy wound up and threw the ball right through the hoop.

"I knew it," Fred crowed. "Look at that. That's it. That is it! That's why you hit so many batters. Freddy, think. When you pitch, what are you looking at?"

Freddy didn't have to think long. "I look at the batter, Dad," he answered.

"I see that now," Fred said. "And from now on, what are you going to look at?"

"The hole?" Freddy blurted out. "No, wait. I mean, the bat. Oh, you know what I mean." Freddy stamped his foot. "I mean the glove, the catcher's glove."

"Right on the money," Fred declared. "Now you see that when I say, 'Throw to the glove,' that is exactly what I mean. Only you have to look at it while you throw. So, try again. Let's see what happens."

Freddy's next pitch sailed through the hoop. Six strikes for nine throws for Freddy that round.

Clyde took his turn and pitched five balls, one after another, straight through the hoop. After the fifth pitch Pump could see his whole body get tight and stiff. He lost his windup. He looked awkward and uncomfortable. Pump felt his heart sink. Here it was again. Clyde was frozen.

"Clyde Jones, stop right there," Fred called out as he trotted out to Clyde, just as if he were going to the mound to talk to his pitcher. "What were we just talking about? Where's the fun? Where's the excitement about getting better? What is going on?"

Fred walked right up close to Clyde. Clyde shook his head. His chin sank so low it practically rested on his chest.

"Look at me, Clyde," Fred Namath said.

Clyde just shook his head again. Fred stayed right where he was.

Slowly, without moving his head, Clyde raised his eyes. Fred smiled and Clyde slowly raised his head. He didn't move his eyes from his coach's face.

"You know what your trouble is, Jones?" Fred asked. "You're just too good too fast. Things come too easily at the beginning. When you realize how well you've done, you have no idea how it happened. You don't really think that you had anything to do with it. Like it wasn't you who just pitched five strikes in a row. So how could you ever do it again?

"Well, if it wasn't you, who was it? Give yourself a break. Be happy with those pitches."

Clyde drew in his breath to say something but Fred continued, "No, you're right. You'll never be able to do that every time. No one could. But it's not magic. It's just you. When it works right, it works right. Loosen up. Let yourself smile. That's it. You threw some great pitches, so where's the funeral?"

Clyde gave one of his big smiles and the tension dissolved like fog burning off in the morning sun.

"You get my meaning?" Fred asked.

Clyde looked straight at him. He nodded.

"Let me hear it," Fred said.

"I get you."

Pump felt like cheering. Instead, he picked up one of the balls and stepped up for his turn at the hoop. He was sure he could throw nine strikes in a row.

Pump did manage two in a row before the ball missed the hoop. Then four in a row. Luke clapped him on the back. Then, Luke relieved Pump of the ball even though he wasn't in the game anymore and threw nine strikes.

"I just had to make sure I could still do it," he said sheepishly.

Fred took Luke, Clyde and Freddy over to the diamond to practice some pitching while Pump and Ken stayed and threw the ball to each other through the hoop. Pump took off the rope that tied the hoop to the brick and pushed the hoop so that it swung like a pendulum. The boys tried to throw through the moving target while the hoop turned as it swung. They dove for balls, rolled on the grass, and tossed the ball from wherever they landed. It was a great game.

They were still playing when the rest of the team started to drift in for practice. Pump and Ken realized how hungry they were. A lot had happened for one day.

Fred drove off. He returned soon after with juice and water and hot dogs wrapped up warm in aluminum foil packages.

With a hot dog stuffed in his mouth, Luke grimaced and slapped his forehead. "O-mig-odd, I've got *my* practice. Hey, Ken, can I borrow your bike? I've got to go."

Ken unlocked his bike for Luke who took off for the Dodgers' practice.

The Second Half

THE MINUTEMEN headed into their second meeting with the Colonists full of confidence and hoping for an easy win. After all, hadn't they won by the mercy rule in the first game of the season? But by mid-season, every team had improved, some more than others. Games that were easily won might not be such easy wins the next time around.

Pump spent the day of the game in school calculating how many runs ahead the Minutemen would be by the end of the fourth inning. Maybe this time it would be a shutout. Maybe even a no-hitter. Pump felt nervous all over again, but it was different from the very first game. These jitters felt good. Everyone looked excited. Pump remembered how tense his team had looked at the start of their first game in April. This was going to be a good game.

This time the Minutemen were the home team. Clyde was back but he was at shortstop. Freddy was on the mound. Fred kept his arms folded across his chest. His face had no expression as he watched Freddy carefully.

Freddy walked the first batter. The second batter watched two strikes go by. On the third pitch he swung and hit a solid grounder that bounded past Clyde and rolled into center field. So much for a no-hitter. Runners on first and third. The third batter seemed like he would be at bat forever. He kept hitting fouls, one after the other. He swung at everything, high or low, inside or outside and he made contact every time. Every once in awhile, Freddy would throw a ball that the batter let go by, just to relieve the monotony. Eventually the count stood at three and two. Since the batter kept hitting foul balls, he seemed in no danger of striking out. He would just keep hitting fouls until the pitcher threw a ball to walk him. The next pitch whistled so close to his head that the batter ducked to avoid it, then threw down his bat and trotted to first. No outs, bases loaded. This was absolutely not the way this game was supposed to go.

Pump told himself things would be all right. After all, the top of the lineup held the strongest hitters. Just let us get past them, Pump silently wished. The next batter swung at everything but hit nothing. Finally, an out. Then a looping fly ball that settled right into Jeff Leonard's glove for a second out.

The next batter was small, a sure sign that they had reached the bottom half of the lineup. But the small batter slugged the second pitch all the way to the fence, bringing in two runs before the ball came back to the infield. What was going on? Was this the same team that the Minutemen beat by the mercy rule just a few weeks earlier?

The Minutemen stiffened up and lost their focus. Their timing was off. Knees stopped bending. Throws were more awkward. The ball seemed possessed by demons that made it extra slippery or bounce in funny zigzags, impossible to field.

Finally, Freddy stopped the Colonists by striking out the ninth batter. Four to nothing after half an inning of play. What had happened?

The stunned Minutemen wandered in from the field. Fred laughed at the looks on the faces of his players.

"Hustle in. Come on, Minutemen, I want to see that hustle."

Fred gathered his dazed team around him and lowered his voice so they had to really pay attention to hear what he was saying. "Listen up. You look like you've all seen a ghost or something. But it's no ghost. It's just a team of kids. What's happening is that you guys started practices way before the season started. Most of the other teams didn't. Like the Colonists. You came into that first game with a lot of work under your belts. That first game was practically the Colonists' first practice. Their experience has come in their games. And they're not bad … as you are finding out. All that means is that this'll be a better game. It's more fun when there's real competition."

That wasn't so clear to the Minutemen. They thought it was plenty of fun to roll over their opponents. Fred smiled.

"Cheer up," the coach said. "This is an annual phenomenon. It just means we still have to work for what we get. No one is going to hand us anything. It means we can't predict the outcome of a game based on our first round experience. That goes for losing as well as winning. Pull together guys. We're gonna make back those runs and then some. So whaddya say?"

"Go, Minutemen!" the team shouted.

"Here we go," Fred held up his clipboard. "Prout, you lead off. We're just trying to get on base. Nothing fancy. The glory is in the basics. Remember that. OK, then, Flagan. Jones. Namath. Maloney, A. Kennedy. Weiss. Leonard. Salvano. Maloney, J., you ready for DH?"

Jill nodded.

"Bednarski and Gerstein, on the bench."

Pump swallowed hard. Lead off?"Don't look so surprised, Pump." The coach had clearly spotted Pump's dismay.

"Nothing big and fancy, Prout," the coach was saying. "Just meet the ball and try to get on base. "

Pump only did half of what the coach instructed. He got on base. A walk. There was no ball to meet. Pump realized the Colonists' pitcher was just as jittery as he was. Leading off wasn't so bad.

Danny Flagan drew a walk, too. Runners on first and second. No outs. Clyde stepped to the plate. The pitcher kicked the mound. He ran in place. He dusted his hands with dirt. His coach walked out to the mound, said a few words and turned back to the third base line. The pitcher nodded. He wound up and threw … a strike. Clyde tapped his bat on the far side of the plate. He took two practice swings. He looked ready. Clyde flowed with his swing sending the next ball deep. It was just too short to go over the fence but it was long enough to bring Pump and Danny home.

The center fielder took a full half-minute to gather up the ball. Clyde would have made it home except that the fielder forgot his cutoff and tried to heave the ball all the way home. The ball was falling into the infield when the pitcher intercepted it. He headed back to the mound just as Clyde rounded third. Play had to stop, leaving Clyde on third.

Freddy took up the bat and sauntered to the plate. The pitcher must have gotten the signal to change the pace because he started throwing pitches that practically landed on the plate. Freddy swung desperately. He couldn't get the timing of those off-speed pitches. He struck out. Annie Maloney didn't swing at those pitches and she got a walk.

Brian Kennedy struck out flailing away like Freddy had done. Jill stood stock still and struck out on a full count. The inning ended with the Minutemen trailing by two runs. Four to two for the Colonists.

The rest of the game was close all the way. The Minutemen were behind until the fifth inning when Freddy walloped a home run to bring in three runs. The Minutemen took the lead by one run and held on to it. Danny came in to pitch the top of the sixth and retired the side with no change in the score, giving his team the win.

Before they lost to the Muskets, the Minutemen had started to feel like they knew what they were doing. But in this second half of the season, everything felt unpredictable, even the weather.

April, known for its showers, had been a pretty dry month. May, on the other hand, seemed to be getting wetter. Pump watched the sky closely whenever he had a game. He was not taking anything for granted. Not the weather and certainly not the Minutemen's opponents. That close game against the Colonists stayed in his mind for the rest of the season. The second half of the season brought more rain and closer games.

Another unpredictable element, even more unsettling to Pump than the possibility of rain, was whether or not his father would show up at the games. Even if there wasn't any sign of him, Pump kept an eye out for him.

The next two match-ups, against the Stars and against the Stripes, were also tight. Pump and his teammates squeaked through the game with the Stars with a final score of 9-8. Then the Stripes put up an even tougher fight. The Minutemen could hardly believe how well the Stripes were playing. Even the tiny kids at the bottom of the line-up were connecting with the ball. The Minutemen dropped behind in the first four innings. Luckily they poured it on in the last two innings. They caught up with the Stripes and then passed them to end the game winning by only one run once again.

By the time the Minutemen faced the Patriots, they were ready for anything. Pump remembered that the Patriots were the first team that had given them any trouble earlier in the season. If the Colonists, the Stripes, and the Stars had all improved so much, Pump didn't even want to think about how well the Patriots would be playing. But then he remembered that in baseball anything could happen.

And it did. The Patriots were all errors and fumbles that day. The Minutemen started off strong for the first time since the half-season mark. They held an early lead straight through the sixth inning.

It was already the last week of May, and the Minutemen still had only one loss for the season. Now there were only three games to go and one of those was with the Muskets. The mighty Muskets, as Ken called his team.

Compared to the beginning of the spring season, just about everyone in Canterbury Little League was playing better. Even with improvement, pitchers still walked in runs. Fielders still chased down hits like puppies chasing their tails. Batters still swung at pitches that bounced in the dirt in front of the plate. Everyone still overthrew. Catchers almost never caught foul pop-ups. Some innings still went through the entire batting order to retire the side. But, in general, every team and every player on every team had improved. The baseball was better.

Pump was having a great time. The Minutemen all seemed happier. Even Bones Bednarski. Not that he stopped complaining. He just didn't seem to really mean it.

Muskets Misfire

THE AFTERNOON after the Minutemen defeated the Patriots for the second time, Pump, his head bent over his homework, heard cleats scrape along the sidewalk. The cleats clacked up to Pump's front door.

"Hey, Prout," Ken Ames said when Pump opened the door.

"Hey," Pump returned. "Who're you playing?"

"The Patriots."

Pump gave a little snort. "The Patriots? We flattened them yesterday. You won't have any trouble."

Ken eyed Pump suspiciously. "You seem like you're sorry we won't have any trouble."

Pump opened his eyes wide in mock innocence. "Who, me?"

The boys' eyes met for a second before they both snickered.

"Can you come see our game?" Ken asked. Then he added, as if to make the prospect more appealing, "Your brother is playing tonight, too."

"Sure," Pump said, "but I have to finish my homework first. I'll get there as soon as I can."

140

Ken smiled. "See ya there," he said as he turned to leave.

Pump sighed and sat back down at the table. Now that he had something else to do, his homework seemed endless. Pump was surprised to find that it had only taken ten minutes.

"What about dinner?" his mother said when he told her where he was going.

"Luke's already gone," Pump explained. "I'll eat with him after the game. We'll get some pizza."

"Oh, that's right. I forgot about Luke's game. Come on, I'll go, too. You want a ride?"

Pump always wanted a ride, but this time he thought he'd rather go on his new second-hand bike. For some reason, he hesitated to say this to his mother. As if it might hurt her feelings.

"I think I'll take my bike," Pump announced.

He closely watched his mother's face. A smile.

"OK," she said. "I'll see you there."

Pump surveyed the field when he arrived. His mom was already standing with the other parents by the fence of the major league field where Luke was the starting pitcher. He saw a Minutemen hat gliding past the line of parents. It was on Josh Gerstein's head. Pump caught sight of Brian Kennedy standing with some other kids Pump knew from school who weren't baseball players.

The teams ran to take their positions. On one minor league field the Colonists were playing the Pilgrims. On the other minor league field, the Patriots were the home team with last ups against the Muskets. Charles Ames was in the on-deck circle ferociously swinging his bat.

Pump met up with Danny Flagan as he strolled toward the field. Danny and Pump passed the rack where Freddy and Clyde were locking their bikes.

"Nice wheels," Danny shouted and gave a long whistle. "Clyde's got a new bike," Danny said to Pump.

Clyde and Freddy joined their teammates.

"Since when are you on wheels, Jones?" Danny asked.

"Since last week is when," Clyde answered. "Sweet, ain't it?"

Clyde hesitated, then he added, "It's Freddy's old bike."

The boys looked back at the rack and saw that one of the bikes was a brand-new mountain bike and the other was old and banged up, just like Pump's "new" bike.

"Sweet!" Danny agreed.

Clyde smiled.

"Boy, you're sure doing a lot of smiling these days," Danny said, laughing. "I don't know if I can recognize you with all those teeth in the middle of your face."

"Play ball," the umpire yelled. The Patriots' pitcher wound up to deliver the first pitch. Pump noticed Jeff Leonard lingering on the fringe of the crowd. Then he saw Bones Bednarski eating chips from a bag. Even Annie Maloney was there and she was wearing a skirt. Pump couldn't believe it. Her sister Jill was hanging around with Penny Weiss. Pump had never seen Jill or Penny anywhere near the field when there wasn't a game or a practice. Annie often showed up to check out the action on the major league field. But never in a skirt.

Willie Salvano came thundering up to Pump.

"What's happening?" Willie panted. "Why's everyone here? We don't play today, do we?"

"Sure we do, Willie," Danny solemnly replied. "Where's your uniform? You know Frank won't let you play without it."

Willie's lips trembled as he said, "But you're not in your uniform either. Are you teasing me?" Willie's voice rose. Danny lunged at him, grabbed him, and spun him around. He clapped a hand over Willie's mouth. Willie's eyes widened looking out over the top of Danny's big hand.

"Shhh," Danny whispered. "I was just kidding, you knucklehead. Why do you think we're all here? Who is the only undefeated team in the league? And who is behind them with only one loss? Seems we're all interested in how the Muskets are gonna do. Whaddya say?"

"I guess that's why I'm here," Willie grinned.

"Aw, Willie, you're here every day," Bones Bednarski said. "The only difference is sometimes you're in a uniform and sometimes you're not, depending on if we're playing or not."

"That's just what I thought," Willie agreed, smiling. "We're not wearing our uniforms so we must not have a game tonight."

"Right on, Mr. Salvano." Danny laughed and let him go.

A cheer from the spectators brought the Minutemen back to the Muskets' game. The Patriots had just retired the Muskets, three up, three down.

Pump loved watching the game with his entire team and he loved the way they had all come together without planning it. The Minutemen really were a team. The only thing that kept him from totally enjoying the game was his disappointment that Ken was a Musket. Pump just couldn't be for that team. He wanted his team to be a half game closer to the Muskets. He wanted the Muskets to lose. The good part of wanting the Muskets to lose was that when they were down, like now, Pump could be happy if Ken made a good play. Even if he hit a home run.

The Patriots were looking good. They were as hot against the Muskets as they were cold against the Minutemen. This time it was the Muskets who were off as they fell farther and farther behind.

In the top of the fourth, the Patriots were leading 13-3. Pump, along with all the Minutemen, was hoping for the Muskets to fall to the mercy rule. If the Patriots could hold the Muskets scoreless in the top of the inning they would only need two runs to mercy the Muskets.

Nevertheless, when Ken came to the plate with one runner on base, Pump cheered for him and shouted out when he connected with a pitch he sent all the way to the fence for an inside-the-park home run. The mercy rule was just that much farther away.

Pump left the minor leagues game to go watch the Dodgers. In the majors, if a pitcher were throwing well enough, the coach might leave him in for the entire game. This usually meant that by the fifth and sixth innings the pitching deteriorated in various ways. It depended on which part of the pitcher was first to fatigue. He might lose his focus, or his arm, or his legs, or his will.

Pump saw right away that Luke had lost his focus. He was distracted, frazzled. This made it hard for him to find the plate. By the time Pump arrived, Luke was walking in a run, just like in the minors. The parents along the fence looked grim. Standing among them, also looking grim, was Pump's father. He was wearing that little hat again, but this time he was right up against the fence next to Pump's mom.

Pump's mother called out, "It's OK, Lukie. You're doing fine."

Pump saw Luke's ears turn pink so he knew his brother had heard their mother.

The coach was on his way to the mound with the catcher tagging along. Pump watched them huddle with Luke, then turn back to the plate. Pump suspected that Luke was not only tired but distracted by his father's presence.

As the coach returned to his place behind the third base line, Pump remembered something that might help. He yelled, "Hey, Prout. Remember the Alamo! Stay with it!"

When Pump was little, he used to pretend he was Davy Crockett. He and Luke both had fake coonskin caps and they'd go hunting together behind their house. One day, Pump was angry at Luke and tried to flush his coonskin hat down the toilet. When Luke found his hat waterlogged at the bottom of the toilet bowl, he shrieked, "Remember the Alamo!" and tore after his little brother, tackling him and pounding him. From that day on, the cry "Remember the Alamo!" was their personal password. It always brought back the sight of the bedraggled hat and a reminder of Luke's superior strength. It always made them laugh.

Luke glanced in Pump's direction and smiled. Luke stretched, shook his arms and wound up to pitch. Pump held his breath. Luke delivered. The batter stood still. The ball thumped into the catcher's mitt. The umpire turned to his right and released his right forearm with his forefinger pointing. Strike one.

Pump saw Luke's shoulders rise and fall in a sigh of relief. Pump felt relieved, too. He saw Luke shoot a look toward their father, who was still there.

Pump stood behind the opponents bench. "What's the score?" Pump asked.

One of the Cubs turned around.

"Five, them. Four, us," he said with a scowl.

"Fifth inning?" Pump asked.

"Sixth."

The top of the sixth. All Luke had to do was keep the Cubs from scoring. The bases were loaded, no outs, one strike. Pump bit his lip.

"Let's go, Luke. You can do it!" Pump shouted.

Pump's parents were standing at the fence behind the Dodgers' bench. He hoped they weren't looking nervous. He was relieved when he thought he could see his mom smile and wink at him.

Luke delivered his next pitch. It was clearly high and Pump groaned to himself. But the batter saved him. Using the old Little League strategy that, if the last ball was a strike, then the next one will be, too, the batter swung and missed. Strike two.

Pump saw a little smile flicker on Luke's lips. Uh-oh. Pump knew what that meant. Something tricky. Luke tried a curve ball. It curved, all right, but it curved outside and never came back. The catcher had to stretch for it. Ball one. Luke jabbed his toe into the hole right in front of the rubber. The batter already had his bat locked on his shoulder. He was certain the next pitch would be a ball.

It wasn't. First out.

Pump heard a small roar from the crowd watching the Muskets' game. He wanted to dash over to see what was happening, but he felt he couldn't leave Luke. While Pump was trying to figure out which team's families had yelled, Luke went ahead in the count, one and two. The batter went for the next pitch and connected with a line drive heading right past Luke who, with quick reflexes, stuck out his hand and caught the ball. Two outs.

Another shout from the Muskets' field. What was Pump missing?

"Come on, Luke," Pump yelled. Please get this over right now, Pump said to himself.

"One more out. Three more strikes. C'mon, Prout!" Pump shouted.

At the three and 0 count, Pump got impatient. Didn't Luke know how much Pump wanted to find out what was going on with the

Muskets? If Luke lost this batter, the game would be tied at best. And at the very least they'd have to play out the bottom of the sixth. It could go on forever.

"Now's the time, Luke," a father's voice rumbled, deep and loud.

Luke threw a slow pitch. The batter went for it and missed. Three and one. The crowd started a rhythmic clapping, which then frayed and stopped. In silence, Luke delivered the next pitch. A foul tip back over the catcher. Full count.

Luke wound up and threw straight. The batter smacked the ball high. It shot almost straight up, then arced its way down into the second baseman's glove. The game was over.

Pump waved at Luke who couldn't have seen him over the heads of his teammates who were swarming around him. Pump was proud to be the brother of the pitcher who won the game. His parents turned and left as Pump sped over to the other field.

"What's up?" Pump asked the knot of Minutemen watching the game together.

"What a game!" exclaimed Danny. "You wanna know the score?" he asked. "I kid you not. It's the bottom of the fifth and it is 18-7. One run away from the mercy rule. Can you think of anything sweeter? The Muskets mercied! That would be so cool."

Josh Gerstein wanted to know if the mercy rule operated like sudden death.

"You know," Josh said. "Does the mercy rule get called the minute there's 12 runs difference between the scores? Or do you wait 'til the end of the inning or what?"

Annie Maloney answered, "Both teams get an at-bat. You can't be mercied 'til the end of the inning. So end of the fourth or end of the fifth. At least four innings have to be played." Annie could be counted on to know the rules. She added, "So we gotta hope the Patriots can do it *now!*"

"What were the big shouts about?" Pump asked.

Bones spoke with excitement, "There was a Patriot on first and their big slugger was up. All he needed to do was bring that run in. First pitch, he hit the ball out of the park and we all yelled, but it was foul. Then he actually laid down a bunt, which got the runner to third.

The batter made it to first, not even a sacrifice. Ames walked the next batter. We cheered then, too. We thought he might walk in a run. No such luck, yet, though."

"You mean you cheered for balls? You cheered for the pitcher's mistakes?" Pump asked.

Bones looked sheepish. "Yeah, I guess so."

Pump realized if it was the fifth inning, Charles probably wasn't pitching anymore. Almost no one pitched more than four innings in the minors.

"Which Ames was pitching?" Pump asked.

"Ken," responded Josh, always pleased to provide information.

"And you cheered when the pitch was a ball?" Pump yelped.

Josh stared at Pump.

Pump squeaked, "You can't do that. You can't cheer because someone blows a pitch. You cheer good plays, not bad ones."

"Whoa, what do we have here?" Danny Flagan joined in. "A dyed in the wool Musket fan? What's with Pumpster here?"

Pump could feel everyone looking at him.

"Ken's a friend of mine," he explained.

"Friend, schmend," Brian Kennedy chimed in. "A Musket is a Musket. They're our enemies."

Pump clenched his teeth. He couldn't find words to defend his friend. Ken was on a different team, a team that Pump, along with all the Minutemen, wanted to see go down in flames. But enemy? No Musket was an enemy, even if it felt that way sometimes. At least Ken wasn't.

"Ken's no enemy!" Pump exclaimed.

"Stop your noise!" Danny ordered. "We gotta concentrate on getting the Muskets mercied. Shhh. While you guys were whining, Ames got a strikeout."

One out, bases loaded, Ken pitching for the Muskets. The next Patriot looked nervous, shifting his weight from foot to foot. On the second pitch, the batter swiped the ball from beneath and sent it softly into a low arc that came right into Ken's glove.

The Minutemen groaned. Pump groaned right with them. Ken made a good play. It was OK to groan.

One more run for the Patriots, however it came, would be enough. They were batting in the bottom of the fifth. Most of the Minutemen hoped for one more walk, just to add insult to injury. The Minutemen held their breath on every pitch. Finally, on a full count, with the batter absolutely frozen at the plate and the crowd in an uproar with every pitch, the batter overcame his fear of swinging and jabbed his bat toward the ball. When the bat connected, the ball dribbled toward the mound.

The runners took off. Ken charged in from the mound. Charles Ames, who had switched positions with Ken, clambered after the ball. The runner from third base kept one eye on the ball as he ran toward home.

"Cover the plate!" shouted the Muskets' coach.

"Run, Run, Tyrone!" shrieked the Patriots' bench.

The players were on their feet bouncing and jumping.

Ken called out, "I got it!" and Charles declared, "Mine," as they reached the ball at the same time, their hands stretching to grab it.

The pitcher and the catcher collided. Ken tripped over Charles and landed on the ground while Charles grabbed the ball and turned toward the plate. But there was no one at the plate, except, a second later, the runner.

Everyone shouted. The Patriots and their families shouted in joy and the Muskets and their partisans in anguish. The Umpire gave the signal to invoke the mercy rule. The game was over. The score was 19-7. The Muskets were mercied.

The Minutemen exploded in ecstatic disbelief. This called for a celebration.

"Pirelli's," the Minutemen sang out. And off they went.

The Revolutionaries

ON WEDNESDAY, the day of the game against the Revolutionaries, Pump woke up to the sound of rain blowing hard against the window. He hurried downstairs to read the weather report. Nowadays he started with the weather, even before looking at the sports section. Rain was predicted to continue all day, even "heavy at times". Heavy rain meant a heavy heart for Pump.

By afternoon the rain had not let up and it was clear the game would be postponed. Nevertheless, Fred didn't call to deliver the bad news until about a half hour before the team was supposed to meet at the field. They were scheduled to make up the game that Friday.

Now that the Minutemen and the Muskets had one loss apiece and the Muskets were only a half game ahead, daydreaming about baseball made Pump nervous. He had plunged into his homework hoping to distract himself from those thoughts and by the time Fred called, his homework was done. Pump went up to his room to sort through his baseball cards.

Pump had kept his Yankee cards in a separate shoebox. He took off the lid and dumped the cards on his bed. All the other cards were sorted into teams with a rubber band around each team. Pump pulled off the rubber bands and tossed the cards, team by team, on top of the Yankees. Using a swimming motion, he stirred all the cards until they were completely mixed together.

"There," he muttered. Sorting his cards would keep his mind off the Muskets.

Pump concentrated hard on what he was doing. A sound at his doorway made him jump. His dad was standing there watching him.

"Mind if I come in?" his father asked.

Pump just widened his eyes and shook his head.

"What're you doing?" his dad asked as he moved closer to Pump. He sat on the bed but was careful not to disturb any of the cards.

"Sorting cards," Pump said. Then he added, "I'm for the Red Sox now, so I've got to rearrange my cards."

"Weren't you always for the Red Sox? You and Luke?"

"Dad," Pump sighed, "don't you remember? I was for the Yankees, forever. And, remember, last year, I *was* a Yankee. In Little League."

Pump's dad looked thoughtful. "I guess so."

They both looked at the bed covered with cards.

"Your mother suggested I talk to you."

Pump felt hot. He was excited and sort of embarrassed.

"She seems to think I should come to your games. So I've come to a few. I saw you once, last year, and one time this year and then I went to one of Luke's just the other day."

Pump just listened. How could his father think this was new news?

"What did you think?" Pump managed to ask.

"Well, I got a real kick out of seeing you and Luke playing out there. You really love baseball, don't you?"

Pump nodded.

His dad continued, "So just because it isn't my favorite thing to do—watch baseball, I mean—it is a great thing to do if you kids are playing."

Pump couldn't keep from asking, "Then how come you never stay and watch?"

"How do you know? Did you see me?" his Dad asked.

"Of course I saw you," Pump said.

"I guess I was just testing it out. Just getting a taste. What do you think? Do you want me to be there?" Pump's father wondered.

"You really want to know?" Pump hesitated.

His father frowned, then gave one of his slow smiles, "Yes, I really want to know."

Pump plunged in, "Yes, I want you to be there. But only if you don't care how I do. If you don't care if I mess up or anything. When you leave, I feel like I didn't play well enough to keep you interested. Or if I blow something, I figure you're disappointed and don't want to see anymore. Or when you look so serious, it looks like you're mad. And I think you've given up on my team. Or on me."

"I'm not mad, Pump," his dad said. "I guess I just look that way. I'll see what I can do. I won't be able to get to all your games, but I'll come when I can. For now, let's go have some dinner."

He reached over and ruffled Pump's hair. Pump still wanted to know why his father always seemed to give up on a team's chances so quickly. But that would have to wait for another time. They got up and headed to the kitchen.

It took another day for the rain to stop. By Friday morning the sky was clear but the ground was still soaked and muddy. The paper was predicting an unseasonably hot weekend. The sun was already warm and by afternoon, Pump's constant inspection of the ground found it to be dry enough for playing. They would play the make-up game against the Revolutionaries.

The days were getting longer. By five o'clock, when the teams assembled, the sun was still warm and the light still bright. The game was shorter than any other game the Minutemen had played except for the one that ended by the mercy rule after four innings. Freddy pitched without hitting one batter. Danny took care of three innings with only six walks, which was a personal best.

Pump was in his element, sliding headlong through the muddy base paths. He was the color of clay and his pants and shirt were the same. Pump's face was striped with mud where he'd wiped his hand on his cheek.

The whole team was on fire. Both Clyde and Freddy hit out-of-the-park home runs. And Jill Maloney shocked everyone with an inside-the-park homer. This momentous achievement started with an accidental bunt and ended with her diving into home as the fielders tossed one wild throw after another. The whole team poured out to welcome her home. The final score was 15-6.

It was a great way to start a weekend. A weekend of practice and a weekend of nerves. The Minutemen would play the Muskets on the following Tuesday.

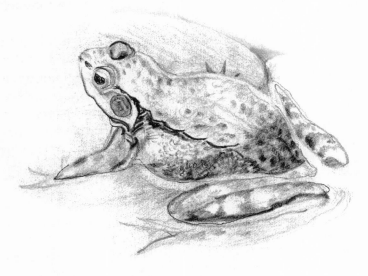

A Day Without Baseball

ON SATURDAY MORNING, right after breakfast, Pump grabbed a wiffle ball and bat and hopped outside to slam the ball as high as he could, trying to get it to bounce off the roof. He was swinging away when his father stuck his head out the window and shouted for Pump to stop making noise. The whack of the ball hitting the house every time Pump missed the roof bothered his father, who was trying to work. Even on a Saturday morning.

Pump felt that funny tightening in his stomach, that came whenever his father disapproved of what he was doing. Like now, playing ball on a weekend. After he and his dad had their talk, Pump realized he had expected his dad to change overnight and that just wasn't going to happen. Pump slammed one more ball right at the house before tossing down the plastic bat. He ran down the block to look for Ken Ames.

Pump spent the weekend immersed in baseball. When he wasn't at a Minutemen practice, Pump was hitting balls with Ken. They made up a game they could play with one of them pitching and playing the whole defensive team while the other batted for each player on his team.

Late Sunday afternoon, the sky steadily darkened. The wind shook the new leaves on the swaying branches of the trees. Pump and Ken looked up wondering if they'd been so wrapped up in their game, that they'd played past dinnertime. A flash of lightning blazed in the sky. A few long seconds later, thunder cracked and rolled. Pump and Ken looked at each other. Another bolt of lightning lit up the sky, followed by another rumble of thunder. The wind whipped the hats off Pump's and Ken's heads. As they scrambled for their hats lightning flashed again.

"Let's get outta here," Ken shouted over the thunder.

As the boys reached their bikes, raindrops started to splatter them. The rain started with slow, big drops. As the boys pedaled furiously for home, the rain grew fiercer and smaller until the drops stung them wherever their skin was bare. The boys were quickly soaked. They dropped their bikes to the ground as soon as they reached Pump's house. Water streamed off their noses. Ken stuck out his tongue and tried to catch the rain. Pump did the same. They laughed at each other as they ran around with their tongues hanging out to catch drops. Still laughing, Pump and Ken stumbled inside.

The rain continued all night. By Monday morning the rain had stopped. The ground was wet. Water streamed in the street gutters, forming lakes where the storm drains were clogged with last year's leaves. On his way to school, Pump saw a lot of broken branches that had fallen from the trees in the storm. Streams of mud worked their way slowly down the sidewalk wherever a yard was on a slope.

Ken and Pump had been riding their bikes together to school every day since Pump's accident. Pump wasn't always sure he wanted to spend so much time with Ken. Like now. Pump wondered if it wasn't bad luck to be getting to be such good friends with an archrival. Ken never seemed to have these doubting thoughts that were so familiar to Pump. Pump met Ken's eyes and Ken smiled. That was all Pump needed.

"Hey, Ken," Pump began.

"Yeah?" Ken answered over his shoulder.

Pump brought his bike alongside Ken's.

"What're you doing after school?"

Ken shrugged. "I dunno. We don't have a game today."

"Neither do we." Pump said. "Want to go catch frogs? I know a good place and after a rain like this, it should be great. Luke's the only other person who knows about it. He showed it to me. You can't tell anyone. Not even one of your brothers."

Pump paused, then asked, "You got that?"

Ken nodded. "Not a soul," he promised.

Ken and Pump met at the bike rack after school.

"Follow me," Pump called as he swung his leg over his bike.

"I'm right behind you," Ken shouted.

Pump led the way. He followed the same route they took every day until the boys passed their street without making the turn. They stopped at a big street that was practically a highway. Several roads came together at this corner and it was hard to tell which way the cars were coming from. Even when the light was red, cars seemed to sail across the intersection from every direction.

"Are you allowed to cross this street?" Ken asked.

"With Luke I am. What about you?" Pump replied.

"But Luke's not here," Ken pointed out.

"It's OK," Pump assured him. "I know what I'm doing."

"That's good," Ken said, not sounding too convinced. "I've never crossed here myself."

Ken and Pump stood on the curb balancing their bikes while they watched the cars speed by. They tried to figure out which signal went with exactly which street and when they could make their move. The cars rushing by made them dizzy. They were so absorbed in watching the cars that they didn't notice one of Pump's teammates pull up next to them on his bike.

The two boys jumped when they heard a loud laugh burst out right next to them.

"Clyde," Ken and Pump cried out together.

"Who else you expecting? You sure jumped a mile when you saw me."

Pump felt relief pour over him. He was really glad to see Clyde.

"Where're you headed?" Clyde asked them. He directed his words to Pump.

Pump hesitated, then said, "We're on our way to catch some frogs." Ken shot Pump a look. Here was Pump, telling his own secret. But it was his secret, after all, so he could tell whoever he wanted. Just because he'd told Ken not to tell anyone didn't mean Pump couldn't say anything. Pump gave Ken a nod that was supposed to say all that without words. Ken still frowned.

"Want to come with us?" Pump invited Clyde. He could feel Ken seethe next to him.

"Cool," Clyde said. "Where's it at?"

Clyde looked more relaxed than Pump could remember.

"Over there, in the cemetery." Pump waved his hand in the direction of a huge cemetery on the other side of the confusing intersection.

"OK," Clyde said. "Let's head out."

The boys waited one more minute before Clyde announced, "Now!" and shoved off to join the cars streaming across the intersection. Pump and Ken followed close behind. Once they were moving, Pump could see the green light that was directing them to go. Suddenly, it all seemed so clear and possible.

As the boys pedaled into the cemetery, they were greeted by a big sign with a list of rules printed on it. No Dogs and No Bicycles were the ones that Pump focused on. He saw an empty bicycle rack. Pump pointed to the sign.

"Guess we have to leave our bikes. Luke and I walked here," Pump said as he dismounted and locked his bike to the rack.

Ken and Clyde followed Pump's lead. Pump led the boys along some pleasant, winding roads. He was pretty sure he could remember the way to the pond. A red car drove past the boys. Pump marveled that cars were allowed here but bicycles weren't. Wouldn't it be better the other way around?

Pump was surprised to find that there were other ponds lined by trees of different varieties. He only remembered one pond. He hoped he'd recognize it if he saw it.

And there it was. Pump's pond was much smaller than the others. It was swampy with long grass growing right in it and muck around the edges. As the boys approached, a male duck with a deep green head and his brown mate quacked in complaint, flapped their wings, and rose off the water.

Mr. and Mrs. Mallard, Pump thought. But he didn't say it out loud.

The sun was blazing after the day of rain. Half the pond was in shade and half was in bright sun. Where the sun was shining the boys saw mist rising off the marshy weeds.

"I don't see any frogs," Ken said after a minute.

"You gotta be patient. Just wait," Pump told the boys.

They waited. Pump took off his shoes and socks and rolled up the legs of his pants. Clyde and Ken followed. Quietly Pump moved toward the pond and quietly he stepped in.

The water was cold. Mud oozed between Pump's toes. His feet sank into muck almost up to his ankles. After all the rain the water was deeper than it had been when Pump had been there with Luke. Pump's pants were immediately wet where they were rolled below his knees.

"Ouff," Pump huffed despite his effort to be silent. His feet stirred up the mud at the bottom of the pond.

Plop. The three boys turned in the direction of the sound. Frogs. Pump grinned. They were still there.

Ken walked in after Pump. Then Clyde moved in cautiously. He made a big splash with his step. Ken and Pump shot him fierce looks.

"You'll scare the frogs," Ken croaked in a hoarse whisper.

"What about you?" Clyde hissed back.

"Shut up, both you guys," Pump laughed. "The frogs're all scared now, anyway. We just have to be still and wait for them to forget we're here."

"I don't know about all this waiting," Clyde said doubtfully. "If we got to wait, can't we do it on dry land?"

Pump lifted his finger to his lips and gestured for the others to follow. He walked a little deeper in the shade. Plop, plop. Two frogs jumped off the shore ahead of them.

"Hey," Ken called, "what are we gonna put the frogs in?"

"Nothing," Pump replied. "We'll catch 'em and let 'em go."

"What?" Ken shouted. "Let them go?"

Clyde looked disappointed, too.

Pump looked at his band of hunters. He nodded.

Just then a frog moved right near Ken who grabbed for it.

"I got him! I got him!" Ken cried out.

He held out his hand dripping with mud and water and slowly opened his fingers. The minute his fingers uncurled, a frog the size of a quarter jumped back into the water.

"Wow!" Clyde exclaimed. "Cool!"

As they moved through the knee-deep water, dipping their arms in, groping through the mud for frogs, Pump noticed that Clyde moved very carefully. He wondered if Clyde was afraid of the water. Ken, on the other hand, pushed through the water as if it weren't there.

They caught only a few frogs and let them all go free in the pond. Only Clyde hadn't caught one.

"There's one," Ken shouted. He pointed right behind Clyde.

Clyde tried to whirl around but the quick move threw him off balance. His arms flailed at the water as his feet slipped in the mud. Down he went. Clyde's arms and hands slapped the water as if he were trying to swim. His thrashing feet churned up the mud. It looked like Clyde couldn't get his head out of the water.

Pump moved to reach for Clyde. His heart was pounding. As he touched Clyde, Clyde's hand grabbed his leg and pulled him down into the water. Pump couldn't get his head up because Clyde gripped him fiercely and held him under. Pump twisted and thrashed trying to get loose.

Suddenly, Pump was standing up, gulping air. He saw Clyde, coughing and spluttering, on the bank where Ken had pulled him to shore.

"Ach, blach." Clyde spat out mud. "Geez."

Clyde blew his nose into his hands, looked at what came out and wrinkled up his nose.

"Yuck," he said in disgust. "Mud!"

He rubbed his hands on the grass, then sat down at the edge of the pond.

"You OK?" Ken asked.

Clyde nodded. He was still catching his breath. Pump and Ken looked at each other with wide eyes.

Clyde sat with his arms stretched over his bent knees, his hands dangling and his head bowed toward his chest. He sat still and silent for a long time.

Without lifting his head he announced, "I don't know how to swim."

In a steadier voice he continued, "I thought I was drowning."

Clyde hesitated. His voice caught in his throat.

"Ken, you—." Clyde paused before blurting out, "You saved my life."

Ken looked away. Then he turned back and said with half a smile, "It would take something to drown in two feet of water. But I hear you're the guy who can do anything."

Clyde lifted his head. He gave Ken an uncertain look and then grinned.

"Yeah, I'm that tough. Hey, Prout, I almost drowned you. You OK?"

Pump nodded vigorously. He stood up as Ken and Clyde did. They looked at each other. Wet and muddy from head to toe.

"Look at you guys," Ken snorted. "Monsters from the deep."

The boys started to snicker, then laughed until they doubled over, breathless. They were smeared with mud and they were fine. As they put on their shoes and socks, they were grinning.

Walking to their bikes, they dripped a trail on the road. They rode in a pack, crossing the intersection that now looked like no challenge at all.

"Here's where I take off," Clyde said. "I just can't believe that I let a Musket haul me out. Don't think for a minute, Ames, that I'm going to give you any breaks for this. After all, baseball is baseball. And we're going to get that title."

Clyde waved and pedaled off. Ken and Pump rode home. Pump was already thinking how good a bath would feel. He hoped he wouldn't have to answer any questions at home.

A Second Shot

TUESDAY WAS BRIGHT AND BREEZY. School crept along at a snail's pace. Pump's eyes constantly wandered between the window, where the leaves played with the sunlight, and the clock whose hands would not move. Pump could hear the muffled tick of the second hand on the big classroom clock as it clicked along, second by slow second.

Finally, he was in his uniform, clicking his cleats on the sidewalk next to the field. He was excited but without the fear that too often came with his excitement. His sense of calm seemed connected to the fright he felt when he saw Clyde thrashing in the pond the day before. Or maybe it was because Pump knew his dad was coming because he wanted to be there watching him. He felt happy to be back playing the familiar game with the team he belonged to. He was even happy to be playing Ken Ames.

"Yeooow!" Pump shrieked.

Something wet and slimy slid down Pump's back. He yelped and jumped around trying to reach his back with each hand.

"Yagh, yaowgh," he shouted. Whatever it was that had joined him under his shirt kept moving even when Pump stopped twisting and turning.

Finally, Pump pulled his shirt out of his pants and something slipped to the ground.

"What the ..." Pump exclaimed as he knelt down to investigate the little frog that had fallen from his shirt. The trip down had stunned the frog. It didn't try to hop away until Pump grabbed it. He covered it with his other hand. Pump slowly raised the covering hand and peeked at the tiny frog. The frog's eyes bulged out as he stared right back at Pump.

As Pump looked at the frog, it sprang out of his hand, landing silently on the ground. Again, the frog froze until Pump scooped him back into his hands. Pump stood up and looked around. The frog felt like a moth fluttering in his hands.

Pump found Clyde standing in front of him. Clyde's mouth was stretched in the broadest smile Pump had ever seen on his face.

"Wow, man, you put on one great show!" Clyde laughed happily.

"You," Pump stuttered, "you ... you ... the frog? Where'd you get him?"

Clyde kept grinning.

"Where d'ya think?" he asked.

"The pond? In the cemetery? " Pump asked.

Clyde nodded.

Pump raised his eyebrows.

Clyde explained, "I went back right after school today. I never got one yesterday, remember? I just had to."

"You went alone?" Pump asked in amazement.

"Not exactly," Clyde admitted.

"Well ... ," Pump prompted him.

"Freddy came, too."

"So now Freddy knows about our place," Pump said quietly.

"I couldn't do it alone," Clyde said. Pump nodded.

"And I didn't fall. And, I caught Papi. Here, let me have him back."

Clyde held out both hands and Pump carefully slid the frog over to him.

"Papi?" Pump questioned.

"You know," Clyde said, "Big Papi seemed a good name for this little guy."

Pump smiled. A Red Sox star.

"Anyway, we'd better get out there. It's time for practice," Clyde announced.

"What're you going to do with Papi?" Pump asked.

"I'm going to put him in his box."

Clyde led Pump to the bench, where a shoebox was sitting with the lid off. Clyde plopped the frog in where he had made a nest of grass with a jar top holding water. He had punched holes in the lid, which he slipped over the box.

Danny Flagan watched the activity.

"I see we have a mascot," he remarked. "A frog? Let's see."

Danny struck a thoughtful pose, his forefinger alongside his cheek, his eyes looking skyward.

"Or is it a toad?" Danny mused, still looking at the sky. "Clyde and Toad Are Friends. No, no, wait, Frog and Clyde Are Friends. Clyde is the toad."

"Oof." Danny coughed as Clyde elbowed him in his belly.

"Who're you calling a toad?" Clyde demanded.

Danny stood up straight and laughed. "I gotta call it like I see it. Clyde is the toad," he repeated.

Clyde dove for Danny. Clyde and Danny pushed against each other trying to throw each other down. They toppled over and wrestled on the ground. Clyde ended up sitting on Danny.

"Give up. Give up, you … you … toad. Admit it. You're the toad," Clyde huffed, out of breath.

Clyde bounced up and down on Danny's belly.

"Ouh, ouph, ouph," Danny hiccoughed. "OK, OK! Just … get … off … me."

"Not until you say it," Clyde insisted, continuing to bounce.

"All right, all right," Danny gasped. "I … am … the … toad." Clyde stood up. Danny eased himself up. He faked a lunge toward Clyde, who stepped back laughing.

"Glad we got that settled," Danny said with a grin.

Pump wished he could be like Danny. Nothing seemed to faze him.

While Clyde and Danny were messing around, the rest of the team had drifted in. Bones Bednarski and Willie Salvano were missing but they were always late. The coaches were talking to the umpire. Fred Namath was laughing while the Muskets' coach scowled.

Pump suddenly knew he needed to find a bathroom. He wondered if he could make it through the game but realized he didn't have a choice. Six innings was way too long.

It was always a drag to get to the bathroom, which was way inside the school. By late afternoon all the doors to school were locked except for the big front door, which was all the way around on the other side of the building. Then, once he'd gotten to the bathroom, he had to undo all the work he'd done at home to get his shirt tucked in and his belt adjusted. Then he had to do all the tucking and belting all over again.

Pump cautiously moved toward the coaches and umpire. He didn't really know how to interrupt them and was hoping they'd stop talking before he got there. He shifted his weight. Pump was afraid he wouldn't last when Fred finally noticed him looking uncomfortable behind the umpire.

"What's up, Prout?" the coach asked.

"I've gotta go and I can't wait," Pump blurted out.

"OK. Just hurry back. Don't be late. I don't trust this ump. He might throw you outta the game." Fred chuckled.

"Better believe it," the umpire growled. This didn't help Pump's situation until he realized the men were teasing him.

Pump jogged to the school building while Fred called the rest of the team together to start their warm-up.

Feeling greatly relieved, Pump ran back to the field. He hadn't felt nervous earlier, which surprised him. But he must've really been nervous after all because his inner workings were all stirred up. Now, he felt better and ready to play. He ran to his position between first and second.

After their turn in the field, Fred sent the team off to run a lap around the three fields.

"Run those nerves out of you," Fred shouted to his players as they took off.

When they came back, breathless, Fred met the team at their bench.

"No talking today," Fred said and was greeted with a cheer from Bones.

Fred shot Bones an icy look but then smiled to maintain the good mood.

"You guys look great, today. That division title is hanging there, waiting to be picked. Who's going to get there first?"

"We are!" the Minutemen yelled.

"And who are we?" Fred called.

"The Minutemen!" everyone yelled.

"And who's going to win this game?" Fred shouted.

"The Minutemen!" the team thundered.

"Let's go, then. Let's see what you can do. Stay focused. Know where the play is," Fred called out last-minute instructions as the Minutemen headed to their positions.

Pump was too excited to hear a word Fred said. All the same, he knew what the coach was saying. He'd heard it often enough.

The Muskets were up first. Pump had been sure that Clyde would pitch this game for the Minutemen. He was surprised to see Clyde jog out to shortstop while Freddy took the mound. Both boys looked perfectly happy with the situation as far as Pump could tell. He trotted to his position and gathered up the ground ball Danny flung at him.

Once again, Ken Ames led off for the Muskets. Pump felt his heart beat faster as he watched Ken, who, to Pump's eyes, looked very self-assured at the plate. Ken let the first pitch go by as though he just wanted to take a look at what Freddy could deliver. Strike one. The next pitch was high but Ken reached for it. He nicked the ball for strike two. Ken watched the next two pitches sail by as high balls. Pump noticed Ken shift his stance and knew Ken was finally nervous. Ken swung with all his might at the next pitch, missed the ball completely, and struck out.

Batting second for the Muskets was a small boy named John Henry Mission. He was replacing Blaster McGarry, one of the Muskets' reliable hitters, who was out with a broken foot. John Henry had start-ed the season just being a short kid. Along the way he had demon-strated real talent with the bat and now he was a kid with a reduced strike zone and an impressive batting average.

Freddy couldn't find John Henry's strike zone but instead of tak-ing a walk, the batter stepped to meet the ball and knocked it be-tween the left fielder and the center fielder. Penny Weiss, in center field, got hold of the ball, caught sight of Pump waving his arms at her and heaved the ball up in the air. Pump sped toward her, inter-cepted the ball before it hit the ground and took off for second. The runner, who had just rounded first, turned back and settled for a sin-gle. Pump started to feel uneasy again. He felt better when the bases were empty.

Freddy poked the mound with his toe, slid off his glove, rubbed his hands, then put his glove back on. Pizza De Souza was up. Fred-dy concentrated hard. He wound up and delivered a perfect pitch. Pizza clouted the ball. It landed in far left field. The impact kept the ball bouncing and rolling toward the imaginary line that determined a ground-rule double as soon as the ball passed over it.

"Let it go. Let it go," Fred Namath yelled urgently to Jeff Leonard in left field.

Jeff kept running. He aimed to intercept the ball, which was slow-ing down as it neared the ground rule double line.

"Let it go. Don't stop it," Fred shouted.

Just before the ball reached the line, Jeff put on a burst of speed, scooped up the ball and heaved it toward third. Annie stretched to-ward the ball, but it flew by, out of her reach. John Henry blazed home to bring in the first run of the game.

By the time Annie had found and retrieved the ball, she turned to cover her base only to find Pizza already there.

"You're fast!" Annie exclaimed.

Pizza tried to catch his breath and smiled.

Now Charles Ames was up. Fred motioned the outfield to back up. The crowd was restless. As soon as Charles stepped to the plate every-thing got quiet for a few seconds. A hum of encouragement started.

"Now's the time, Freddy," the coach called out. "You can do this."

"You da man," Mr. Bednarski growled.

The Muskets' bench started to chant, "Cha-rles, Cha-rles, Cha-rles!"

Charles swung his bat fiercely. Pump swallowed hard. Charles looked scornfully at the pitcher.

Pump knew he would cower before such a look. Luckily, Freddy didn't seem to share that feeling. The first pitch blazed right over the plate. After watching the speed and riveting straightness of the first pitch, Charles slashed at each of the next two pitches. He went down swinging.

Two outs. Two Ames outs.

After his brilliant display of control against Charles Ames, Freddy hit the next batter, Ben Bracken, and walked the one after that. Bases were loaded.

The Muskets' lineup now presented the increasingly small strike zones that always gave Freddy a hard time. He threw slowly and carefully which didn't mean a lot of strikes but did tempt a batter to go for the pitch, no matter where it was headed. The next batter stuck his bat way out in front of him to try to meet the ball. He barely made contact, which resulted in a perfect, but unintentional, bunt. The ball simply dropped. It had no forward momentum.

Pizza charged home, his only hope being to knock over the catcher. But Brian grabbed up the ball and stepped back onto home plate. Then, like a matador, he nimbly slipped out of Pizza's way. Pizza dove to the plate.

As Pizza lay sprawled across the plate, his coach walked over to him, leaned down and muttered, "Forced out, De Souza. But nice dive."

Pizza slapped his forehead and lay his head down on his arms.

"Side's retired," shouted the umpire. Muskets, one run.

Charles Ames glowered from the mound as Pump approached the plate. Pump thought he had gotten used to the idea of leading off, but once again found himself wishing he could bat safely after someone else had started. He tried not to look at the pitcher. He also tried not to look at his dad standing at the fence along the first base line. In the brief glance he shot at his dad, Pump saw him stick up his thumb and smile.

Pump stepped up to the plate, then moved back out of the batter's box. His mouth was so dry his lips stuck to his teeth. Pump took some practice swings. Fred Namath's voice right behind him made him jump.

"Whoa. Take it easy," the coach said with a laugh.

Since when was Fred Namath so calm, Pump wondered. He acted as if he were always this cool.

"You look stiff as a board," Fred said. "Loosen up. Relax. Just meet the ball."

Pump was as amazed by Fred's easy mood as he was by his dad's thumbs-up and by the way his own swing became smooth.

As it turned out, Pump didn't need a swing since he faced four balls in a row so far out of his reach he wasn't even tempted to try for them. Tossing his bat aside, Pump trotted to first base. He kept his eyes on the ground so no one could see how relieved he was to draw a walk.

Charles Ames on the mound was not a pretty sight. His face was clouded with anger. If he hoped to intimidate the batters, Pump thought, he'd have to do it with his pitching and not his ferocious faces.

Pump watched from first base as a warlike Charles Ames missed the plate again and again to put Danny on and move Pump to second. This time it was Clyde who stood at the plate while the pitches hit the dirt in front of the plate. Another walk. Bases loaded.

Freddy was up next. The pitcher's cheeks were pale with a pink flush on each side of his face. His first pitch found the plate. Freddy watched it sail by. Strike one. The runners sensed they had to wake up. They stretched and shifted on the bases. The fielders hunched over to be ready.

Freddy went for the next pitch with a mighty swing that knocked the ball so high in the air Pump lost sight of it against the bright sky. It reached the top of its arc and gathered speed on its way back to Earth.

The Muskets' center fielder and right fielder converged toward the spot where the ball would land.

"Move it," shouted Fred Namath. "Run, run," he yelled waving his arms to provide some motion. "Get moving!"

The base runners watched with open mouths as the soaring ball descended. They were so sure it would be caught, they didn't dare run despite the coach's loud orders. Fred was counting on the likelihood of an error. Instead, the runners waited to tag up when the ball was caught. Pump caught a glimpse of the pitcher sprinting toward the outfield.

Pump was more afraid not to obey his coach than he was afraid of being put out. He started toward home, hesitating about halfway there. He saw Charles Ames totally out of position calling for the ball. The outfielders froze. The ball dropped. None of the outstretched gloves touched it. The ball smacked to earth and bounced a jagged path away from the fielders.

Pump scored, Danny followed and Clyde crossed the plate. Chaos broke out on the field. Charles followed the ball, grabbed it and, without bothering to aim for a cutoff, heaved it to the infield. The ball rolled past the mound where Ken ran to retrieve it, then headed back toward the plate, which he'd left unguarded. Ken's speed forced Freddy to hold up at third. Three runs, no outs, and the Muskets in confusion.

Pump couldn't stop smiling. What a start to the most important game of the season! His grin broadened as he let that good feeling of scoring the first run surge through his whole body.

The Muskets' coach was pacing up and down behind the third base line. "You gotta play first-place ball to be in first place," he shouted. "That was last-place ball I just saw. Shape up, Muskets."

Charles Ames, his shoulders hunched up to his ears, stalked back to the mound. Their coach, Tony, made his way out to the mound to talk to his pitcher. Pump drank some water from the big team jug and focused on the game again. He glanced at his father who now stood with Pump's mom. No frown. Pump could forget about him for now.

The Muskets had been on top for the second half of the season. In a funny way, Pump and the rest of the Minutemen had found it easier to play good ball when they were a game behind. They got stronger and stronger, while it looked like the Muskets were starting to unravel.

The way the Muskets were playing reminded Pump of the beginning of the season. Annie and Brian were walked. The bases were

loaded again. Penny Weiss came up to bat and her walk brought in Freddy's run. Jeff Leonard managed to get put out by a foul tip that sprang off his bat right into Ken's glove. Willie Salvano, with his impossible strike zone, decided he needed to start getting some hits. He swung mightily at three balls and missed them all, just the way they all missed his strike zone. Two outs.

Jill Maloney stepped to the plate. Charles Ames gave her his most evil eye and, with a pitching motion that looked more like a tantrum, hurled a pitch directly at her. Jill stood frozen in the path of the oncoming ball. It hit her in the thigh.

The onlookers gasped. Jill stood for a moment before grabbing her leg. She crumpled to the ground and whimpered. With the help of Fred, Louie and the umpire, she got up and, sniffling, took some tentative steps.

Jill's father shouted encouragement, "Walk it off. Keep moving. You'll be fine. You're OK."

"You brought in a run," Butch Flagan called to her.

Cheers poured forth as Jill walked to first base. This brought her sister, Annie, home. Five runs for the Minutemen.

Bones Bednarski, batting as DH, swaggered to the plate. Pump wondered if Bones remembered that, no matter what, he would be the last batter of the inning. Bones heaved some mighty practice swings. He tried to look menacing.

"Get on base, Bones," his burly father called out. "A walk's as good as a hit."

Pump cringed. Fred made it clear that a hit was always better. No one on the team could get away with saying what Bones's dad said. To Pump's relief, Fred wasn't paying attention to anything but his team.

It didn't matter what Charles Ames threw; Bones was going for broke. He swung mightily at three pitches in a row, missed them all, and brought the inning to a close.

Fred called the Minutemen into a huddle.

"I just want to remind you guys about something. That little line that determines the ground rule double? You know about that? If you see a ball headed for it, what do you do?"

No Minuteman was willing to offer any answer. Fred was out for blood.

Fred looked with meaning at Jeff Leonard. "Nothing. That's what you do. Don't go for the ball unless you're sure you can get the runner out at second. And that's something you can never be sure of. Not yet. If you field it, the runner can get a triple or even a run. So stay out of the way. Or is that too much to ask?"

Fred had started to sound cranky, but then changed his tone again.

"OK, boys and girls, let's show them how baseball is played!" Fred clapped his hands and sent the Minutemen into the top of the second inning with the score 5-1.

The Muskets' big hitters were out of the way. From here to the end of the lineup the batters became progressively smaller and were Freddy's biggest challenge. As usual, Freddy's best bet was to reduce the speed of the ball in order to tempt the batters to swing. At this end of the lineup, a swing often missed.

Freddy threw slow pitches as close to the plate as he could get them. The first batter fell for it and reached for everything until he struck out. The second batter followed the statue technique and drew a walk. In trying to get the ball closer to the plate, Freddy hit the next batter, who took his base. Runners on first and second.

The fourth batter stuck out his bat as if he were just trying to touch the oncoming ball. He did this three times in a row and struck out. All three pitches would have been balls. Two outs. The Muskets' DH was next up. She was very small but marched to the plate with a huge bat over her shoulder. Pump didn't see how she would be able to swing such a bat. But he knew that the Minutemen better get out of this inning without bringing Ken up to bat. This had to be an out.

Freddy tried a slow pitch but the batter wouldn't take it. Pump decided her bat was too heavy to lug off her shoulder for a slower ball. Freddy must have made the same assessment because he fired a fastball that was high and outside but got that big bat moving. Strike one.

The next pitch was in the dirt in front of the plate. No action. Two balls. Freddy concentrated on getting the ball high, aiming toward that big bat, coaxing it to move. It worked. Two more pitches, two more strikes. The Minutemen held the lead at 5-1.

The Minutemen were up, with Pump leading off.

"Ball one," the umpire called out.

Pump was relieved. He'd been so lost in the thought of not getting rattled by Charles Ames that he hadn't even noticed that Charles had started pitching. Luckily, the pitch was way outside. Pump focused on the ball. He swung sending a high fly out to right field.

The ball soared so high that there was plenty of time for the center fielder and right fielder to converge under it. For a while neither of them called it. They stood still under the falling ball until each fielder stuck out a glove. The center fielder shoved his hand above his teammate's and the ball dropped into his open glove only to bounce out again and fall into the right fielder's glove that was waiting below. The ball stayed balanced on the right fielder's glove. The Muskets cheered.

Pump made it to first. He couldn't tell what had happened and figured he must be out. Fred was spinning his arm wildly instructing Pump to keep going. He sped off to second. As far as Pump could tell, the ball was still somewhere in the outfield. Fred gestured for Pump to keep going, so he rounded second and headed for third.

Pump could tell there was some action now at the mound and Fred signaled for him to stop at third. Bewildered and breathing hard, Pump slid into third. His slide calmed him down. Pump stood up and dusted himself off while the Muskets' fans unleashed a storm of protest as the Minutemen's fans cheered wildly.

The Muskets' fans were shouting and screaming, "He's out! He's out! That was a fly ball! You've gotta be kidding, ump. You're blind. That was an out! For crying out loud!"

While the Minutemen's fans chorused, "Great hit! Attaway, Pump! Runner in scoring position on the first hit! He's safe! He's safe!"

"Where's instant replay when we need it?" yelled Danny Flagan.

The Muskets' coach stalked out to the umpire, who stood behind the mound. The umpire was tall and heavy. The coach was short and heavy and breathing hard. He shoved his face right up to the umpire's chin. The umpire wouldn't look down.

"For Pete's sake," Tony growled. "The kid is out, Mel. We all saw it. My fielder caught that ball."

"Which fielder?" the umpire wanted to know.

Tony sputtered and the ump concluded, "I rest my case." He paused and then roared out, "Batter up."

The crowd settled down a little, but a drone of muttering continued.

Danny Flagan began to swing his bat and Ken Ames crouched behind the plate. Charles Ames wound up and delivered a strike.

After such a complicated beginning the rest of the inning started to feel anticlimactic. Danny didn't put much energy into his swing and struck out. Clyde came up to bat. He took some slow practice swings that were as lackluster as Danny's had been.

Pump called to him from third base, "Hit one for Papi!"

A smile curved Clyde's lips before he threw his weight into the next swing and sent the ball over the fence to bring Pump and himself home.

The crowd cheered and stamped their feet. 7-1, Minutemen lead. Freddy took the bat and sent the first pitch looping into the field over the heads of the pitcher and second baseman. Pump could feel the excitement as his team gained momentum. He knew that could change at any moment, but right now the Minutemen had the momentum. Anything could happen.

Annie Maloney was up. She looked as confident and determined as Pump had ever seen her. Charles Ames glared at her from the mound. His face twisted with an angry grimace as he wound up. He hurled the ball with such force that his brother couldn't hold on to it. Force does not do much for accuracy, Pump thought, as Charles kicked dirt all over the mound when the umpire called a ball.

Two more sizzling pitches evaded the plate and bounced off Ken's catcher's mitt. Three balls.

Annie rearranged her fingers on the bat as she waited for the next pitch. Her strong legs were bent at the knee, her body coiled for action. Another ball sailed in low. Annie couldn't wait for a walk. She swung with all her might. The ball flew off her bat, Freddy took off for second, and Annie stared after her hit. It arced high over the field, then over the fence. Her first home run ever. The crowd roared. The Muskets stared blankly at the sky where the ball had been.

"That was Annie. Did you see that?" Mr. Maloney shouted as he pounded Mr. Gerstein on the back. "Way to go, Annie. Way to go!"

Charles Ames's face was splotched with red. His eyes were damp and glazed. Tony headed to the mound and Ken followed behind. Charles stamped his foot, turning his back on his coach and his brother. Tony's face became tense and unmoving.

"What kind of a prima donna are you, Ames? You think you're the only guy who ever gave up a home run to a girl? You look at me when I talk to you," Tony ordered.

The pitcher turned to face his coach.

"I was just coming out to help you settle down," Tony said, "but now I'm just going to take you out. Switch places with Ben. And no making faces behind my back. You got something to say to me, say it to my face."

Ken trotted back to the plate. Pump could tell he wanted to keep out of his brother's way. Charles took Ben Bracken's spot at shortstop and Ben started warming up on the mound.

Pump had never seen Tony say anything to Charles about his tantrums and fussing. He'd certainly never seen him pulled out in the second inning. This was turning into quite a game.

Nine to one, one out and Brian Kennedy was up. The Minutemen lost some of their certainty at the plate after the pitching change. Ben was calm and businesslike and pitched straight, clean balls. Nothing fancy, nothing very fast. The drama was gone for now. On the two-and-two pitch, Brian hit a cautious fly ball into left field, which was caught for the second out. Penny Weiss took the plate, got to a count of three and two by observing rather than swinging, and then struck out. The side was retired.

The Minutemen ended the inning still in front, 9-1. Pump kept feeling electric excitement shiver through him whenever he thought about the score. He knew he'd have to stop thinking and stay focused on the game. The whole thing could turn around so fast. But at 9-1, how could they lose?

"Nine to one, Minutemen," Fred said. "Sounds good. But you know what? We still gotta work for this one. Don't let up. Now's the time to play harder, maximize our advantage, increase our lead. You can never be too far ahead of a good team.

"The Muskets were nervous. Now they're the ones with nothing to lose so they'll relax. It's our job not to tighten up. You're making me proud. Keep it up."

How to Clean a Musket

PUMP FELT A GLOW INSIDE as he trotted to his position. Freddy was on the mound loosening up. Danny threw Pump a hard, energetic grounder. Pump crouched and managed to catch the ball as it took a hop off the ground. He caught sight of Clyde watching him. Their eyes met for a second before Clyde looked away.

"How long you gonna hold on to that ball?" Danny called from first base.

"Sorry," Pump said as he fired the ball as hard as he could to Danny. The throw missed the first baseman, who had to run down the ball. Pump was mad at himself and hoped Clyde had stopped looking at him before he made the bad throw. Pump still felt a little shy with the older boys. He felt apologetic about his errors, as if the older guys would never make mistakes like he did.

The Muskets were back to the top of their lineup and Ken Ames was at the plate. Ken was looking for a hit. He turned the first two balls into strikes by swinging hard at them. He must have realized that the pitches were missing the plate, because he stopped swinging and watched the next four pitches give him a free trip to first base.

John Henry Mission stepped to the plate. His stance was full of determination. He was poised to hit. He caught a piece of the next two pitches. Two fouls. Then he, too, seemed to realize that the pitches were not in the vicinity of the plate. He stopped swinging and was walked.

Pizza De Souza followed. His batting skills went untested as well. He took his base on balls.

"That's looking 'em over, Muskets," Tony called to his players. "Good eye."

On the bench Bones leaned over to Willy and snickered, "Yeah, real good eye. You don't need any eyes to get walked when Namath's in a rut. You know every pitch is gonna be a ball."

No outs, bases loaded. Charles Ames took up the bat and sliced the air with smoking practice swings. Ken, John Henry, and Pizza hunched over, ready to run. Charles swung mightily over the low pitch. Strike one. He banged his bat on the plate in a loud challenge to Freddy to give him something to hit. Freddy did, but Charles missed his chance. Strike two. The next pitch was slow and loopy. Charles stood and watched as it passed over the plate.

"Strike," growled the umpire.

Charles threw his bat off to the side and stormed to the bench. The umpire called him back.

"You don't throw bats on my field, son," the umpire said sternly. "You'll never do that again d'ya hear? Now pick up that bat."

Charles Ames glowered at the umpire. Pump thought for a second that Charles was about to really lose it. At that instant, Tony calmly came up behind Charles, grabbed him by the back of his shirt and pulled him away.

"Get that bat, Ames," Tony hissed. "To the bench, double time."

Tony gave Charles a shove, turning him toward the bat and away from the umpire. Pump knew the last thing Tony wanted was to see his strongest player ejected from the game.

Freddy started rushing his pitches. In a matter of minutes, two runs were walked in with the bases still loaded. Nine to three. One out. The Minutemen started to get restless. The pitcher was the only player to get any action and none of it looked good.

Pump knew that Fred usually tried to let a pitcher get through three innings no matter how things were going. Pump could practically hear Fred saying, "Figure it out," which is how he would let you know he had faith that you could do it yourself. This time, however, Fred walked to the mound, with Brian trailing after him. After a brief conference, Fred and Brian left Freddy, who twisted the ball in his mitt.

The next batter was nervous. His wrists churned so that the vertical bat made circles at the top. Freddy sent his pitch toward the plate. The batter swung and missed. He repeated the sequence with the next pitch. Strike two. On the third pitch, the batter drew his bat back, swung and sent the ball to right field. Jeff expended no energy on this routine catch. He ambled toward the descending ball, opened his glove, and missed the ball completely. Suddenly everyone was awake. The runners were running. The crowd was roaring and shouting. Jeff scrambled after the ball while Pump, the designated cut-off, readied himself for the play. As Jeff moved toward the ball he managed to kick it farther out of reach. The crowd screamed; the Minutemen yelled. The runners were coming home. One, two, three. Only the batter was left turning the corner at third when Jeff managed to catch up to the unruly ball and heave it to Pump.

Pump threw the ball to Brian, the catcher, but Brian missed the throw. Pump felt his heart sink. Was his throw off? Was it too hard? Was it his fault when Tony waved the runner on and the kid chugged all the way home? Brian got hold of the ball and reached out toward the runner, but not in time.

The crowd on the Muskets' side went wild. Cheers and whistles rained down on the exuberant Muskets who bounced and slapped each other and bounced some more. The Minutemen's side fell silent.

Pump closed his eyes. When he opened them again, another small batter at the plate faced Freddy. Still just one out. Minutemen nine, Muskets seven. Pump wondered if they'd ever get out of this nightmare inning.

The batter stood straight up and didn't move a muscle. Pump

knew Tony coached the bottom of his lineup to just stand there as much as possible, always figuring that a base on balls was a better bet than trying to hit the ball and striking out.

As Pump watched Freddy throw a mix of balls and strikes he realized that the Muskets were on their eighth batter. That meant they only had two more batters to go before the side would be retired. Maybe it just made sense to walk them rather than giving them anything to hit. After all, even three walks wouldn't bring in a run. Anything else was risky. But that was thinking like Tony. To Pump playing things so safe felt cowardly. But he really didn't want this game tied up.

Freddy, at a three-two count, threw a last strike. Two outs. Then, maybe thinking the same as Pump, he walked the last two batters and trotted in to the bench.

"It ain't over 'til it's over," Danny said as he slapped Freddy on the back. Danny gave Pump a high five just as their coach started to speak.

"So we've seen a little shift of momentum. That's all it is. Remember, their pitcher came out in the middle of the last inning and our pitcher got us through the third. Good work, Freddy."

Fred patted his son's shoulder for the first time in history.

He continued, "Now we'll do our talking with our bats. We blew plays we shoulda made. But that's just nerves. Look at the score. We're still ahead and we're batting. Here we go, Minutemen. Leonard, you're up. Gerstein, on deck. Jill Maloney, double deck. Now who's going to get some runs this inning?"

"The Minutemen," the team shouted, excited again.

"Who's going to win this game?" Fred called out.

"The Minutemen," everyone yelled.

"You bet!" Fred exclaimed. "Now get to the bench and let's hear some noise. Jeff wants to know his team is behind him."

The Minutemen settled down as Jeff Leonard carried his bat to the plate. Ben Bracken's practice pitches were unhurried and pretty accurate. This was one steady pitcher. Pump hoped that Jeff realized that.

"Be ready, Leonard," shouted the coach. "Don't spectate!"

Pump knew you couldn't wait for walks from Ben.

Jeff watched the first pitch sail by. A slow strike. Jeff assumed, what Danny called, "Leonard's batting trance." He seemed mesmerized by the pitcher. Pump couldn't figure out what Jeff was looking at, but it sure wasn't the ball. He swung slowly at the next pitch and missed. Strike two. Pump wondered if Jeff decided the next two pitches were balls or if he just needed a rest because he didn't swing and the balls missed the plate. Two and two.

"Let's hear a little chatter, Minutemen," Butch Flagan called over his shoulder to the bench.

Danny obliged. "Give it a ride, baby. Let those Muskets eat our dust."

"Raaaal-ly! Raaaal-ly! Raaaal-ly!" chanted Brian, immediately joined by the entire Minutemen bench.

Jeff hunched over to go for the next pitch. He went down swinging.

"Good cut," Butch Flagan called to Jeff. "Good try, buddy. Next time."

Josh Gerstein moved to the plate for his first at-bat in the game. He stood so far away from the plate that only the tip of his bat stuck over the plate as he swung. "Move into the box, Gerstein," Fred Namath called to him. "Get your bat *over* the plate, not sniffing at it."

Josh moved in closer to the plate. His expression looked like he was pleading with the pitcher. What for? Not to throw the ball anywhere near him? To give him a good ball he could swing at? Josh was frozen. But somehow it worked and he drew the first walk from Ben Bracken.

Jill Maloney, now playing DH, looked worried at the plate. She stood straight up and swiveled her bat around. She only swung her bat at one ball but she managed to hit it. A cheer of amazement swelled and abruptly stopped. The ball went right to the pitcher who easily caught it for the second out.

Pump was up next. He had the feeling that something extra was expected of him. If Josh could get on base, then Pump should be able to do as much. If Pump could get a rally going, the Minutemen could save this lousy inning. The top of the lineup would be ready to knock in some runs. In fact, Pump was the absolute top of the lineup. He was supposed to provide a reliable bat. Here goes, he thought.

Just like Jeff, Pump watched the first pitch go by. It was a good one and Pump promised himself he would be more active on the next pitch. He knocked a foul backwards over the backstop and into the street. He swung at the next pitch, a faster ball, and ticked it for another foul. The bench was quiet with held breath.

"You gotta piece of it. Now get the whole thing, Prout."

Pump recognized the voice of Brian's father, Coach Kennedy. Pump slashed through two practice swings. He was ready. He swung with all his might.

Clap. The ball landed in Ken Ames's glove. Strike three.

"Good cut, Prout." Coach Kennedy smiled over the fence at Pump as he collected his mitt to head out to the field. "Sweet swing you got there," he said.

A lotta good it does, Pump thought to himself. His heart was almost too heavy for even Coach Kennedy to raise his spirits. But he met Coach Kennedy's eyes and couldn't stop a smile.

"Good work, Prout. You're developing nicely. I knew I had a find the first time I saw you. Hey," Coach Kennedy said quietly so that Pump had to step closer to hear him, "don't let a strikeout get you down. You're too advanced for that. You're still ahead.

"Go on now. I'll be watching," Coach Kennedy finished with a wink.

Pump wondered if he would feel more tense because he knew Coach Kennedy was there. But as he jogged to second he realized he felt better knowing that his old coach was watching. Pump felt himself settle down.

It was the top of the fourth, and Clyde took the mound. Danny was at shortstop, and Freddy was on first base. Clyde moved into his warm-up pitches. He looked OK, Pump thought. His face seemed pretty relaxed. Pump saw none of that vacant look he'd gotten to expect from Clyde.

"Batter up," the umpire called out.

Ken Ames stepped to the plate.

This time Clyde didn't get rattled by a ball or two. He just kept pitching and seemed to be liking it. Pump felt he could read all this in Clyde's windup and delivery. At the three and one count, Clyde threw a beauty, right down the middle. Strike two.

The Muskets started to stamp their feet in rhythm. *Stomp ... stomp ... stomp.* A few of them whistled. Ken frowned and swung the bat with determination. He swung hard at the next pitch. Clyde struck him out.

The Minutemen cheered. Pump felt a wave of relief pass over him. Clyde bit the inside of his cheeks to try to look serious and get rid of his smile.

As Pump watched Clyde pitch to John Henry, he understood that what he was watching was not ordinary Little League baseball. Everything was relative. Compared to each other, some pitchers in the league were better than others but not by much. No one had much control. Just getting the ball the 46 feet from the mound to the plate was clearly a challenge. Then getting the ball over the plate was no easy accomplishment. And if over the plate, there was still the task of keeping the ball in the strike zone.

Distinguishing balls from strikes required a lot of creative interpretation by the umpires, who often felt sorely misunderstood by angry coaches and parents. Of course, they called smaller plates and smaller strike zones for the better pitchers. It was all seen as part of helping a pitcher develop. The pitchers and their coaches never saw it that way. They saw it as persecution.

Pump had watched Luke move from the minors to the majors. Even now, as one of the best pitchers they had and in his last year of the majors, Luke was not reliably consistent. He tried to throw some different pitches that rarely worked. There was an element of uncertainty with every pitch.

Clyde was one of the oldest boys playing in the minors, but that wasn't enough to explain what Pump was seeing. Clyde was throwing the ball like no one else. Right before Pump's amazed eyes, Clyde found his groove and tossed every pitch precisely to Brian's glove. Some of his pitches were slow, some were fast. All were reasonably accurate.

Pump figured that this was what Fred Namath had seen all season. The coach had known Clyde's potential before Clyde had any idea of what he could do. Then Fred had rushed things. He had gotten ahead of Clyde, ahead of the Minutemen and ahead of his own better judgment.

As Clyde kept throwing strikes, Pump watched the strike zone shrink. Each time the umpire called a ball that a few pitches ago would have been a strike, Clyde would frown, squint his eyes and smile when the next pitch was a called strike. After two strike outs and a walk, Clyde's last pitch of the inning produced a pop fly to right field where Jeff redeemed himself by making the catch.

The Minutemen were full of chatter as they tossed aside their gloves and settled onto the bench. Fred Namath moved toward the third base line without saying a word to his team. Pump felt the excitement he was sure the rest of the team was feeling.

"Let's go, Minute-men." *Clap—clap—clap-clap-clap.* "Let's go Minute-men." *Clap—clap—clap-clap-clap.* Annie started the cheer and the team kept it up.

Danny walked to the plate with assurance. He had plans for this at-bat. But Ben Bracken had a way of messing up the plans of the Minutemen batters. In fact, it was easier to get on base against Charles Ames.

As a pitcher, Ben was quiet and simply delivered. He just presented a tempting pitch. It was up to the batter to find a way to hit it. Ben threw his share of balls, but he threw just enough strikes to force the Minutemen to keep swinging. At everything.

The strongest trio of the batting order, Danny, Clyde and Freddy, went down in flames. The crowd groaned. None of the batters had the patience to look the ball over. Everyone just wanted to swing, and swing hard.

The game moved into the fifth inning with the Minutemen still two runs out in front.

Fred brought out his clipboard.

"Willie," Fred called out, "you take over for Josh in center. Gerstein, you stay in the lineup as DH. Jill, fine work today. You take a rest now, over with Bednarski on the bench.

"Remember—from here on there's no limit to the batters. We gotta keep 'em under control. Tighten up our defense. Defense is critical now. You can't expect it all to come from the pitcher. Don't forget—he's got a team behind him. And what team is that?"

"The Minutemen," shouted the Minutemen, full of excitement.

Ben Bracken led off. He studied Clyde's pitch that sailed by him for a strike. On the next pitch, Ben met the ball with a smooth swing, sending it deep into center field. Ben ran. Fielders scrambled. A stand-up triple. The next two batters struck out. The batters were getting smaller. Clyde walked the next batter. Runners on first and third.

The next batter, without a breath of a backswing, held his bat straight over the plate. The ball struck the bat and bounced to the ground right in front of the plate. Brian tried to swing off his mask and grab the ball at the same time. Somehow his mask caught on his ear. He had to grope for the ball with his mask hanging in front of his face. He grabbed the ball and threw it in the direction of first.

Freddy was clearly not expecting the throw. Holding the ball at home to prevent a run was a better bet than trying to make the out at first. Freddy had to chase down the ball and missed the out at first. The other runner made it to third, while Ben brought in the run.

Pump suffered a shiver of doubt. Clyde wasn't invincible. How quickly he had started to think Clyde would win this game all by himself. The rest of the team had thought so, too. Isn't that what happened at the beginning of the season? And look what that led to.

Clyde showed no sign of dissolving. Instead, he threw three strikes in a row to the tiniest strike zone the Muskets could offer. The side was retired with the Minutemen ahead by one run.

Annie led off in the bottom of the fifth. She smashed the ball past the shortstop and it hardly slowed down as it bumped and bounced over the ground-rule-double line.

Brian Kennedy put more energy than usual into his practice swings. Pump figured he wanted to show his dad what he could do. Instead, he got walked. Two Minutemen on. No outs. Penny Weiss followed, did not attempt to swing, even for practice, and struck out. Jeff Leonard swung extra slowly and missed three pitches in a row. Two outs.

"Willie, bring 'em home," Danny shouted.

"Wil-lie. Wil-lie. Wil-lie. Wil-lie," the Minutemen chanted.

Willie Salvano slashed the air with his practice swings. He wanted to bring those runners home. A swing and a miss. Strike one. He set his body squarely facing the plate. On the next pitch, he swung and connected. The ball went straight up. Willie took off, his short legs churning as fast as they could. Annie shot toward third and Brian lunged for second.

The ball came straight down. Ken Ames, his head back to look straight up, swayed beneath the ball as he waited to make the catch. He held both hands ready. The ball fell into his thick catcher's mitt, then immediately rolled out before he could bring his right hand over to cover it. The runners reached the bases safely but could not advance since the ball was lying right next to home plate. It was the first time Willie got on base with something other than a bunt.

Disgusted, Ken picked up the ball and threw it to the pitcher.

Bases loaded. Josh Gerstein was up. Until now nothing seemed to faze Ben Bracken. His pitching was not what Pump would call inspired but it certainly was effective. Unusually effective for the minor league. Maybe it was the ghostly pallor on Josh's cheek, or the terror he could read in Josh's frozen stance, but for the first time since he'd taken the mound, Ben looked shaken. He'd walked Josh his last at-bat. Pump wondered if that had gotten under his skin

It wasn't that Ben hadn't given up his share of walks, but he had an uncanny ability to get his pitches over the plate. Now, he couldn't find the plate. After four awkward pitches he lost the batter. After the umpire called the last ball, Josh still gripped his bat. He continued to breathe quick little breaths through tightly pursed lips. He looked exactly like a fish out of water trying to breathe.

"Take your base, son," the umpire boomed behind him.

Josh leapt forward, dropped his bat and sprinted to first base. His walk brought in a run. Pump was up.

He had to remind himself that he wasn't leading off and that the team was ahead. Not exactly safely ahead, but ahead all the same.

As Pump approached the plate, the crowd woke up and started calling for him to bring in the runs. That, indeed, would put the Minutemen ahead, safely ahead.

"We've got 'em where we want 'em. Go get 'em, Pump. Show them you've got the right stuff."

Pump swallowed hard. He heard Fred yell, "Easy does it. Nothing fancy."

Pump was thinking fancy. The possibility of bringing in a few runs at one blow was an irresistible cue to imagine great glory. Not to mention the grand slam he tried not to think about, but there it was, beckoning.

Pump knew enough to take a few deep breaths to control his pounding heart. Besides, once a pitcher loses the plate it's not so easy to find. Ben's first pitch was a strike that Pump, hoping for a ball, let sail by. No easy bases this time. Maybe if Pump could look as nervous as Josh had, he would rattle this pitcher. He tried to think scary thoughts but found he didn't really want anyone to see him looking scared. The next pitch was another strike. Pump realized he'd better get busy. "Don't spectate," went through his head.

"Good eye, good eye," Butch Flagan called out as Pump let a ball go by. By then he had planned to go for a hit and it was hard to let the pitch go.

Pump threw himself into his swing at the next pitch and sent the ball out of the infield in the air. He started to run. The runners, forgetting that on the last out you run on a fly ball no matter what, hugged their bases.

"Run," shouted Pump as he bore down on Willie. Willie looked startled and took off. Pump looked out beyond Willie's running form and saw his ball fall into the glove of the right fielder who held on to it as he whooped and jumped up and down.

At the end of five innings, the Minutemen led by two runs: 10-8.

Ken Ames was the lead off batter in the top of the sixth. Pump felt agitated for the first time in this game. It seemed like the game was lasting forever. Usually Pump wanted baseball to last forever, but now he just wanted this endless game to be over.

It felt like bad luck to have Ken lead off. Pump felt in his bones that Ken was going to do something big. Ken looked like he had the same feeling as he strode to the plate. As the game got longer, the sun got lower in the sky. Now it was directly in the eyes of the batters. Ken had put on dark sunglasses, which made him look very cool and very menacing.

Much as the sight of Ken made Pump feel queasy, it seemed to have no effect on Clyde. His warm-up pitches were stronger than ever and more precise.

Brian stood up and yelled to Clyde, "Take it easy, big guy. I can't catch half an inning if you wreck my hand before we start."

Clyde responded with a lopsided grin.

Ken stepped to the plate, took some impressive swings and waited for his pitch. The third pitch was his and Ken sent it high into the outfield. Pump thought it might make it over the fence only it came down just inside, hit the fence and rolled back into the field toward Willie who was in center field.

Ken tore around first as fast as he could. He made the mistake of looking to see what was happening to the ball. He slowed up to watch the ball hit the fence, and he stayed slow when he saw little Willie running to retrieve the ball. No rush, he clearly thought.

Willie sped to the ball and deftly scooped it up. He forgot he had a cut-off in Freddy or Pump and, with all his might, threw the ball in. Pump knew that all of Willie's might wasn't very mighty, so he ran toward Willie and dove for the ball. Pump spun around and whipped the ball all the way to Annie at third.

Ken had already passed second base and was on his way to third, when he saw Annie catch Pump's throw. Ken was so startled to see the third baseman with the ball that he didn't immediately stop running. Annie started running toward him. Ken jumped around only to see Freddy coming toward him, ready to receive the ball. Ken spun back to try his luck at third. With short but rapid strides, Annie was on him and tagged him out as he turned back toward second. One out.

The crowd and the bench went wild. John Henry stepped to the plate while the noise died down. Clyde wasn't smiling, now. He looked determined. He pitched a full count. John Henry fouled off the next three pitches and it seemed like he planned to stay at bat forever. The next pitch was a ball and he walked.

Even Pump could read Tony's signal telling Pizza to lay down a bunt. Tony regularly told his kids to bunt. He counted on the opposition to bungle the ball and saw the bunt as a great offensive weapon.

The Minutemen were ready when Pizza went for a low ball and

tried to bunt. He missed his first try. Tony asked for the same. This time Pizza stood with his bat in position to bunt even before the pitcher started his wind-up. He poked his horizontal bat forward and jabbed the ball. It took a short hop toward third. Brian got to the ball before Annie. He grabbed it with his bare hand and threw to first. Danny kept his foot on the bag and stretched for the ball, which didn't make it all the way to him but bounced, then rolled in his direction. Danny left the base to get the ball just as Pizza crossed first. Runners on first and second. One out.

"Let's go, Muskets. Now's your chance. Let's go," the Muskets fans shouted and clapped.

Charles Ames swaggered to the plate. He stared directly at Clyde as he swung the bat for practice. Clyde met his stare and stayed cool. Every muscle in Pump's body was ready to move. Clyde wound up and delivered a slow, looping pitch. Charles slashed at it with his bat and missed. Pump saw a smile flicker on Clyde's mouth. The next instant Clyde's face was without expression. He pitched a ball high and outside.

The Muskets' bench chanted, "Bring them home! Bring them home!"

The Minutemen countered with "Two more outs! Two more outs!"

The two chants mingled and Clyde threw another high ball, which the batter swung at and knocked foul.

"Settle down, Ames," Tony bellowed.

Charles shot a look at his coach, then riveted his eyes on the next pitch. With a huge swing, he drove the ball straight back at Clyde. Clyde doubled over and dropped to his knees. The cheers and shouts fell silent. The umpire, from his position right behind the pitcher, reached Clyde first. As he bent down to help the fallen player, Clyde raised his face showing a wide grin to the crowd. He uncurled his bent body and pulled out his gloved hand, which held the ball! Relief was loud in the umpire's voice as he announced forcefully, "He's out!"

The cheers and yells from the Minutemen were deafening. The Muskets looked horrified. Charles Ames spat and hissed before he turned back to the Muskets' bench.

Two outs brought Ben Bracken to the plate. Pump knew that in his steady, quiet way Ben was more of a threat than Charles. Pump felt uneasy but excited. One more out meant a win. One more run meant, well, a closer game. Two runs … don't even think of it, Pump warned himself. A tie. Of course, there was always the Minutemen's last ups.

Pump's thoughts were interrupted by a roar from the crowd responding to the ball Ben had just hit into right field. It bounced toward Jeff Leonard, who waited for the ball to reach him. The ball slid right through his legs. By the time Jeff found the ball, Ben was practically at first, Pizza, puffing hard, was on top of second and John Henry had rounded third. Pump ran into right field to be sure Jeff could see him and remember that Pump was his cut-off. Jeff spotted Pump and threw a slow ball toward him.

Pump barely managed to snag the ball. A roar from the Muskets' side told him that John Henry had crossed the plate. Pump spun and threw to third as fast as he could. Pump's throw beat Pizza by a split second. Annie moved off the base to make the catch. In a continuous motion she brought both hands and the ball down on top of Pizza's head just as he tried to slide into third.

"He's out," the umpire roared. Pizza De Souza burst into tears. The Minutemen fans whistled and cheered. The Minutemen shrieked and pounded each other on their shoulders, backs, and heads.

It wasn't easy to contain themselves enough to file past the Muskets and skid Minutemen palms across Muskets palms. Then they erupted again in delirious whoops and shouts.

Pump saw Ken among the Muskets, looking tired and slump-shouldered.

Fred beckoned the Minutemen back to the side of the field.

"Great game, guys. Grrrreat game!" Fred beamed. "But we gotta let the losers maintain a shred of dignity."

Fred winked, "Let's keep our celebration under control, at least as long as the Muskets are still around. After all, they are a fine team … a fine team *that we've just beaten!*"

"We won," Bones yelled and startled everyone by heaving himself into the air and shouting, "Wahoo!"

"We're in first!" cheered Willie springing into the air again and again.

"Hey, all you jumping jacks," Danny called out, "if you can bounce so high why is it so hard to snag fly balls? I gotta know."

Fred, who rarely found anything that Danny said funny, laughed until tears glistened in his eyes.

"When you find out," Fred Namath said with a smile, "let me know, will you?"

Still chuckling, Fred gathered the team together and they sat down in a bunch for their post-game wrap-up.

"Boy, Fred is really excited we won," Danny whispered to Clyde as Fred was talking to them. "I don't think I've ever seen him laugh out loud. And what I said wasn't even all that funny."

"You're right," Clyde whispered back, "it wasn't that funny."

Danny jabbed him and Clyde leaned back to dodge the poke. Danny's momentum left him sprawled across Clyde's lap. The two boys were trying not to laugh but choked snorts escaped from their noses.

"Hey, Minutemen," Fred said, all business again, "time for joking is over."

Everyone fell silent and Fred continued his recap of the game. Pump wondered if anyone was listening. He knew he wasn't. He couldn't let go of the savory thought that they had beaten the Muskets. He no longer cared *how*, only that they had.

The Taste of Victory

WHEN FRED NAMATH finally released his team, everyone stood up and stretched.

Clyde ran over to check on Papi the frog. The Minutemen all got a chance to hold him before Clyde slipped the stunned frog back into his box.

"I'm starving!" Danny announced. "We'd better do something and we'd better do it fast!"

"Pirelli's?" Josh, emboldened by victory, asked, loudly.

"Right on," Danny yelled. Josh's parents, looking on as always, beamed proudly.

"To Pirelli's!" the Minutemen yelled and hooted. And off they went.

Pump waved to his mom and dad who were talking to other parents near the fence.

"Great play, Pumpkin," his mom called over to him.

Pump closed his eyes. How could she call him that? Especially now. He knew there was no answer.

His dad strode over and held up his hand for a high five. That was a first! Pump slapped his hand.

"Great game," his dad said.

"Thanks." Pump grinned. "See ya later."

Pump turned to join his teammates. The Minutemen had all gone on ahead. Pump saw Ken waiting by the bikes and met up with him.

"Some game!" Ken exclaimed, as if he hadn't been a part of it.

"Yep. Some game all right," Pump agreed.

Pump unlocked his bike and said, "Everyone's going to Pirelli's. You want to come?"

Ken looked pleased. "Sure," he said.

The two boys rode, Pump behind Ken, to Pirelli's.

Pizza never tasted as good as it did at Pirelli's, and it never tasted as good at Pirelli's as it did if the team had just won a game. But the taste of Pirelli's pizza after beating the Muskets was probably the most delicious taste in the world.

Louie Pirelli himself had been at the game, rooting for the Muskets. Now, there he was, behind the counter, smiling and humming as he brought out from the oven hot pizzas topped with cheese and sausage and pepperoni. The players wolfed them down as fast as Mr, Pirelli could cook them. Minutemen uniforms mingled with Musket uniforms.

True to his name, Pizza De Souza was packing away more than anyone else. He had jammed himself into a booth full of Minutemen. He had managed to squeeze in next to Annie Maloney who was trying to match him piece for piece.

"So what if you guys are in first?" Pizza said with his mouth stuffed full. He chewed awhile before adding, "We play on Wednesday and you play on Thursday. We'll roll over the Stars and the Pilgrims will roll over you. Sounds good, don't it?" Pizza swallowed. "Then we'll be tied and have a playoff. And, man, will we be out for revenge."

Then he exclaimed, "More pizza!"

"That's not gonna happen, man," Clyde called over from another booth. "This was it. The big game. There's no way we're not holding on to our lead."

Pump slid into the booth where Clyde sat. Clyde reached over and scuffed his hand over the top of Pump's hair.

"My main man here agrees with me, don't ya, Prout?" Clyde asked.

Everyone looked at Pump.

Pump gulped and nodded.

"Sorry, Pizza, but we've just become invincible," Danny Flagan announced, pulling the spotlight back to himself, much to Pump's relief. Danny, sitting between Clyde and Freddy, put an arm around each of them. With one quick move he brought both of their heads down and sideways so they clunked together.

"See"—Danny chuckled—"we're too tough to crack." Danny laughed out loud while Clyde and Freddy rubbed their heads.

Mr. Pirelli gave free packages of cookies to all the players before they left. Pump and Ken headed home together.

When Pump got home, his whole family was in the kitchen eating dinner.

"Is that you, Pump?" his mother called out.

Pump came into the kitchen, which smelled of the garlic his mother used in almost everything she cooked. His parents and Luke were sitting at the table. A place was set for Pump. Still dirty from the game, he sat down without washing his hands. For once, no one seemed to care.

"Great game," Luke greeted Pump.

Puzzled, Pump stared at Luke. Luke sounded serious but that was uncharacteristic of him. Pump waited for the teasing.

Luke added, "No, I really mean it. I wasn't even bored watching you amateurs fumble your way to success. It was a good game. I was even proud of my little brother."

"Yes, Pump," his father said, looking at Pump over the top of the half-glasses he always wore around the house, "your mother explained to me that your last throw saved the game. Luke said the score would've been tied if that run had ever come in. Nice work."

Pump slid down in his chair. He blinked like an owl at his father. His father was learning about baseball!

Pump basked in the memory of that play—Jeff Leonard trying to locate the ball, the runners trying to make it around the bases and

Annie, ready and waiting for the throw while time was running out. Pump remembered how it took Jeff about an eternity to throw him the ball. He remembered how fast he had to throw to third, without even having time to take aim. He remembered holding his breath when Annie stretched up to make the catch. He hadn't breathed again until she had put Pizza out.

"It was Annie's catch as much as my throw," Pump said, finding it hard to absorb his father's praise. He wasn't used to it.

"Well, you certainly did your part. That's the good thing about team sports. Everyone has the same goal and you work together to achieve it."

Pump thought his dad was sounding a lot like Fred Namath.

"So, boys, you're turning your old man into a baseball fan. What do you make of that?" their dad said smiling.

This left Pump open-mouthed and speechless. He felt Luke kick him under the table.

His dad continued, "When's your next game? I understand it's your last and I don't want to miss it."

"The game's on Thursday," Pump replied.

"Who're you playing?" Luke wanted to know.

"The Pilgrims," Pump answered.

"How'd you do against them the first time? You beat 'em, didn't you?"

"Twelve to eight," Pump said. "But they weren't bad. I'll bet they're even better now. Everyone seems to be."

"Except the Muskets," Luke laughed.

"Except the Muskets," Pump echoed with satisfaction.

Pump's father pulled out his cell phone.

"Hmm, Thursday," he said as he checked his calendar. "I'll just shift some things around at work."

"Do you want some dinner, Pump?" his mother asked.

"I bet he had pizza at Pirelli's," Luke put in.

"Let Pump answer, Luke," his mother said.

"Luke's right," Pump agreed. "We all ate at Pirelli's. I had a lot but you should've seen Pizza De Souza. He's a Musket. He ate more pizza than I've ever seen anyone put away at one time."

"At least the Muskets are good at something," Luke said.

"Everyone is good at something," their mother said gravely. Then she smiled. Her eyes twinkled.

"Yes, Mom," the boys said together.

"Now, why don't you both go show us how good you are at home-work," Pump's father commanded.

Luke put his dishes in the sink and took off to do his homework. Pump went to take a bath. He needed some more time to replay the afternoon's game to himself before he could begin homework. The bathtub often served as a ballpark for Pump. He would lie in the tub and pitch his wet washcloth at the opposite wall. Even though he would wring out the cloth, spray flew when it hit the wall. While the washcloth slid down the tiles, the fielders fielded and the runners ran. Once the cloth slid back into the tub, play stopped.

He filled the tub with water as hot as he could stand so it would stay warm enough for him to pitch a long game.

The Pilgrims

THE END OF THE SEASON was as nerve-wracking as the beginning, only in a different way. In the beginning everything was unknown and that made Pump nervous. In the end, it seemed the only unknown was the outcome, which made Pump nervous, too.

The weather added an element of uncertainty. Days had gotten hot, but rain was always a possibility. The morning of the game with the Pilgrims, Pump could see it was drizzling outside. The sky was a seamless gray. The paper predicted "unsettled" weather. *Unsettling* was more like it, Pump thought.

On his way to school Pump caught up with Ken who was wearing a bright yellow slicker. The sky was getting lighter and Pump could see the sheet of grey soften into outlines of clouds. The drizzle had stopped. It was hot and steamy with a fine mist in the air.

"OK, Pump, you ready for the bad news?" Ken asked as they pedaled along together. It was clear to Pump that Ken had been pedaling very slowly waiting for Pump to get on the road.

"I guess so," Pump said. "Let's have it."

"We beat the Stars. No problem."

"What was the score?" Pump asked. Not that it mattered.

"Fifteen to six. We crushed them. And I ... ," Ken hesitated.

"Yeah? You what?" Pump took his cue.

"I hit an out-of-the-park homer."

"Hey, that's great. How many runs?" Pump asked.

"Two. Me and a kid who'd walked."

"Wow. I still haven't hit any homers and you've had two," Pump said wistfully.

"You will," Ken assured him.

"So now we have to win today or else we have to play you guys again," Pump thought aloud.

"That's what we're hoping for. We wouldn't let you beat us twice," Ken said emphatically.

"*Let* us beat you? Hah! You didn't *let* us beat you," Pump sputtered. "We practically creamed you. Forget it! We'll do it again if we have to."

Pump was surprised how angry he felt. He really didn't want to play the Muskets again. He kind of agreed with Ken that the Muskets would beat the Minutemen if they played again. But what kind of an attitude was that? Not useful. He could hear in his head Fred Namath saying, "Think positive. That makes the difference in a tight situation."

"Nah," Ken went on. "You guys were just lucky. Let's see if we get the chance to prove it to you. Which we will."

Ken looked over at Pump and grinned mischievously. Pump realized that Ken had no idea he was irritating Pump. Ken probably had more faith in the Minutemen's capacity to beat the Muskets than Pump let himself have.

"We're not going to give you that chance," Pump declared as they locked up their bikes in front of school. "I'm just hoping it doesn't rain again."

"That's OK," Ken said. "I'll bring an umbrella."

"You coming?" Pump asked.

"Are you kidding? I wouldn't miss it. I'll be there."

"Who're you going to be for?" Pump blurted out.

"What do you think?" Ken looked wounded.

"OK, OK. Sorry I asked. Forget it," Pump said.

"I'll even stand behind your bench just so you'll know," Ken laughed.

Pump managed a strained smile. "Thanks," he said. "See you."

The sky was ominous all day but the rain held off. The air was damp and chilly but the field was dry enough to be played on. The base paths were soft in spots, but not slippery.

The Minutemen started out playing like a totally different team from the one that defeated the Muskets two days earlier. Everyone was tight and edgy. The Minutemen were playing a game they were afraid to lose rather than a game they wanted to win. They made more errors than they had since the beginning of the season.

Luckily for the Minutemen, the Pilgrims were nervous, too. They had been overwhelmed by the news of the opposition's win over the Muskets. The Pilgrims' coach knew that not being expected to win could be very liberating, because the underdog has nothing to lose. He tried to convey this to his team but despite his encouragement the Pilgrims played like they were all expecting to lose. Each time the Minutemen made an error—and there were many errors—the Pilgrims were surprised which made them lose precious time before trying to capitalize on the error.

The Pilgrims' coach was going wild. He screamed, "Run, run," until he was hoarse but still his players froze like startled deer each time the Minutemen overthrew the bases or missed easy plays.

Pump saw his father watching with a furrowed brow as though he were puzzled by what he was seeing. This game was more like a circus than a baseball game. Pump himself had missed an easy play when he dove for a ball hit right toward him and came up empty-handed. Another time he overthrew to Brian at the plate and a run came in on his error.

The Pilgrims finally relaxed and by the bottom of the fourth inning, the Minutemen were down 8-3. As the Minutemen glumly came in from the field, their coach called them into a huddle.

"OK, Minutemen, that's enough of this doom and gloom. Where's my team from the day before yesterday?" Fred asked.

The players shrugged or shook their heads or just looked uncomfortable.

"I'll tell you where that team is," Fred exclaimed with enthusiasm. "That team is right here in front of me. *You* are still that team. You are still the Minutemen who have had a great season and come as far as any team in Canterbury history. I know you're not feeling that way right now, but it's time to change that. And we can.

"We're going back to basics. You're playing like you're spooked. Like the Red Sox with the Curse of the Bambino. It's all in your heads. Tell me, who here thinks we can win this game?"

There was an uncomfortable silence as the teammates twitched and scratched and squirmed, shuffled and sniffed. Heads were lowered. The Minutemen were all inspecting their feet.

"I do," Clyde said with energy. "You're right, Coach. It's like we're holding a glass ball and we're afraid if we move we're going to break it. Sounds weird but that's how I've been feeling anyway."

"Me, too," Danny agreed. "I feel like this division championship is right in our hands and we'd better not do anything to lose it. Or break the glass ball, like Clyde said. It's like we don't dare move or we'll lose everything."

The Minutemen were all nodding in agreement. Even Bones.

"It's hard to play when you're holding your breath," Annie sighed. She took a loud, deep breath and her teammates followed with deep breaths of their own.

"What's going on, Namath?" the umpire shouted. "Play ball!"

"Oh, yes, baseball," Fred said with a laugh. "I almost forgot."

"Who's gonna win this?" Danny yelled.

"The Minutemen," everyone shouted as they headed for the bench.

"Leonard, you're up," ordered Fred. "Salvano on deck. Bednarski, double deck. Let's go, Minutemen. I want sparks flying off those bats."

Jeff Leonard approached the plate with more determination than

Pump had ever seen in him. He was awake and full of anticipation as he addressed the plate.

After two energetic swings that missed the ball, Jeff retreated to his usual loopy batting. He swept his bat under the next pitch and scooped up a nice hit that landed between the second baseman and the right fielder. With his gangly stride, Jeff made it to first base.

Willie swung his bat with determination. He'd been longing to get the ball out of the infield at least once this season. No one could do it for him. It was up to him and he knew it.

The pitcher couldn't get the ball in Willie's strike zone and by the third ball Willie's whole body was taut with eagerness. He did not want to walk. No one could find his strike zone with regularity so he felt he needed to help out the pitchers. As the fourth ball came toward him, he took a quick hop forward and struck the ball. It rose into the air, sailed over the pitcher's head and landed in short center field.

The center fielder moved slowly so the shortstop dashed to field the ball and made it to second in time to greet Jeff with an out. Willie was safe on first, where he bounced around and hugged himself. One out.

Bones lumbered to the plate. Pump, in his batting helmet, stepped into the on-deck circle and took some swings to loosen up. Unless Bones hit into a double play, Pump would be up this inning.

Bones took his swings. He seemed to tilt ever so slightly forward, which meant his weight was tipped forward instead of back on his heels. Bones usually swung late so any ball he managed to hit headed toward right field. This time, with this new forward tipping, Bones's swing threw him forward even though he missed the ball. The Minutemen watched in amazement. They'd seen Bones fall back so many times, it seemed as rare as a solar eclipse to watch him fall forward. The next pitch was a ball. Bones attacked the following pitch with all his might and walloped the ball deep into left field.

Willie took off like a shot. Bones lunged toward first, tripped in his eagerness, pulled himself up and ran. The fielders swarmed after the ball. Willie zoomed around the bases and was home before Bones had rounded first. Fred waved Bones on and he chugged toward second. The ball was finally gathered and thrown to the shortstop cutoff.

Bones made it safely to second and looked relieved when Fred signaled him to hold up there.

The crowd was cheering Bones's hit and Willie's run as Pump approached the plate.

"Go Pump!" Pump recognized his father's voice as he took some swings. He took some more swings just to calm himself down.

The team had come alive. Somehow Pump couldn't stay with them. He still was plagued by ambition. It wasn't the Pilgrims he was thinking about. It was his father. Pump wanted to show him his best baseball, something that would convince his father how great baseball was, maybe even how great he, Pump Prout, could be.

Pump felt stiff. The pitcher didn't know that. All he knew was that the Minutemen were hitting, something they hadn't been doing since the beginning of the game. So the pitcher tried to put a little something extra into his pitches. Naturally, this gave Pump a base on balls.

"Good eye," called out Butch Flagan.

Pump shivered as he crouched at first. The sky was darkening. He felt a few drops of rain. Nothing serious. Not yet.

Danny Flagan walked up to the plate swinging his bat. He was chewing gum. He gurgled and hawked and spat a big wad onto the ground. Danny took two balls, then swung at the third pitch. The ball sailed to the fence. Bones heaved himself toward third. Pump had to slow down in order not to overrun Bones. Danny had to hang around first. He jumped in place hoping that his hit wouldn't be limited by Bones' pace. But it was. Bases loaded, one out.

Danny called to Clyde, "Make it a homer, Clyde, baby, or Bednarski'll never get home."

Bones's face was red and sweaty from his efforts at running, but Pump could still see the blush that flushed his neck. Bones nodded in agreement.

Clyde was only too happy to oblige. He smacked the first pitch over the fence. A grand slam. Bones struggled home followed by Pump right on his heels, then Danny and finally Clyde.

The runners fell into the waving arms of their teammates. The Minutemen were cheering and roaring. They patted and pounded the heads and backs of the runners. Fred calmed everyone down and sent Freddy out to bat. Freddy's vision was clouded by ambition, too. He wanted to equal Clyde. Pump bet he wanted to show his father what he could do.

Pump felt a wave of sympathy for Freddy, who was always quiet and hardworking, and had to play for his father, the coach, every day. Pump found it a strain just to have his dad there watching. He could imagine what it must feel like to Freddy. Lucky for them all, but especially lucky for Freddy, Fred seemed to have undergone some kind of change over the course of the season.

The pitcher was rattled and became even less consistent. Freddy drew a walk. Annie followed with a foul pop-up that the Pilgrims' third baseman caught. Two outs. The pitcher regained enough composure to strike out Brian Kennedy and retire the side.

At the end of the fourth inning, the Pilgrims and the Minutemen were tied at eight apiece.

The fifth inning brought Josh Gerstein in for Willy. Bones stayed in as DH to reward his amazing accomplishment in helping tie up the game, but also to save Jill Maloney who had come down with the flu after the Muskets' game. She didn't want to miss the game, but her eyes were sunken and circled by deep shadows. She sat on the bench wrapped in a blanket, but insisted she was ready to play.

The sky darkened further. Pump shivered in the damp air. The top of the fifth went by quickly. Danny was pitching and he met no resistance. Three batters up, three batters down.

The batters of both teams seemed to be trying for too much. A base hit would be fine, only they wanted a homer—just to be sure. The Minutemen sent Penny, Jeff and Josh against the Pilgrims' very mediocre pitching. Only Josh made it to first and he was walked. Even Penny, the immobile Penny, was looking for runs and swung the bat at thin air.

Bones presented himself at the plate looking for that same satisfying experience of a long, hard drive. Pump noticed that Bones had already forgotten to lean forward and into the ball. There he was, back on his heels, late again. Bones slashed the air with his eager bat and came up with the third out.

Just before he took the mound again to pitch the sixth, and

hopefully last, inning, Danny said to Pump and Clyde as they walked to their positions, "Hey, guys. You know what I've been thinking? This is the last inning I'll be pitching in this division. We're gonna win this game, and then no more Muskets or Pilgrims for me. Clyde, we're going to the majors next year. Makes me kinda nostalgic."

Danny warmed up looking as casual and undaunted as ever, but Pump could tell that Danny was very focused.

The Pilgrims' coach must have pointed out to his team how fruitless it was to attack every pitch in hopes of smashing a masterful hit to break the tie. In the top of the sixth, the Pilgrims were restrained. They were looking for walks.

"Make him pitch to you. Wait for your pitch," the Pilgrims' coach shouted.

Danny gave them their pitches. He was on a roll. The Pilgrims, however, were having trouble recognizing their pitches. Every batter stood stock still, afraid to swing at a pitch that wasn't his or hers. It began to drizzle.

Danny was clearly enjoying himself. He was calm, focused and throwing right to Brian's glove. He gave up two walks, struck out two rigid batters and sent a third down swinging. The game was still tied.

"Minutemen," Fred called to his team. "it's getting wet out here and it's going to get worse. No point in staying out here any longer than is absolutely necessary. So bring in some runs. Just one run is all we need. Watch the ball and go for it if you get the chance."

The sky grew a shade darker, the drizzle continued.

Pump led off in the bottom of the sixth. As he took his practice swings he had to shake off the thought that he would hit a solo home run and be the hero of the season. He just needed to get on base. That was his job as lead-off. The thought of having a job to do helped Pump settle down.

Even though Pump felt settled, the pitcher didn't and he walked Pump.

"Good eye," Pump heard his father shout.

He's really getting into this, Pump thought with amazement and pleasure as he jogged to first.

Danny wasn't interested in waiting for a walk. He swung at two low balls for two strikes. He waited out two more balls but got impatient again. He swung at another low ball, scooped it up for a short fly ball just over the head of the shortstop, who reached up for an easy out. Danny was mad. He kicked dirt as he scuffed to the bench.

Clyde can bring me home, Pump thought as he watched Clyde's smooth swing slice through the air. Now that he couldn't bring himself home, Pump didn't care who did it. With Danny, Clyde, Freddy and Annie following him at bat, one of them would surely bring him home. Not Danny, though.

Clyde clearly wanted to bring in the winning run. He forgot about patience and focus. He swatted at the pitches as hard as he could. He struck out. Clyde threw down his batting helmet. He gave Pump a sheepish look and shrugged his shoulders. Pump tried to smile to let Clyde know it didn't matter. Freddy was up next. Maybe he would do the job. Two outs. Not looking as good as before.

Freddy knew he had to be patient and he let himself be walked. The pitcher was definitely having trouble. Once on second, Pump felt more hopeful again.

Annie came to the plate. Finally a pitch crossed the plate. She was ready and swung. Foul ball. She must've liked the feeling of a swinging bat because she went for the next ball, too, even though it was high and outside. She missed it. Strike two. On the next pitch she swung again but got too close and caught the ball with the neck of her bat. The ball landed and stayed right in front of the plate.

Annie took off for first, Freddy sped to second and Pump flew to third. He was ready to keep going but Fred waved him off. The catcher had gotten hold of the ball and wasn't letting go. He didn't want to risk a throw so he just held the ball at the plate to thwart any attempt at bringing in a run. The deciding run.

The game-ending, division-winning run, in the shape of Pump Prout, stayed on third. Bases loaded and Brian Kennedy was up.

Brian coiled up waiting for a ball to spring at. He saw one and went for it. He struck a bouncing grounder right to the pitcher who managed to catch it on the bounce. With no strike zone to worry about, the pitcher threw the ball right over the plate into the glove of the catcher. The crowd was screaming all around. The catcher jumped up and down on the plate. "You're out," the umpire yelled, adding insult to injury.

Pump knew he was out and didn't want to be told.

The side was retired. The game went into the seventh inning.

"Great jawb!" the Minutemen heard the familiar voice of Coach Kennedy calling encouragement to them.

The coaches were in a huddle with the umpire. Fred Namath was gesturing heatedly as he spoke. He broke away from the others and approached his team.

"OK, Minutemen," Fred said, "the Pilgrims wanted to call the game. It's not wet enough underfoot to require stopping, but it's going to be that way soon. Let's make this inning ours, Minutemen. Let's hear it for the seventh inning."

The Minutemen yelled and hooted and the few who could whistle—Pump wasn't one of them—did.

Clyde took the mound, Danny went to first and Freddy moved over to shortstop. The ball was wet and Clyde rubbed it on his damp pants to try to dry it off. Clyde's face was relaxed. He looked like he wanted to be there on that wet mound, with rain starting to replace the drizzle. He glided through his warm-ups. He was ready.

Pump was not the only one who was mesmerized by Clyde. Everyone watched as Clyde threw a sequence of pitches across the plate. A few pitches caught one corner of the plate or another. Pump believed that Clyde intended them that way.

The Pilgrims couldn't resist after the first batter just stood and watched himself be struck out. They started swinging. They went down swinging.

Bottom of the seventh.

Penny went rigid at the plate. She looked hypnotized and only emerged from her trance when the umpire said, "Take your base."

Penny had done her job as the lead-off, Pump observed, grateful that the pitcher had helped her out.

Jeff Leonard, gangly and hopeful, swung placidly at the first pitch.

He was not going to just stand there and watch the pitches go by. Someone had to hit the ball and he wanted to be that someone. Instead, he struck out.

The rain was falling in earnest. Parents and friends were standing under plastic bags and umbrellas, any protection they could find. Pump saw his father and Ken Ames, in his yellow slicker, sharing a big plastic bag they held over their heads. His mother and Luke had their jacket hoods up and stood with their shoulders shrugged up to their ears and their hands shoved deep in their pockets.

As Josh went to the plate Pump put on his batting helmet. He was on double deck. Josh swung at the first pitch and hit a ball that bounced foul over the third base line. The next three pitches were balls. Throwing his usual caution to the winds, Josh risked another swing and missed. On the next pitch he instinctively played the odds, stood motionless and walked.

The Minutemen on the bench were all standing at the fence that separated the bench from the field. The crowd had thinned out substantially. A lot of the parents had sought shelter in their cars. Everyone left watching was hanging on the fence and making a lot of noise. The Pilgrims fans were cheering on their pitcher and fielders. The Minutemen fans were chanting and yelling encouragement to the batters. Everyone was wet.

"Give it a ride, Bednarski. Just like before. Bring Weiss in. Get us out of this rain, would ya please?" Fred.

Willie was jumping up and down behind the fence.

"Go, Bones. Go, Buddy. I seen ya do it before. I know you can!" he yelled. Pump remembered what it felt like to be a rookie. He bet it was even tougher this year. They really gave each other support.

Bones hadn't entirely forgotten about trying to meet the ball. His chest and arms folded forward to reach toward the ball, but he kept his weight on his heels so the whole lower half of his body hung back. This left him a little off balance. Bones swung and missed and fell over backwards onto his rear end.

"Ouff." The impact knocked the air out of Bones. He got back up, shook himself off, knocked real mud off his cleats and resumed his stance at the plate. The Minutemen cheered him. Strike one.

Pump noticed Fred put his hand over his eyes for a minute. It was the first indication that Fred was on edge, too. That made Pump nervous. He was up next. What if he struck out, just like Bones seemed about to do? In two more swings, Bones was out. Two outs. Runners on first and second. Pump was up.

Pump assumed his batting stance at the plate and loosened up his tight arms by taking some swings. He found he was holding his breath and made himself exhale hard. Luke always said, "If you make yourself breathe out, don't worry about breathing in. You gotta do that. The trick is to breathe out when you're nervous."

Luke was shouting at Pump, "Here you go, Pump. Give it a ride. Bring 'em in."

The fans were clapping and whistling. All the noise suddenly stopped as the pitcher wound up. Ball one.

"That's lookin' 'em over. Good eye." Pump heard Coach Kennedy's deep roar.

Pump's mouth was dry. His face was wet from the rain and from sweat. He looked at the pitcher. Pump silently pleaded for a walk, but then realized he had to go for the next pitch coming right over the plate. Strike one.

Pump's thoughts were jumping around when all he wanted was to focus and watch the ball. His imagination was spinning from wildly brilliant hits to lousy strikeouts.

Pump swung and his bat ticked the ball which fell foul. The catcher scrambled after it.

"You got a piece of it," yelled Butch Flagan. "Now get the whole thing."

Pump was so busy trying to calm his thoughts that he barely saw the next pitch, which hit the dirt in front of the plate for a ball. The count was two and two.

This time the crowd kept up its cries straight through the pitcher's windup and release. Pump swung. The ball took off in a high line drive that rose over the pitcher's head and landed beyond second base in center field. Penny and Josh started running. The center fielder tried to follow the ball that was bouncing through the wet grass.

Pump passed first base and moved toward second. He realized he'd hit a solid double.

Penny ran as fast as she could. The crowd was screaming and shrieking. She thumped the plate as she crossed it. The crowd, yowling and yelling, poured onto the field. The rain poured onto the crowd. The rest of the Minutemen leaped on Pump and Penny and anyone they found. Everyone was jumping up and down. They had done it. The Minutemen had won the division championship!

The teammates jumped up and down, slapping and hugging everyone, hooting and hollering. Fred Namath, beaming and grinning, yahooing until he was hoarse, finally got his team lined up to slip their wet hands over the equally wet hands of the disappointed Pilgrims.

"Hey, Pilgrims," Danny yelled, "don't look so glum. You're our favorite team!"

Pump grinned. This was his team. They were the division champs. Next week they'd play in the City Cup playoffs with a chance to be first in the city against three other divisions. But that's next week. Right now the Minutemen were winners and Pump felt every inch a Minuteman.

"We'll skip the wrap-up," Fred announced as rain dripped off the tip of his nose. "I know everyone is soaked but I think I could go for a trip to … "

"Pirelli's!" the Minutemen shouted.

"Don't you think the kids should dry off first?" Mrs. Gerstein wondered.

"Aw, Mom," ventured Josh, "maybe *you* should … just … dry … up!"

For a flicker of a moment everyone fell silent. A look of doubt clouded Josh's face. Pump heard people suck in their breath. Josh's mother and father looked startled. And then, of all people, Pump's father started to laugh. Mrs. Gerstein broke into a smile. Everyone laughed and shouted again.

"To Pirelli's!"

Pump was jumped from behind by his brother, who caught Pump before he fell over.

"Little sprout," Luke said, as he danced like a boxer around Pump.

Luke sprang at Pump and gave him quick jabs in the arm. "Very nice work. Now, *that* was real baseball!"

Pump's mother came over and gave her wet son a hug.

"What a great game!" she exclaimed. "What a super hit!"

Pump's father approached with more decorum. He put his arm around Pump's shoulders and squeezed him.

"Now I see why you like baseball. You're good at it. Great hit, there," his father said gruffly. "Now we've got to get home. Are you coming with us?"

Pump shook his head. "I'm going to Pirelli's with the team. We always do that, but especially tonight." Pump had a note of pleading in his voice.

"Well," said his father, "I want to dry off. Pizza isn't exactly what I think I'd like right now. Why don't you come with us?"

"Dad, it's OK. I'm going, too," Luke said. "Everyone does after the last game."

"Even when you're wet?" their father asked.

"Dripping wet," replied Luke. "See you guys later."

Luke put his arm around Pump's shoulder and turned him toward Pirelli's.

"Whadya think about double cheese?" Luke asked as he pushed Pump along through the rain.

Double cheese sounded just right to Pump.

THE END

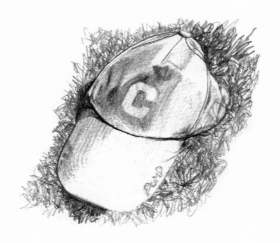

About the Author
A. R. Pressman lives in Cambridge, Massachusetts where her two sons played Little League baseball. When one of them ran out of baseball books to read, he said he wanted one "with a lot of baseball in it," so she wrote that book and here it is.

About the Illustrator
Peter Aldrich is a short-statured Cantabrigian who takes delight in the heroics of scrappy small players of any game. He is a retired businessman who has traveled the world, but always returns to Fenway Park or the West Cambridge, Massachusetts Little League fields.

About the Designer
Jeannet Leendertse designed many serious books since she swapped The Lowlands for the USA. She had great fun working on her first children's book.

oligopoly regulates
the Regulators
diverters — regulates
role by rule of
benefit the protection
of the oligopoly
lawyers opinion
It's a Big Charade

Made in the USA
Charleston, SC
08 May 2011